# Keep This Off the Record

### Arden Joy

Text copyright © 2023 **by Arden Austin**

All rights reserved. For information regarding reproduction in total or in part, contact Rising Action Publishing Co. at www.risingactionpub lishingco.com

Cover Illustration © **Ashley Santoro**

Distributed by **Blackstone Publishing**

ISBN: 978-1-990253-55-3
Ebook: 978-1-990253-61-4

FIC027250 FICTION / Romance / Romantic Comedy
FIC027210 FICTION / Romance / LGBTQ+ / Lesbian
FIC027020 FICTION / Romance / Contemporary

#KeepThisOffTheRecord
Follow Rising Action on our socials!
Twitter: @RAPubCollective
Instagram: @risingactionpublishingco
TikTok: @risingactionpublishingco

*To Bill Rheinhardt:*
*I never knew how to thank you other than to publish this book*
*and dedicate it to you.*

# Keep This Off the Record

# Chapter 1
## *Abby*

A SINGLE CHERRY FLEW THROUGH THE AIR.

As it gracefully somersaulted across the space between Abby and Freya, "The Blue Danube" started playing in Abby's head. At first, she couldn't figure out why that particular song had popped into her mind, but then she remembered that scene in 2001: *A Space Odyssey.* Wasn't there something in the beginning with a bone flying through the air to the tune of "The Blue Danube?" That had to be the connection.

The cherry, a shade of, well, cherry red that could have only been achieved through years of genetic modification, was trailing slightly behind the rest of her drink. *That would make sense,* she told herself. The cherry had sunk to the bottom of her glass, so, naturally, it would come out of the gate a little slower than the Blue Envy Tequila-tini itself.

The Blue Envy: tequila, blue curaçao, pineapple juice, a splash of Sprite, and yes, a maraschino cherry. It was the orangey sweetness of the curaçao and sugary goodness of the pineapple juice that made the drink dangerous. Those two candy liquids created a beverage sweet enough to go down like a soft drink instead of a stiff drink. As she watched the bluish liquid speed toward Freya, it rippled and undulated in a way that reminded Abby of the sculptures she had seen in the Chihuly Garden and Glass in Seattle.

Abby wasn't entirely sure how this moment—her drink about to hit her mortal enemy in the face at their high school reunion—had come about. The Blue Envys were partly to blame for that. She was on her fourth. Although, to be fair, the fourth one was about to make contact with Freya. Still, she'd never been able to hold her tequila very well, such that inhaling three Blue Envys would be ill-advised on a good day, let alone on a day that was definitely not.

She hadn't expected to have so much to drink. Then again, she hadn't expected a lot of things that had happened this evening.

Like Freya.

Naomi had promised her that Freya would absolutely *not* be at the reunion.

"She's doing a whole series on the refugee crisis in the EU. She's not even in the country!" Naomi had assured her.

Yet, here she was. She was not only at the reunion, she was being *honored* at the reunion. According to the evening's program, which Abby had been handed by alumni president Puja Kapoor when she finished writing out her name tag, Freya was receiving an "Alumni of Distinction" award for her work in journalism on *Nightly Global News*.

Abby had always assured herself that one day, Freya would be the cellulite-ridden, oily-skinned hoarder who had peaked in her teens. That thought, that promise, had become a security blanket of sorts that had gotten her through high school. Sure, she didn't use it very often all these years later, but there were still times when she'd find herself lying awake in the middle of the night, thinking of the perfect response for something Freya had said more than a decade ago. In those moments, she would reach for her blankie, well-worn and comforting, and drift into the familiar fantasy of a blubbery Freya sitting on her ripped sofa, covered in Cheeto dust, and surrounded by stacks of magazines. Instead, here she was, looking like time had forgotten to take a toll on her body, being recognized for her great achievements.

Still, it's possible Abby could have avoided this drink-flinging moment, if that was all that had happened. Then, her best friend since the first day of Hebrew school had decided to flirt with Will.

Why did it have to be Will? She was thrilled that Naomi was actually connecting with someone. But Will? *Really?* There were at least one hundred of their classmates packed into their high school gym, including Michael Weinberg (who had been Naomi's crush for their entire high school career and who had shown up not only alone but sporting the kind of well-manicured beard that was right up Naomi's alley). Abby would have done a victory dance to see Naomi flirt with any of them.

Instead, she had hit it off with Will while she and Abby were waiting to spend their drink tickets at the bar. Will, was neither a classmate nor a classmate's date, as he would explain, but Freya's associate producer, who was only here because he and Freya were headed out to do an interview immediately after she accepted her award. Naomi appeared unphased by his nefarious connections, though, and her small talk turned to giggles and fingers twirling in her hair when he offered to spend one of his drink tickets on her until she walked off with him, the two of them practically leaving sparks in their wake.

Maybe returning to high school was bringing back Abby's teenage angst, but mingling with the enemy's side-kick felt like a complete and total breach of BFF protocol.

Not that she would go so far as to admit that out loud.

What else was Abby supposed to do but drink? She was already at the bar when Naomi walked away with Will. It seemed like the best decision. Have a drink, and get the hell out of there.

She would have gone for a simple glass of wine. One glass.

If it weren't for the bartender.

Why was she such a sucker for Southern accents? She hadn't even given the bartender a second glance until she asked Abby what she'd have to drink, and a sweet New Orleans drawl languidly drew out her words like a stripper slowly, seductively, sliding down a pole.

Abby found herself leaning onto the bar, in that way that all humans seem to instinctively know how to do when they want to show interest, saying, "Why don't you surprise me?"

The bartender leaned too. "Well, let's see. You seem like a tequila girl to me," she said with her luscious accent, now enhanced with a hint of playfulness. She brushed her pony-tail away from her shoulder, and a tattoo teased its way above the neckline of her bartender's uniform. Abby didn't stand a chance. Tattoos were traditionally frowned upon in the Jewish tradition, which shouldn't mean much to her, theoret-ically. Although she had been raised in the Jewish faith, her Jewish identity had evolved over time and as an atheist, she now considered herself a cultural Jew who was proud of her heritage and participated in many of the traditions, but also didn't adhere to any practices that were restrictive or exclusionary. However, for some reason, the tattoo taboo had wheedled its way into her sexual psyche at a young age and never left.

After finishing her third Blue Envy, she thought that perhaps this night was redeemed. It seemed likely, very likely, that she was going to find out exactly how far down that tattoo went before the evening was over.

"So, I'm thinking," the bartender had said, setting down a fourth drink before Abby even had to ask, "that when I finish up here, maybe we can—"

"Umm, excuse me. Can I get a drink over here?"

Although she didn't know it right then, that was the moment. The moment when the countdown to 2001: *Space Odyssey* pineapple, flying Chihuly Blue Envy Tequila-tini began.

As Abby turned, her vision lagged slightly so that everything seemed to have a tail, like a shooting star across the night sky. Up until that moment, she hadn't thought she was intoxicated—comfortably buzzed, maybe. The kind of buzzed that was like wearing a pair of noise-canceling headphones when all the background clatter is reduced to a low thrum. As she waited for the world and her thoughts to come into focus, she realized she may have sped well past comfortably buzzed.

She blinked twice, and her eyes finally settled on Freya. Her blond hair was pulled back into a chic and professional tight bun, the kind that made Abby, by comparison, look like an angry schoolmarm. She was dressed in a black pantsuit made of a thick and luxurious fabric that expertly hugged every single curve of her body. There were no out-of-place curves, no bumps or flaws, not even a single line across her immaculate milky face, that Abby could see.

Freya let out a sharp chuckle, a single, breathy note in the minor key that said she knew she had caught Abby off guard. She put a French-manicured hand on her hip and lifted one perfectly-shaped eyebrow, like a matador raising the red flag and inviting her to charge. "Oh my God. I should have known it was you holding things up."

Abby remained still, but mentally slammed her head against the bar. She should have been ready for this. She'd had a lifetime to prepare. If not a lifetime, then at least the last hour, from the moment she'd seen Freya's name on the program. If they were going to have one final rematch, she was not going to go down without a fight. She only needed a minute to get her footing. That was all.

Much like the spark that caused the Big Bang, the origin of the feud between Abby and Freya remained a mystery. The reality was, even Abby wasn't entirely sure what had started it—but she was sure it was Freya's fault. It was true Abby had never liked Freya. From the moment she had laid eyes on Freya on the first day of high school, something about her come-hither stride mingled with her cheerleader smile had rubbed Abby the wrong way. Still, she was sure that it was Freya who had fired the first shot. While she wasn't one to start a fight, Abby wasn't one to lose one either. Whatever the spark was, it led to four years of a Capulet-and-Montague situation with none of the romance and all of the endless cycles of revenge.

The feud had only ended because high school had ended

6

—or so she had thought. Standing here, fifteen years later, she knew she had been wrong. They were about to pick up right where they left off.

"Honestly." Freya laughed and tossed her head. "I have to admit this isn't far off from how I imagined you'd end up. The sad, lonely drunk at a bar."

"I'm not—"

"Let me guess. You live alone. With your cat."

"Yes, but—"

"I knew it!" There was that laugh again. Someone once said it was musical. Abby thought it was musical the way a child banging on a piano senselessly is musical.

This was not going well. She felt like she was trying to run up an avalanche. Abby looked down and took a deep breath. She could see the unmistakable Christian Louboutin red peeking out from the soles of Freya's shoes.

"No, hold on. Let me keep going. You're still attached at the hip to that girl ... What was her name? Nicole?"

"Naomi. But we're not—"

"Abby?" Someone touched her shoulder and she turned around to see Naomi standing there, wearing the exact same expression she used to put on when she would try to intervene in their arguments in high school.

"Oh. My. God." This time Freya actually clutched at her stomach as she laughed, her hand covering a Chanel belt, cream-colored with the distinct double C buckle in white. "And there she is, right on cue."

"Hi, Freya," Naomi said in a polite but placating tone. It was the same tone Abby used when approached by Greenpeace volunteers on the street. That sort of *it's nothing against you personally, but I don't want to get involved, so I'm going to smile and say hi and keep walking.* In true, sweet-natured, Naomi fashion, she had never been pro- or anti-Freya, despite Abby's best attempt to convince her of Freya's dark nature. Although loyal to Abby, Naomi had remained mostly neutral on the subject of Freya Jonsson. Her biggest hope was that everyone would get along. Barring that, at least find a way not to fight. It seemed nothing had changed there either.

"Abby," Naomi said again, a little more forcefully. "Can I steal you for a second?"

Before she could respond, Will appeared next to Naomi. Had they been talking to each other this entire time? Why was he standing so close to Naomi? Was he touching her? Abby couldn't exactly tell. Her vision wasn't clearing at all. In fact, it seemed to be getting blurrier. The adrenaline she was feeling only seemed to be making things worse, as her heart beat quicker, and seemed to be fast-tracking the alcohol into her bloodstream.

"Ahh." Freya sighed contentedly, plump lips spreading into a wide smile. "Honestly, this is exactly how I imagined it. You, peaking in high school—if we could even call it peaking—and ending up as an old cat lady who is still obsessed with your 'friend' from high school."

The bartender, who had stepped away to serve someone drinks, wandered back in their direction. Abby felt a flush of embarrassment warm her cheeks.

"I am not—"

"Freya, um, I think they're getting ready to start the program," Will said, each word punctuated by hesitation. Or was that her imagination? Everything felt like it was starting to move slower. Like when she accidentally hit the button that made her podcasts play in half time. "Maybe we should head over to the stage."

"Finally," Freya said. "It's certainly been a pleasure. For me, anyway."

*No.* This couldn't be how things ended.

"See you at the next one, then? I seriously can't wait." Freya's voice dripped with sickening glee.

*No. No. No.*

Freya couldn't walk off with the last word. She couldn't say all those things and then disappear, thinking she had won. Thinking she was right. Thinking that Abby was some sad, lonely loser.

It was too late. Freya was putting her purse on her shoulder. She was about to leave—and Abby had nothing to say. No cutting remark that would put her in her place. No biting comeback that would let Freya know she wasn't the victor.

Abby looked down at the drink in her hand and realized something important.

She didn't have to worry about detention. She didn't have to worry about going to the principal's office. She didn't have to worry about her transcript. She didn't have to worry about getting references for college. She'd done all those things. She was an adult who could do whatever she wanted. She could finally put Freya Jonsson in her place, and no one could stop her.

With one swift motion, she lifted her hand, and tossed the contents of her glass.

# Chapter 2
## *Freya*

As a global journalist, Freya was no stranger to having liquids unexpectedly spilled on her. She'd been soaked by sake on a private jet with one of Japan's billionaires, by her coffee on a bumpy mountain road up the Alps, and even by vomit when a dignitary at a presidential dinner forgot to mention to the staff that he was allergic to quinoa. A little cocktail wasn't a surprise to her.

As she looked down at the beads of turquoise liquid rolling down her jacket, what did surprise her was just how good it felt. Her lip gave a threatening twinge upward, and she forced it back down. She could never let on that she felt this way.

She could never let people know that even after all these years, she had always wondered what would happen if she ran into Abigail Meyer again someday. Or that it had always bothered her that the end of high school left them in a stalemate, with no clear winner. Or that she'd secretly been hoping to run into Abby at the reunion so that she could finally close this chapter once and for all. Or that it had all gone better than she could have imagined, because Abby had just turned her private loss into a very public display of failure.

Now, everyone knew what she had always known: Abby wasn't the witty, funny, cute, nerd she'd portrayed herself to be in high school. She was an inarticulate, immature, toddler, who threw things when she didn't get her way.

It was absolutely and completely exquisite.

"Ohhhhh ..." Naomi held the word so long it sounded like she was a robot losing power.

Freya instructed every muscle in her face to remain neutral as she lifted her head. Abby was looking at her squarely. Somewhat squarely. It was clear from the glaze across her hazel eyes that she was not entirely sober. It was also clear that she looked pleased. Like, pleased-as-punch. Not embarrassed. Not sheepish. Not horrified or despondent or even slightly perturbed. Most certainly not like someone who thought they had lost. She looked like she thought *she* had just won.

This irked Freya, and the fact that she was irked, irked her even more.

Abby let out a tiny, but unmistakably devilish, giggle.

Freya didn't have to command her face muscles anymore. Forehead, eyebrows, mouth, all plunged downward. "Really?"

The giggle grew in size and volume, until it was a full, wide-mouthed, howl of laughter.

Naomi placed a parental hand on Abby's shoulder. "I think we're going to, um, head out now; come on, Abby. Let's go this way."

Abby accepted the directive and allowed herself to be

guided towards the double doors of the gym, letting out a loud, almost post-orgasmic sigh. "Don't be mad, Naomi." She leaned into Naomi, causing the two of them to list like a ship on a stormy night. "You can't be mad. I had to. I finally got to show everyone—"

"Napkin, honey?" The bartender held out a generous stack of white cocktail napkins.

Freya didn't respond, hoping she could catch the end of that sentence. Finally got to show everyone *what?* It was too late. The din of the crowd had overtaken their conversation.

Will took the napkins from the bartender. "Here, let me," he said. He hesitated, then pressed the entire stack onto her arm so lightly that it barely brushed the fabric.

Freya applied a reassuring smile and took the napkins from him. "I'm fine; it's just a drink." She set the pile of napkins on the bar, then took one and began to dab along her arm. "I'm pretty sure cleaning drinks off my clothes was not in your job description."

Will shifted his weight from right, to left, to right again. She wanted to tell him to spit out whatever it was that was making him do this nervous dance, but at the same time, she didn't. She knew he wanted to ask a question that he knew better than to ask.

His baby-faced features belied the fact that he had years of experience under his belt, nearly all of which he'd spent by Freya's side. It was that very baby face coupled with his homegrown midwestern mentality that made him her go-to producer for *Nightly Global News*. He was the yin to her yang, the *piano* to her *forte*. When she walked into a room, everyone noticed. When he walked into a room, no one noticed. He was unassuming and disarming. Most importantly, he knew how to use all that to his advantage and get things done. Also, it wasn't horrible having someone genuinely nice around. It was not a common personality trait in her field of work. Genuinely trying to step on you to climb the ladder, genuinely trying to steal the story, genuinely trying to get the dirt on you, yes, but genuinely nice? No. She wouldn't even qualify herself as that. But, that was also part of the job. She wasn't supposed to be kind; she was supposed to get the story, no matter the cost.

Will never seemed to judge her for that. She knew that she could sometimes be curt, demanding, or lacking in giving praise. For the most part, he didn't appear to mind. Sometimes, it seemed like figuring her out was one of his favorite parts of his job. If she had to be honest, he'd done fairly decent work. He knew when she needed help, and when she needed to be left alone. He knew when she needed coffee, and when what she really needed was bourbon (and her favorite orders for both). He knew how to get her to take a break, and how to motivate her when she felt stuck. Most importantly, he knew to keep their conversation focused on work and to never ask personal questions.

Will gave in and went for it. "Are you ... okay?" Even when Will screwed up, it was still because he was genuinely nice.

"Yep." She didn't look up to answer. "Good thing I wore black, huh?"

"It's just..."

Keeping her head down, she flicked her eyes up at him. "It's *only* a drink, Will. I'll be fine."

"I think what your friend here is trying to say is, we're all dying to know what just happened." Freya had forgotten that the bartender was still there. But there she was, holding up her hands in a sign of peace. "I know it's none of my business, but I work a lot of these reunion-type events, and that was a first for me."

"You're right. It is none of your business," Freya said so fiercely that everyone was taken aback. Freya cleared her throat, attempting to buy herself a few seconds to collect her thoughts. That delectable feeling she'd been savoring only minutes earlier had started to curdle, spoiled by these questions and by that image of Abby's triumphant, albeit lopsided, stare. She dabbed at her arm and gave a warm smile. She needed to keep this a funny story the bartender would tell her friends tonight and not have it turn into a twelve-part tweet that would end up on Gawker. "To be honest, you know about as much as I do. Um, what was your name again?"

"Caroline, but Lena is fine."

"Lena," she said, securing it to her short-term memory. "Thanks for the napkins, by the way. I think I was able to get most of it off me before it soaked into my jacket too much. As I was saying, I wish I had more to tell you. I came over here to get a drink, we exchanged a few words, and then ..." Freya placed a handful of blue stained napkins on the bar to finish her sentence.

"Oh, I get it." Lena slid the napkins off the bar and tossed them into the trash. "You two dated or something? Bad breakup?"

Freya braced her core like she was about to do a deadlift. "No," she said, with as much measure as possible, glad she'd had years of practice masking her reactions to distasteful subjects. "Abby and I didn't date. There's no history."

"Oh, these two have history," a familiar voice said.

"Can you say, 9021-oh my God, drama?" a second speaker added.

Freya didn't need to turn to see who was talking—she could never forget those voices. Out of politeness, she faced them anyway, her eyes landing on her high school girl gang, Penny and Ashley, as they approached. Freya gave her best enthusiastic gasp of delight, but they brushed past her, directing their attention to Will and Lena.

"Listen, you want the *goss*?" Penny crooked her finger, inviting Will and Lena to come closer. To Freya's annoyance, they both did.

"It's simple," Ashley was next, squeezing in beside Penny. "In high school, Freya here was a queen. Little Abby over there, she was jealous. It was so obvious that she wanted to be popular."

"Exactly." Penny again.

"She reminds me of those yappy little chihuahuas that always bark at the bigger dogs," Ashley said.

"Oh my God, exactly," Penny said, giving her a little push. "And Naomi was always hanging on to her like a bad case of fleas. The whole thing was bizarre."

"Yeah, it was so sad. But also kind of entertaining. Like four years of binge watchable, so pitiful you can't look away, d-r-a-m-a." Ashley looked at Penny. "Pen, stop me if I'm wrong."

Penny gave a shake of her head. "Nope. Can confirm, that is one hundred percent accurate."

Freya could confirm that she one hundred percent did not miss this routine, though Ashley and Penny had been the right people to keep by her side in high school. They were both beautiful and popular, but not enough to outshine her, and while she wouldn't exactly have described them as loyal, they had been enthusiastic about being her chosen companions. She also wouldn't have described them as particularly enjoyable to spend five days a week with at school, but then, like now, she wasn't about to let on how she really felt about them. Instead, she laughed. "Will, meet Penny and Ashley, my absolute best friends from school who know a little something about drama themselves." She crinkled her eyes as she smiled. "You two haven't changed a bit, have you?"

"Not where it counts!" Ashley said, in the same high-pitched voice from a decade ago. "We're as pretty and as catty as we were freshman year."

That one got a real laugh out of Freya. "If I had a drink, I'd cheers to that, but I got interrupted," she said. She'd barely had a moment to wonder if she should explain why, before Penny spoke up.

"Oh, we know," she said, with the seriousness of a doctor delivering a terminal diagnosis.

"Why do you think we made a beeline over here?" Ashley said, then quickly added, "Not that we weren't excited to see you anyway, but that kind of sped up our timeline for coming over here."

"You saw it?" Freya asked.

"Are you kidding?' Penny said. "Abby drink slapped you. Everyone saw it."

"Everyone," Ashley confirmed.

*Good.* Then she remembered Abby's giggle. Abby's proclamation that she finally got to show everyone—what? No, it didn't matter.

Penny turned her attention back to Will and the bartender. "I wish I could say I was shocked, but I'm not."

"Not in the slightest," Ashley continued. "If I were on the reunion committee, I can tell you that I would have lost her invitation, that's for sure. It seemed inevitable that she was going to do something to try to ruin this for you."

"Guess I dodged a bullet, then," the bartender said, collecting a few empty glasses that had accumulated on the bar. "I was about to give her my number."

"I was about to give my number to Abby's friend too," Will said. "Things went, um, south, before I could."

Freya's throat constricted so tightly, she let out a little cough. The idea that her most trusted colleague could be dating Abby's best friend made her entire body cringe. Tonight had been her chance to put this chapter of her life to rest. Instead, she had nearly given it a case of Red Bull.

"Okay, what?" Ashley said.

"Um, no." Penny pointed at the bartender, then to Will. "And no."

"No?" Will repeated, with a soupçon of disappointment.

"Weren't you listening?' Ashley said. "Yappy chihuahua's fleas? *That's* Naomi."

"I'm sure Naomi is a perfectly nice human being," Penny insisted with a wave of her hand. "But if she's stayed friends with Abby all these years, and it seems she has, imagine what kind of Stockholm Syndrome she must be living with."

"Wait a minute," Ashley said, when Penny paused to take a breath. "If you were going to get Naomi's number, then that means you and Freya aren't here together." She ping-ponged her eyes between the two of them.

"Us? No, no, no," he said so quickly that Freya could see Penny and Ashley's eyebrows begin to lift.

Freya laughed reassuringly. "You think I'd bring a date in a T-shirt?" she asked, gesturing to his Dunder Mifflin shirt. She hoped her comment wouldn't land too poorly on Will. He knew she barely tolerated his insistence on wearing graphic tees but he also knew barely tolerating was more than she would do for anyone else in the office.

Ashley and Penny mimicked her laugh.

"No, of course not," Penny said, though she clearly meant otherwise. For all their talk of Abby being jealous, those two had always been on the lookout to claim the throne. It wouldn't surprise her if Penny and Ashley hadn't been busy engaging in some 'goss' about her and Will before coming over here.

"Will is my Associate Producer," she said, applying a sprinkle of her on-camera voice. She wanted to make sure that they and anyone else listening heard her clearly. "We're heading out to London tonight for the G7 Summit right after I accept this award. He offered to wait in the car, but I said he should come in and have a few drinks."

Penny and Ashley shrank just the tiniest bit, enough to reinforce to Freya that they knew that she was, in fact, still the biggest dog around.

"Speaking of the award," she opened her purse and rustled around for a moment before continuing, "I need to head over to the stage. But it was a highlight to see you both. We should catch up soon! Lena, it was wonderful meeting you." She extended her arm and handed her a tip, a single folded bill.

Lena accepted it and then looked down. "Did you mean to—ma'am this is a hundred dollars."

Freya was already walking away; her fingers dancing a goodbye before anyone could say another word. She hoped the tip would help stop, or at least shape, whatever story the three women were probably already posting about.

With each step away from the bar, she began to feel more like herself again. Abby, Ashley, Penny ... they were from another lifetime. What had she been thinking, giving Abby even a second of her time? She hadn't really. When the woman who had been monopolizing the bar turned around and it was Abby, Freya had experienced a loss of control. Her high school self slid into the driver's seat and pressed the pedal to the floor. Being transported to that girl again, with her skin buzzing like an electric fence, was exhilarating, and a waste of time. She wasn't that person anymore, and she had more important things to do than spend one more brain cell on something that didn't matter from so long ago.

Despite his long legs, Will nearly had to jog to keep up with her. "Your friends seemed ... nice," he said, his voice rising at the end into an almost question.

She gave a dismissive shake of her head. "They were right about one thing: they haven't changed one iota. They're still as shallow as a kiddie pool."

"I mean they're your friends, so I wasn't going to say it, but ... yeah. I mean, who says 'the goss'?"

Something about that made her smile. It must have been bad if the genuinely nice guy could make fun of them. "They were good friends to have in high school."

She assumed the conversation was over, but Will said

hesitantly, "You think they were right about Naomi too? She seemed pretty ... amazing."

Freya forced herself to keep walking, to keep looking forward. "I don't know, but it's too late now, anyway, isn't it?"

"Yeah, I guess so. It's too bad. She seemed like something special."

# Chapter 3
## *Abby*

HELLO MY NAME IS ABIGAIL MEYER.

Bleary eyed, Abby stared at the crinkled name tag sticking to her arm. The letters jiggled and wobbled in her vision, like fruit stuck inside a Jell-O mold. She waited until the letters stopped dancing before trying to make out the clock beside her bed.

*6:58 a.m.*

She wondered why she was awake so early on a Saturday morning, and with a Macy's-Thanksgiving-Day-Parade-sized hangover marching through her head.

Her field of vision continued to expand as her brain powered up, allowing her to eventually get her answer in the shape of the tall, birdlike, frame of Riley Tahara at the foot of her bed. The soft morning light coming in from her bedroom window—contrasted with their black tight jeans, even tighter button-down shirt, and thick, black eye-liner—made their honey skin practically glow. A large red bag was slung over their shoulder and in their hands were two to-go cups of coffee.

"Good morning, love!" Riley grinned and gave an excited shimmy with their shoulders. "I brought you coffee!"

"Riley?" The word came out more like a croak. "What's going on?"

"What do you mean? I brought you coffee!" Riley held one out to her.

"At six in the morning?"

"It's almost seven; don't be so dramatic. Now wake up, sleepy head!"

"Go away. I'm dying." She knew it was too late. She was too aware of the pain in her body to go back to sleep. With a groan, she rolled over and pushed herself up to sit.

On the other side of the room, the mirror reflected something out of a sci-fi movie. With her body entangled in green chiffon, white tulle sprouting from different angles, and black eyeliner streaking across her pale face in every direction, she was pretty sure she'd seen an alien like it in an episode of *Dr. Who*.

"There you go," Riley leaned over the bed and handed her the coffee. "Drink up."

She took a sip and while her stomach roiled in protest, a few more synapses in her brain fired up. Memories of the evening flashed through her mind like a 1980s movie montage. The reunion. Freya. The drink. She looked at the coffee in her hands and then at Riley, "Oh, my God. She told you."

"Who? What? Told me what?" Riley placed a hand on their chest in a woefully unconvincing attempt to feign confusion.

Abby set her coffee down on the nightstand, tossed the blankets aside, stood up, and wobbled. Then she ambled, zombie-like, toward her front door. As she opened it, she snatched her keys from the hook by the door.

The rustling of her dress was drowned out by Riley following behind her, repeatedly calling her name. She ignored them and kept walking to the third door on the right, where a small, ornate, pink mezuzah was attached to the door frame. She lifted the key ring and squinted to focus her eyes enough to find the right one.

"Abby, let's talk about this," Riley pleaded. "There's no need to go in there. She's probably sleeping. Why bother her about something that isn't even a thing?"

The apartment door next to them squeaked open. Abby didn't need to turn to know that Mrs. Pachenkis, their elderly neighbor whose only hobbies seemed to be letting her cats escape from her apartment and calling in noise complaints to the building, wore a disapproving scowl.

Abby located the correct key, unlocked the door, briefly touched her fingers to the mezuzah and her lips, and stormed in.

The apartment was laid out exactly like hers. The front door opened into a spacious living room with two large windows at the far end that looked out at a small boulevard below. Directly to the right was a long hallway, with doors to the bathroom, bedroom, and the kitchen. Without hesitation, Abby walked down the hallway and straight into the bedroom, and turned on the light.

"You told them," Abby said, each word punctuated like a staccato pluck on a violin string.

Under a tangle of luxurious black curls and light blue sheets, Naomi let out a squeak of protest. She rolled over enough to peer out at Abby and Riley from under her arm. "What is happening right now?"

Abby remained in the doorway, but she could feel Riley hovering behind her. "Riley broke into my apartment and woke me up in the middle of an ungodly hangover sleep because of you. So, now you are facing the consequences."

Riley let out a small gasp. "I did *not* break in."

Abby glanced over her shoulder at Riley. "Did I invite you in?"

They paused to straighten their wheat-colored bow tie, then said softly, "What am I, a vampire? You gave me keys. I assumed that was an invitation."

Abby's hazel eyes made a full rotation along the edge of her eyelids. "I gave you my key last week because Naomi and I were both out of town, and I needed you to feed the cat."

"Yes, and I made a copy then. You know, for emergencies."

Abby waved her hand towards Naomi. "Please, enlighten Naomi as to what the *emergency* was that brought you into my apartment at 6:58 a.m. On a Saturday."

"I never got to say what it was because you were busy jumping to conclusions about God knows what."

"I know what," Abby interjected.

"As I was *saying,*" Riley said. "I needed to tell you that I'm in love. It happened last night. I stayed late at work doing some last-minute fittings for a Fassi runway show we're doing next week." When Abby looked back at them, a playful smile danced across their thin lips.

Riley was the creative director at the headquarters of Fassi, a popular chain clothing store that promised: "Couture Not

Cost." While this position still meant more data entry than designing, they occasionally got the chance to—as Riley put it— "play with fabric swatches and models," which made the position tolerable. "Then I stayed even later doing ... was it Ethan? No, Evan. Well, whatever his name was, he was a Greek god, wrapped in a Roman god, smothered in the nectar of the gods."

Abby whirled around, rocking slightly on unsteady feet. "That was last week, and his name was Eric."

Riley inspected their well-manicured fingernails and mumbled, "I mean, fine, maybe I also wanted to hear more about how you Real Housewife'd a star."

Abby faced Naomi again. "Like I said, you told them."

Naomi wriggled herself into a sitting position, tucking her sheet under her arms. Her jaw shifted a millimeter. To the untrained observer, it would be a meaningless gesture, but Abby knew it meant Naomi was biting down on the tip of her tongue to keep a straight face.

"I see it, Naomi! I see you biting your tongue. The jig is up. Admit that you told Riley."

Naomi threw her head back in defeat. "Riley! You swore you wouldn't say anything!"

Riley jutted their chin out indignantly. "I didn't! I showed up with coffee. I handed Abby the coffee. Literally the most innocent and friendly thing a person can do."

"Let me get this straight," Abby said to her. "You're yelling at Riley for not keeping a secret when you swore to me last night you wouldn't tell a soul?" The ride back from the reunion had sobered her up just enough to realize that throwing drinks wasn't her proudest moment and definitely wasn't something she needed anyone else to know about.

Besides her entire graduating class, of course. That seemed like more than enough people for a lifetime.

"Says the woman who used her spare keys to break into my apartment because she's mad that Riley used theirs to break into hers." Naomi looked more amused than she should.

"Ah ha!" Riley swung an arm around and pointed a finger at her. "J'accuse!"

Abby opened her mouth in protest, but nothing came out.

Naomi was visibly trying really hard not to laugh as she spoke. "I'm sorry, okay? But I had to tell someone. It was killing me!"

"Laughing while you apologize is not super convincing."

"It's hard to do anything properly without coffee," Naomi said, swinging her legs out of bed. "Can I please go make some before we continue this?"

"Yes." The mention of coffee reminded Abby of the throbbing in her, well, everything. "Please go make some."

"Oh no, you don't. No more delays," Riley said. "There is perfectly good coffee in Abby's apartment that I brought specifically to facilitate this conversation. Naomi, you can have mine. Let's get a move on."

Ignoring their death stares and whining, Riley shooed the two out of Naomi's apartment and down the hall. "Come on now, chop chop," Riley called to them from behind, clapping their hands.

Naomi scurried towards Abby's door, pulling down on the oversized T-shirt that barely covered her tanned thighs. "You could have at least let me change first!" she protested. The commotion brought Mrs. Pachenkis to her door again— or maybe she had never left.

When they were herded into Abby's apartment, Riley closed the door and whipped around to face them with tornado-like speed. "Story. Now."

Naomi walked toward the sofa. As she passed Riley, she glared at them defiantly. She was barely over five feet tall and had to drop her head to her back to meet their gaze.

Riley, in turn, had to nearly touch their chin to their chest to present Naomi with their offended face. "What?" they demanded.

"You are in so much trouble," Naomi said, plopping onto Abby's sofa and pulling a blanket over her lower half. "This doesn't seem like appropriate behavior on Shabbat." She pouted.

"You're right," Abby said. Naomi's Judaism, like Abby's, had evolved over the years. It was one of Abby's favorite things about Judaism—everyone's relationship with being Jewish was personal and unique. In Naomi's case, she continued to fully embrace the faith she had been raised with, although much more casually than her parents. Except for moments, like this, when she suddenly became much more observant. "Which is why you were home lighting candles instead of out drinking and cavorting last night."

"Cavorting!"

"Spoilers! You have to start at the beginning," Riley interrupted. They took a seat at the other end of the couch, leaning back and crossing their legs on the coffee table. They opened their mouth to speak, but their words turned into a gargle when Abby's cat, Lancelot, leapt onto their lap.

"No, no, Lancelot." She could hear Riley say as she walked into her room to get the two, now very lukewarm, cups of coffee. "I hate to rain on your parade, good looking, but I'm in all black and you're in all silver and never the twain shall meet."

Abby returned and handed Riley's cup to Naomi, then looked at Lancelot who was sitting on the coffee table, staring intently at Riley with his kelly-green eyes. "Are you tormenting Riley again?"

"Yes!" Riley replied.

"Good, get 'em," she said.

"Here, Lancey, come snuggle with me." Naomi patted her blanket. Lancelot's eyes flicked toward her but locked back onto Riley. Like all cats, he only wanted to be where he wasn't welcome.

"Enough distractions!" Riley said. They crossed their legs, pressed two fingers to their lips, and closed their eyes, a habit they had picked up after watching the Cumberbatch version of *Sherlock Holmes* "I'm ready. Fill me in."

Abby cut a sharp glance at them. Their eyes were still closed, but she glared anyway. "Freya emerged from the depths of the netherworld and started doing that same goddamn thing she did in high school, where she picks apart and belittles my entire life. And I was a few drinks in."

"A few?" Naomi stopped her. "I believe you told me you were four, *tequila* drinks in."

Riley's eyes flew open. "Oh, sweetie, you've never been able to handle your tequila."

"I'm aware." Abby pressed her palms to her temples. "So yes, my tequila-soaked brain made a less than stellar decision. A decision I'm comfortable putting away in a vault and not talking about ever again. But if we're locking it all in a vault, then I get to add how amazing it was, that after all these years, I *finally* got to put Freya in her place. For the first time in my life, I left her speechless. It felt so good. And now we close the vault door forever."

"You can sleep soundly knowing that you have made many seasons of reality television stars very proud," Riley said. "And now that I am comfortably sated in my need for gossip, I decree it is time to go shopping."

"I really need to work today," Naomi told them.

"On a Saturday? What kind of totalitarian regime do you work for?"

"An accounting firm in the middle of the busy season."

Riley clucked their tongue. "Naomi, the three of us—we've gone through something big together. Fingers were pointed and lies were stripped away. Now we need to heal. There's no better way than through shopping."

"I really should—"

"Excellent! I'm glad we're agreed on that."

"I'm sorry," Abby said. "Do I not get a say in this shopping trip? I could have plans. Or work."

"Abigail Meyer, I know you well enough to know that you would never book clients during the sacred hours reserved for hangovers and the walk of shame. Besides," they said, their dark eyes taking on an amused sparkle. "I peeped your calendar when I met you at your office for lunch yesterday, so I know you've got nothing planned."

～

AFTER A FEW MORE CUPS OF coffee, they were ensconced in a boutique clothing shop on Milwaukee Avenue. Naomi immediately went to the jewelry section. Riley mined every corner of the store while Abby absently inspected a rack of shirts, a well-worn shopping ritual that she and Riley had established years ago.

Abby had met Riley in college, and they quickly had their own established *things*: their own way of communicating, their own jokes, and definitely their own rituals. Like this one. It wasn't that Abby didn't enjoy shopping, but this was not "shopping." This was "shopping with Riley," which really meant "watching Riley shop and admiring their choices."

After a late-night *Sister Wives* marathon, Riley joked that the situation is eerily similar to theirs and Naomi's with Abby—each having a relationship with Abby while having relationships with each other and the group as a whole. In response, she'd punched them in the arm, but moments like this made her secretly agree. Although she had *things* with Riley, Naomi always belonged, and vice versa.

Naomi held a pair of silver hoop earrings to her cheeks. "Feels?"

Abby looked up at her, unable to keep the gnawing question to herself any longer. "What do you think she meant, 'this is exactly how I imagined it?'"

"What who meant?"

"Freya. You were there. She said, 'this is exactly how I imagined it.'"

Naomi put the earrings down. "I mean ... does it really matter?"

Abby pursed her lips. "No, you're right. It doesn't matter."

Naomi nodded and reached for another pair of earrings.

"Except," Abby continued. "She makes it sound like she's been harboring this fantasy about me growing up to be some sad, friendless, cat lady. I mean, who does that? How immature."

Naomi leaned forward to inspect a necklace.

"And," Abby continued, "apparently, I managed to live up to whatever it was she's been picturing all these years. Right? Isn't that what that means? 'This is exactly how I imagined it?' But I'm not some sad, friendless cat lady. I'm proud of who I am. I'm a successful therapist who owns my practice, I have plenty of friends, and seriously, the internet wouldn't exist without cats, so the whole cat lady thing needs to be put to rest."

"Exactly," Naomi confirmed, turning back to face Abby. "You're an amazing person, and you should be proud of what you've accomplished."

"Right, but she doesn't know any of that." Abby's eyes squeezed together into a squint. "As far as she knows, I'm *exactly how she imagined.*"

"Okay, so maybe that's true. Not to open the vault again, but an hour ago, you said throwing a drink at her righted those wrongs. That you finally got to," —she held up air quotes, —"'put her in her place.'"

Abby shifted uncomfortably and tugged at her necklace, a small, silver Star of David that had been a Bat Mitzvah gift from her Bubby. "Yeah."

"But?"

"But, did I? Really? She probably thinks I threw the drink on her because she was right." A frustrated rumble emanated from Abby's throat. "Except she's *not.* And meanwhile, she's nothing like I ..."

"Like you imagined?" Naomi finished for her.

Abby's eyes narrowed, but she didn't argue.

"You couldn't have been totally surprised by her. She's kind of ... famous."

Abby made a sound between a gurgle and a gag. "Famous for like, people my mom's age, famous maybe. She's a journalist on TV. I mean, who even watches TV to get their news anymore except people our parents' age?"

"About our parents watching Kent James? No, but that doesn't mean she's not famous."

"I don't see HuffPo doing any *Top 10 Freya Jonsson Moments* lists."

Naomi slipped her phone from her back pocket and googled Freya's name. "I think she's a little bigger than Buzzfeed. Here, look," she said, reading off her Wikipedia page. "She's won two Emmys for her coverage of the Syrian refugee crisis. She wrote a New York Times bestselling book called *She Speaks*—"

"Oh my God." Naomi looked up to see Abby on her own phone now. "She has 4.2 *million* followers on Instagram? How—"

"I told you. She's *famous*."

Abby draped herself over a rack of clothing. "All these years, I've lived in my happy little bubble, getting my news from *The Skimm* and Twitter headlines. How was I supposed to know karma was completely slacking off?"

A piano version of "Poor Unfortunate Souls" emanated from Abby's purse and her already stormy expression darkened a few shades more. Naomi had helped Abby pick out that ringtone, so she also knew it meant Abby's sister was calling. There's always a crisis when it comes to Becca.

"Hello?" Abby answered. "Hello?" she said again, with an added snarl, before abruptly hanging up.

"Pocket dial?" Naomi asked.

As if in response, the phone lit up in Abby's hand. She answered, not even bothering to say hello, and held the phone to Naomi's ear so she could also hear the hum of engines and the rhythmic rustle of phone against pocket. After a few seconds, Abby took the phone back and hit the red icon to end the call.

Instantly, it was active again and beckoning her to answer.

"I swear on all that is good and holy," Abby moaned.

Forcefully, she jabbed at her phone, declining the call, and then poked several times to pull up her contacts. With one angry tap, she initiated the call.

A honey-sweet voice answered, "Hello dearest sister of mine!"

"Rebecca, can you please, for the love of God, lock your phone? Or at least, change my name so that I'm not your first contact? You pocket dialed me again!"

"Honestly, Abby, I don't see why you hate it so much that you get pocket dialed all the time," Rebecca chirped into the phone.

"Well, do you have any idea how annoying it is to have a seventeen-minute message from the inside of someone's pants?"

Curiosity got the best of Naomi, and she mouthed the word "speaker" at Abby. It was no secret she liked being on the sidelines of the Abby and Becca show too.

Abby obliged, holding out her phone and turning it on speaker.

"Someday, you'll get a pocket dial, and it will be someone plotting to rob a bank, or someone getting murdered," Becca was saying. "Or at the very least, someone having sex. Isn't that possibility worth it? It would be worth it to me."

"I accept your apology."

"I am not apologizing for what my phone did without my knowledge."

Abby's head dipped down, and she propped her forehead against her fingers.

"Although," Becca said, with added pep, "this does work out perfectly, since I was planning on calling you anyway."

"Where are you? It sounds like you're standing in the middle of a runway."

"I might as well be. I'm over in Bucktown."

Abby checked the time on her phone. "Bucktown? What are you doing there at 10:30 in the morning on a Saturda— oh, please tell me you weren't doing what I think you were doing."

Becca hesitated before responding with a mousy, "Umm ..."

"Becca!" Abby scolded loudly. Several customers turned to glance in their direction. Naomi smiled apologetically at them. "You told me you ended it with him! I thought you were on the straight and narrow!"

"I was," her sister exclaimed. "But then I met Amos. He's a dancer for the Joffrey Ballet. You'd love him, Abby."

"Does the wedding band on your finger mean nothing to you?"

"Sure it does! Just ... not ... all the time."

In nearly every respect, the Meyer sisters had nothing in common. Abby liked chocolate, Becca liked vanilla. Abby liked cats, Becca liked dogs. Abby liked red wine, Becca liked white. Abby liked girls, Becca liked boys. It seemed the only thing they did share was a dogged confidence in the things they liked and an indefatigable will to pursue them.

When it came to pursuing boys, Becca had jumped right in at the ripe age of three, when she toddled home from preschool announcing that she had a boyfriend. That relationship, like all those afterward, lasted only a few weeks before she was on to the next, and most people, including Abby, assumed that this would be a lifelong pattern for Rebecca—until five years ago when, without warning, she came home sporting an engagement ring the size of the moon on her finger.

Abby suspected that Becca's recent graduation from college had been the reason behind the engagement, and that in the face of impending adulthood, Becca had turned to the only thing she really knew how to do well: find a man. The man who she had found was Peter Rhein, CFO of Lynch Mortuary Services, one of the nation's largest funeral home supply companies. While his profession, personality, and small stature were a complete one-eighty from Rebecca's usual type, Abby always assumed it was his large bank account and blind adoration of Rebecca that attracted her to him. Everyone liked Peter, and they had all hoped that his devotion and unlimited credit would be enough to keep Becca faithful to him. It had taken less than six months for her to fall off the wagon, although Abby wondered if she had ever really been on it at all.

Lost in apparel bliss, Riley was the only one in the shop who had failed to notice Abby's earlier outburst and they beckoned to her, from where they were buried under a mound of clothes.

"Ready," they sang with delight before bounding toward the dressing room.

"Coming," Abby sang back.

"Who are you talking to?" Becca asked.

"Riley," she answered, heading to the dressing area.

"Who is she talking to?" Riley asked Naomi before stepping into a small booth and sliding the curtain shut.

"Becca," Naomi said, as she and Abby took a seat on a small bench across from Riley's dressing room.

"Is that Naomi I hear too?" Becca asked. "Where are you all?"

"We're in Wicker Park," Abby said. "And you're lucky; if you had woken me up with this news—"

"Wicker Park!" Becca exclaimed. "That's perfect!"

"Apparently," Naomi said, continuing to talk to Riley, "she was out philandering with another one of her—"

"Wait, what's perfect?" Abby cut in.

"You! Being in Wicker Park!" Becca said. "Cause I told Peter I was out with you and—"

"You what?" Abby shouted, this time receiving a warning glance from the cashier.

Riley poked their head out from behind the curtain. "Wait, she was out with another one of her boy toys? I thought she was going to—"

"So did I!" Abby said. Riley *tsked* in disapproval and vanished behind the curtain again.

"From the sounds of it," Naomi added, "she's not only back to it, she wants to use us as an alibi."

"What!" Riley shrieked.

"No!" Becca exclaimed. "It's not like that. I told Peter I was going to hang out with Abby. I didn't say when or where or for how long. So, I want to see you for a few minutes. At least that way I won't be lying. I'd feel so guilty otherwise."

"Your sense of morality is a shining light in this dark world," Abby said, rubbing the visibly taut muscles at the nape of her neck.

Riley pulled back the curtain to reveal a pair of tight, yellow pants. They cocked their head, waiting for Abby's response. Abby could tell by the look on their face that they didn't like the pants. Abby responded accordingly.

"I don't know. These pants don't say," Abby searched her barely functioning brain for the appropriate outlandish phrase, "deity of the sun to me."

Riley contemplated, tapping their finger against their chin.

"Hmmm ... goddess of the sun, goddess of the sun..." they repeated, inspecting themselves in the mirror. "You're right, I am not a goddess of the sun in these pants."

Abby tapped mute on her phone and looked at Naomi. "I've officially hit that hangover zone where I'm caffeinated, exhausted, hungry, and nauseous at the same time. I literally cannot with her today."

Naomi put an arm around her and gave a squeeze. "I think it's in your best interest to get some food and give in to your sister. Tell her to join us for brunch."

Abby let out a sigh that sounded like a balloon losing air. She unmuted the call. "Okay, fine, Becca. We're going to get brunch, and you can come."

"Yay!" Becca exclaimed.

"Meet us at Tragically Hip on Milwaukee." Abby rotated her head to get a better view of the pile of clothes Riley had taken with them. "From the looks of it, we'll be here for a while. So please ... don't rush." Abby ended the call and dropped her head into her hands with a moan.

"When Becca gets here, I am going to give her a piece of my mind about this whole affair business," Riley said over the rustle of clothes being removed. "Don't get me wrong, I'm all for a little extramarital excitement, but only when I'm the extra in the marital. Either that girl needs to end it with Peter, or get her thruple on, because sneaking around is ridiculous. And frankly, it's stressing me out, and I am not willing to waste my limited facial elasticity on her."

"I think you telling my sister to have a threesome is not really the best route to take here. How about you let me handle it?"

"You're acting like she would listen to either of you," Naomi said.

"Touché."

As long as Abby could remember, her younger sister had used her beauty, intelligence, and resourcefulness to neglect developing skills like responsibility and a moral compass. It seemed that no matter how bad the situation, Becca somehow managed to masterfully pilot her way out and emerge unscathed. It didn't seem to matter if she was late for the twentieth time or never called you back or even if she was the one who hit your car. All she had to do was look at you with her big eyes, smile sweetly and say ...

"Oh, you are such a darling, Abigail. What would I do without you?"

Abby looked up to see Becca gliding toward them. Rebecca Rhein was six years younger than Abigail and, for all intents and purposes, identical to her sister. Despite being the same height, shape, and similar skin tone, Becca somehow managed to wear her attributes differently and come off looking smaller, curvier, and perkier than Abby ever had at any point in her life.

Becca was clothed in a sequined tank top, a short denim mini-skirt, and black, knee-high boots. She flung herself onto the dressing room bench next to Abby and exhaled. "What a day it's been! Not quite what I was hoping for so far, but now that I'm here with you, I think it's starting to turn around, don't you?" She looped her arm around her sister's.

"Hello, Naomi!" Rebecca leaned toward Riley's dressing room. "Hello, Riley!"

"Hello, love!" they called back. A moment later, the curtain flew open, and Riley emerged wearing a black, fishnet, long-sleeved shirt. Their eyes sparkled with delight.

"Oh, look at you!" Rebecca said before Abby could get in a word. She shot up from her seat and circled Riley enthusiastically. "You skinny thing! Only you could pull something like this off. I mean, honestly!"

Riley was soaking up every word like a dry sponge, and Naomi could literally see their plans of speaking their mind drowning in her compliments. They clapped their hands with glee. "You think so?"

"Oh, absolutely! You have to get it!"

"Done!" Riley announced, sliding the curtain closed.

Her work complete, Rebecca returned to her seat next to Abby. "How do we all feel about mimosas?"

"I'm in!" Riley called out. "I want to celebrate finding the perfect shirt."

Rebecca turned to her sister, eyelashes fluttering.

"Sure," Abby agreed with the zeal of a full-fledged curmudgeon.

"Great!" Becca exclaimed, clasping her hands in delight. "Oh, but would it be possible for you to spot me? I think I left my wallet at Amos'. Awkward!"

"Oh, that's the awkward part?" Abby looked at Naomi for approval of her zinger, but Naomi was staring at her phone like it was a traffic accident. "You okay, Naomi?"

Naomi looked up and then wordlessly handed her phone to Abby. She looked down at a string of texts from an unknown number. The first two words made her feel like Sandra Bullock in *Gravity,* as if she were tumbling untethered through space with no safety line.

> UNKNOWN NUMBER: Hi Kiwi

There was only one person who called Naomi that.

The messages continued, piling on top of each other like Tetris blocks.

> Did you go to the reunion last night?

> I didn't but I kept thinking about it.

> Kept thinking about you.

> Thinking about all the good times back then. Remember when we won that dance contest?

> Wish I could have been there and danced with you one more time.

> I miss you. I know I shouldn't but I do.

> I know you miss me too.

She scrolled down to read the last one.

> I can see it in your eyes when I watch you.

Finally, Abby managed, "Oh my God."

"Ooh, what is it?" Becca asked, trying to get a look at the screen. "I need the tea."

Riley's face peeked out from the curtain. "Tea? What, what?"

"No gossip." Abby stood up and held the phone out. "Simon."

A bare arm snaked out from behind the curtain and grabbed the phone from Abby. Their eyes flitted across the screen. "Let's get out of here." Still clutching Naomi's phone, they dipped back into the changing room.

When Abby looked back at Naomi, her horrified look had been replaced by tears. It was her turn to put her arms around her friend's shoulders. "We'll meet you outside," Abby said to Riley. As Abby led Naomi out of the store and down the street, she sagged like a ragdoll in her arms. Abby set her down on a small bench nested under a maple tree.

"I know 'it's going to be okay' is the worst platitude in these moments," Abby said, running a hand along Naomi's back. "But it really is going to be okay. Not because of him, but because you're not alone. We're all here with you. Well, I don't know if Becca is ever really here for anything, but Riley and I are here." She hoped she'd made the right call by throwing in a little humor.

It seemed to work, because Naomi's sobs subsided

enough for a laugh. "Sorry," she said eventually, wiping her eyes. "I know I shouldn't let him get to me like this, especially not after all these years."

"Yes, I definitely think shaming yourself is the right call," Abby said.

Naomi let out another laugh-sob and then buried her face in her hands. "I wasn't expecting it, is all. I haven't heard from him in, what, six months? I had started to think that maybe ..." She bent over, wracked with more sobs.

"I know," Abby said softly, her own eyes brimming at the sight of her best friend's pain.

They sat together, not speaking, until the jingle of the boutique doors broke the silence.

"What?" Becca was saying as she and Riley exited the store. "You're not even going to get the shirt?"

"You know what they say, Becca," Riley replied. "Hoes before clothes."

"Who is this Simon? The name is not ringing a bell."

Riley sniffed. "And Abby says I'm the self-absorbed one."

"Riley!" Becca's voice rose to a sweet but desperate pitch. "Tell me!"

"Simon Phillips?" When Rebecca gave no response, Riley continued. "Does high school sweetheart, turned abusive and cheating husband, turned restraining-order ex-husband sound familiar?"

Abby looked up to see Rebecca, now only a few feet away, cock her head like a curious puppy. "High school sweetheart? Oh right! I remember him. Wait, they got married? And divorced?" Rebecca stepped in front of Riley to block their path. "So, what happened?"

Irritably, Abby stood and moved her out of the way. "We don't have time to indulge you right now, Becca!"

Riley took Abby's place beside Naomi. "You doing okay?"

She nodded, wiping at her damp cheeks. "I'm better. It caught me off guard."

They handed her phone back to her. "I searched the number. It came up right away on one of those text spoofing sites. There's no way to trace it to him."

"Of course," Abby said.

Without any proof that Simon was violating his Order of Protection, there was nothing they could do. They had been through this a dozen times since the divorce. Simon would disappear and then reappear exactly like this, out of nowhere, with vague threats. As an attorney, Simon knew the loopholes that would let him reach out to her in ways that beat the system. Each time, Naomi contacted the police. Each time, the police told her that their hands were tied for one reason or another.

Naomi let out a sigh.

"You know what you need?" Rebecca patted Naomi on the knee. "You need one night of really good sex. After that, you won't even be thinking about this loser; trust me."

"Rebecca," Abby said through gritted teeth, "I think you should—"

"Should what? Stop giving good advice? Please, Abigail," Rebecca said, propping herself up against the tree. "If there's anything I know about, it's boy troubles."

"And don't forget me," Riley added eagerly. "I mean, if you think about it, of the three of us, you're the only one without any boy experience. So really, it seems like Becca and I should take the lead here."

Rebecca nodded. "You know, Riley, you have a point there. The two of us—we're like the dream team of boy advice."

Riley brought their hands together in front of their chest. "You're right! We should have a podcast!"

"Yes! Oh my God, people would lose their minds. We could call it, um, Dicks for Days."

"Ooh! Cock O'Clock."

"Why not go simple and just call it Penis, Penis, Penis?"

"Okay, we'll figure out the name later. But regardless, Naomi, my co-host is correct. The only way to get over a boy is to get under another one. Or at least near one."

"I... uh ..." Naomi stammered. "I suppose ..."

"Trust me," Rebecca assured her in a clinical tone. "This is exactly what you need."

Naomi chewed on her lower lip and then glanced up at her friends.

"Uh-oh." Rebecca grinned. "I know that look. You've got someone in mind, don't you, you naughty girl? Who is it?" She leaned forward in anticipation.

"Well." Naomi hesitated. "I met this guy last night..."

Abby's jaw unhinged and swung open like a screen door. "Freya's minion?"

Naomi's face flushed in response.

Abby puffed out her cheeks, trying to stop her protestations from flying out of her mouth.

"Perfect!" Rebecca exclaimed. "Text him."

"That's the problem. He was reaching into his pocket to

give me his card. But that's when, well ..." She glanced at Abby. "Suffice it to say, things got a little crazy, and I never got his info. All I know is he works with Freya at *Nightly Global News*."

"Freya from *Nightly Global News*?" Rebecca said. "As in Freya Jonsson? As in *People*'s Sexiest Woman of the Year? As in the face that has brought many lonely people great happiness in their beds at night?"

"Yes, as in Abigail's archnemesis," Riley added.

Abby made a growling noise. "She is not my archnemesis."

"Wait a minute." Becca's brow furrowed as she began piecing together the information. "That's the same Freya? The girl from high school who she always used to complain about?"

"One and the same!"

"You never told me that you were friends with a celebrity!" Rebecca said to Abby, her eyes bulging.

"That's because I'm not," Abby grumbled.

"It doesn't matter anyway," Naomi said. "Like I told you —no number. I don't even know his last name."

"Naomi, Naomi," Rebecca chided. "Let me show you how it's done."

Rebecca had reached into her purse and pulled out her phone. After a few swipes, she nodded. "Here we go. *Nightly Global News*, main line." She tapped the phone and put it to her ear.

"Wait!" Naomi gasped, her face registering the terror of someone who realized the carnival ride had started and their seat belt wasn't working.

Rebecca made a show of clearing her throat and tossing

her hair back confidently. "Hello!" she said to someone on the other line. "I was hoping you could help me out."

Abby blinked, moderately impressed at Becca's professional tone. "Yes, I've been trying to get in touch with NGN's..." She put her hand over her phone and whispered, "Wait, what's his title?"

"Producer?" Naomi said haltingly. "No wait, associate producer. That was it."

"Associate producer," Becca repeated into the phone. She paused again and lowered the phone. "What's his name?"

"Will!" the entire group said in a whispered shout.

"Will. He works directly with Ms. Freya Jonsson," she said calmly into the phone. "Yes, Will Quinn. I believe that's him. He gave me his business card, but I seem to have misplaced it. I know it's Saturday and all, but this is a rather urgent matter regarding an upcoming interview."

Abby looked at her friends and saw they were as taken aback by Rebecca's performance as she was.

Rebecca paused and nodded. "Oh, you could, could you? That would be wonderful, thank you."

Another pause. Naomi, Abby, and Riley remained silent, staring.

Obviously relishing the attention, Rebecca pretended to ignore them by slipping a tube of lip gloss from her bag and applying a generous helping to her lips.

Riley was the first to give in. "What? What's happening?"

Rebecca smacked her lips and dropped the lip gloss back into her bag. "She's transferring me to his work cell. She said

—oh, hello! Is this Mr. Quinn? Yes, how are you today? This is Naomi Hoffman's personal assistant, Rebecca."

Panic-stricken, Naomi pleaded with her eyes to stop, but Rebecca only smiled mischievously. "You met Ms. Hoffman at the ... yes, the reunion last night." Becca winked at Naomi.

Riley leaned in toward Naomi. "Well, that's a good sign."

"Oh really?" Rebecca was saying into the phone. "I see. Well, Ms. Hoffman was wondering if you would be interested in having dinner sometime in the next ... Tuesday? Six o'clock? Could you hold one moment while I check her calendar?"

She looked up at Naomi who gave the barest of nods in confirmation.

With another theatrical flip of her hair, Rebecca returned to the conversation. "Yes, it looks like she is available during that time. Bella Luna. On Halsted. Of course. Yes, yes, thank you. Have a wonderful afternoon."

Hanging up, Rebecca tossed her phone into her purse and smiled.

"Becca ..." Riley said, their voice hushed in awe. "Personal assistant—it's brilliant. Abby will you be my personal —"

"No."

"Damn you."

Apparently exhausted from her show, Rebecca sighed heavily. "Well, dearest Naomi, Tuesday, six o'clock at the Bella Luna."

"Thank ... you," Naomi said, still trying to process everything.

"Oh, it was nothing," she said graciously. "I hardly had to

do anything. He's clearly smitten by you already. You heard me! I couldn't even finish my sentences."

"I don't think we talked enough to move to smitten ..."

"Trust me, I know when a boy is smitten. I also know when I am owed a drink for services rendered. Let's go."

# Chapter 4
## *Freya*

FREYA STOOD IN A DIMLY LIT ROOM, ONE HAND ON THE chair of the editor who sat in front of her. As she watched footage from her latest interview, she engaged in the time-honored dance of the high heels: lifting her left foot out of its shoe and wiggling her toes before slipping it into the shoe and switching to the other foot. These were sit-at-your desk, in-your-car, on-the-airplane, for-an-interview shoes. They were definitely not stand-in-an-editing-room-for-an-hour-and-talk-through-how-to-revamp-something-that-was-already-done shoes.

"Stop there." Freya pointed at one of the screens in front of her. The image froze on her, leaning forward as she prepared to ask a question. On screen, her frosty blue eyes, a gift from her Icelandic parents, locked solidly on the man sitting across from her as she prepared for her gotcha moment. She let out a sigh. "Let's take out everything up to that point. Then move this part back to the—"

"Section from the—yep—already on it." This was the first time Freya had worked with Janet, the paperclip-thin editor who had joined *Nightly Global News* only a few weeks ago, but this marathon session had bonded them like soldiers on the battlefield.

"If you decide to make a massive career shift and become a clairvoyant, I will absolutely pay $9.95 a minute for your mind-reading services."

Janet didn't look up as she said, "I'm pretty sure that's not a thing anymore."

"Let's just pretend it is and I'm not aging myself."

"You got it, boss."

There was a knock at the door, and a sliver of fluorescent light as someone inched it open.

"You in here?"

She knew it was Will even before he slipped his head through the crack to peer into the room.

"Under duress," she said. She gave Janet a collegial pat on the shoulder. "No offense."

"None taken," Janet said as her fingers flew over her keyboard.

"I definitely want more on that, but you're late to record promos for the Costa Rica segment," Will said, his unattached head still floating like a buoy in the doorway.

"Damn, really?" She wanted to be annoyed at the time crunch this edit had put her in, but her toes were tingling with anticipation at the mention of getting to sit for the next hour. "Okay. We're almost done here. Give me just two minutes."

"Here we go," Janet said as Will closed the door. "How's this?"

Janet replayed the video without the section that Freya had identified for the digital cutting room floor.

"That's perfect. I think we're good to go. And with the amount of time we were given, if Brian doesn't like it, he can ask his proctologist to go look for the better version," Freya said. She held up her hand in an invitational high five. "Teamwork makes the dream work!"

Janet reciprocated, though with some hesitation that suggested that she didn't want to be on record supporting anything referencing her boss's boss's rectal area.

There was another knock at the door.

"Yes! Coming!" Freya grabbed her stack of notes and stepped out into the quiet hallway. *Nightly Global News* was nestled on the 12th floor of the 42 story WNO Tower in Streeterville, steps from Lake Michigan and the popular Magnificent Mile. The World News Organzation, which had started as a radio station in the late 1920s, was now WNO, one of the largest entertainment groups in the world. It encompassed radio and television networks providing hundreds of hours of content a week. WNO Tower was the company headquarters, and it housed most of the business operations as well as studios for some of its most famous programming, including *Nightly Global News*. However, unlike nearly all the other programs filmed at the Tower, *Nightly Global News* had been allotted its own floor, giving them access to more resources and, Freya's favorite, fewer people.

Will stood outside the door. To the untrained observer, he might appear to be calmly waiting for her, but the slight upturn of his eyebrows told her he was anxious to get her to her next appointment.

"I know. I'm sorry," she said. "Let's move."

"What was that all about?"

"Ugh," she said both in response to his question and to her feet, which protested with each hurried step she took. "Brian stopped by my office an hour ago."

She probably didn't even need to say more. Will knew all too well that any time Brian, one of the show's executive producers, ambled out of his office, there were no happy endings. "He'd seen the interview with Governor Hadly and he said I couldn't include anything about the Amerilife Gas Pipeline on Native lands."

Will dropped out of lightspeed and looked at her. "You've got to be kidding me. That was fifty percent of the interview. And it was important. People need to know that he's going to—"

She held up a hand. "You don't have to tell me. Or him. Because I definitely did. But he said Amerilife is a part owner of WNO, which I appreciate him failing to mention to me before we went ahead with this story. So essentially that means that we can dig up whatever dirt we want on him, but not about that."

The muscles around Will's jaw twitched in frustration. "I'm feeling very conflicted right now," he said, which Freya knew was his polite way of releasing a fury of expletives.

"Nothing makes you feel better about your job than learning it's partially owned by a company that has a well-documented history of violating human rights around the world and being forced into protecting a civil servant who is doing the same thing, does it?" They had reached the door to the makeup room, and she pushed it open without pausing. "The good news is, it's over and done with. I've taken care of it. Bye bye, Amerilife. Hello, Mimi." She waved to the makeup artist who was leaning against a wall, tapping on her phone and sipping an iced coffee.

"Jonsson, you are late," Mimi, generally chipper and propelled by caffeine, said as she came over.

"I could have done the edits. You've got a full day," Will said.

Freya took her seat at Mimi's makeup chair and released an internal sigh of relief as she lifted her feet off the floor. "I've been doing the 'Placate the Cis Old White Men Upstairs' tap dance for years. I knew exactly what Brian wanted, I figured it would be faster to do it myself and get it over with." She kept her face still as Mimi wiped the makeup off and then applied a base coat of primer. "And we'll live to fight another day. Just not about this."

"I have no idea what you're talking about," Mimi said as she made quick brush strokes. "But I can confirm that the tap dance is real and sometimes a necessary survival skill."

In the mirror, Freya could see Will walk over to a seat in the corner and sit down with such force that the chair let out a squeak of protest. Freya simultaneously wanted to comfort him like she would a sad puppy and scold him like a misbehaving one; luckily, her situation afforded her the opportunity to do neither. It was sweet that he was upset, even more so that it was because the actual message in their work was about to be lost. At the same time, it was obnoxious that he was so taken aback by something that was a daily part of her life. There were Brians and Amerilifes around every corner. She'd spent her life learning to navigate them, not pouting about it in corners.

"Speaking of a full day," she said, changing the subject.

"Talk me through tomorrow. Are we good to go with the prime minister?"

He nodded. "Security checks are complete, and I confirmed with her team this afternoon. We're set to arrive at 1930 hours, which I pretended to know, and then looked up later."

"7:30 p.m.," Freya said.

He gave her a single-finger gun. "Correctomundo."

"So, we'll leave from here at 6:45?"

His expression reorganized into something resembling dismay.

"You think a little earlier?" she said, trying to guess the source of his distress. "You're probably right, we need to give ourselves some wiggle room with traffic."

He leaned forward, resting his elbows on his knees. "I was thinking we would go separately and meet there."

"Why, if we're both leaving from the office? That's more time wasted if they have to sweep two cars."

He hemmed. "I kind of have ... something right before."

She watched his reflection. "Something?"

"Yes, a, um, date."

"Oh, details, please. That's more interesting than prime minister schedules," Mimi said, her burnt orange lips inches from Freya's face. "Close your eyes."

"There are really no details," Will said. "She and I met only briefly, but we hit it off and are going on a first date."

"There are always details," Mimi said. "Where did you meet? Who asked who out? What did you like about her?"

"We met at ..." his voice trailed off.

Freya stared into the blackness of her lids and tried to follow the thread of his discomfort. While she never talked about her personal life with him, she also never discouraged him from talking about his. In fact, his anecdotes about bad dates and broken hearts had gotten them through long flights and late nights. She enjoyed hearing about his romantic escapades, and as far as she knew, at least up until now, he enjoyed talking about them. What about this particular situation could be causing him to suddenly clam up? Why would he be uncomfortable talking about a woman he barely knew …

Her eyelids flew open like a set of broken window shades. "You're going on a date with Naomi?"

Mimi trilled with interest. "Ooh, Naomi? Who is that? Close your eyes, Jonsson. We're short on time here."

She couldn't see Will, but his uncomfortable groan was enough to confirm her suspicions. "She called me. Her assistant did, actually. Called the front desk, I guess. Anyway, she wanted to know if I wanted to go out—and I said yes. I don't know, it seemed like a good idea in the moment. Afterward, I started panicking because I remembered what everyone was saying and about what happened and now I—"

Mimi laughed. "Slow down, hon, I feel like I missed an episode and now I need a 'previously on' recap. And Jonsson, relax a little. I can't get this eyeliner on when you're scrunching your eyes like that."

It wasn't only her face that she was wrinkling. It felt like her entire circulatory system had stopped any blood from flowing through her body. Will, to Naomi, to … Abby. The splash of cheap tequila, that triumphant laughter, her gleeful declaration that she had shown everyone … *what?* Memories of Friday night washed over her like high tide. There wasn't supposed to be a need for a "previously on"—Friday was supposed to be the series finale. But Will was going on a date with Naomi. A date could mean more dates; it could mean *dating*. It could mean getting to know Naomi's friends. It could mean that Will, her favorite associate producer, her friend, could find himself in Abby's crosshairs, like the scorpion and the frog, destined to be poisoned because as she had shown, a scorpion cannot change its nature.

She gripped the armrests of her makeup chair and took her best yoga cleansing breath. If she could handle Brian and Amerilife with aplomb, she could certainly handle Will and ... Naomi.

"That's better," Mimi said to Freya, then directed her voice at Will. "Tell me about Naomi."

"We met, briefly, at a thing. Then, another thing, happened," Will said with so many pauses it sounded like he was making a William Shatner impression. "And she had to leave before I could give her my number."

"That's a lot of ... things. But I think I'm following, sort of. Then she found you; that's kinda cute, right?"

"I thought so. But her friend and Freya have kind of this, well, thing."

"There are so many things flying around. This story is turning into a Dr. Seuss book."

"There's no *thing*," Freya interjected sharply, eyes still closed. This was exactly what she had wanted to avoid. This one date was turning into a rumor breeding ground for her staff. She needed to get ahead of the story and, thankfully, that was something she was good at. "We bumped into some of my friends from high school on Friday. That's where Will met Naomi, and I learned that my high school girl squad was still stuck in high drama mode. They were trying to dig up gossip about Naomi to scare off Will. It was pathetic, honestly, don't you think, Will?" Mimi had moved to her lips, so Freya opened her eyes. Will was staring intently back at her.

"Uh, right. Exactly," he said.

"What is it with some people getting stuck in high school? The best time of your life is being a pimply bag of raging hormones in a sea of confused half-adults? I will never understand it," Mimi said. She stepped back to inspect her work on Freya, and it seemed she was entirely off the scent. Until she looked up. "You're still going to see her, this Naomi, right? To decide for yourself?"

"I guess, if it's okay with ..." Will looked at Freya.

Freya looked at herself in the mirror and summoned her most pleasant but disinterested smile. "Of course, why would it matter to me if you see her? And it's no problem; I'll plan to pick you up after your date on the way to the interview."

*It doesn't matter*, she assured herself. What Will did with his personal life, in his own time, didn't affect her. Even if dates led to dating, and then to spending time with Abby, that didn't change anything. It's not like *she* would be spending time with Abby. That part of her life was officially and completely over.

# Chapter 5
## *Abby*

BECCA: Soooooooo...

ABBY: So?

RILEY: What Abby said

BECCA: So what time are we meeting at the restaurant?

ABBY: Restaurant...?

RILEY: I once again second what Abby said

BECCA: OMG seriously? To the Bella Luna. Naomi's date tonight?

RILEY: I'm well aware of Naomi's date. I helped pick out her dress.

BECCA: I want to see how it goes.

RILEY: OHHHH. I like how you think.

ABBY: What?! What is happening right now? No one is crashing Naomi's date. Who even does that?

BECCA: We do.

ABBY: Who is the WE in this sentence? And WHY would we do that?

BECCA: The we is us. Well definitely me. As for the why, I got them together and now I want to see what happens. Besides, I'm bored.

RILEY: It's incredibly hard to argue with that logic.

ABBY: Actually it's super easy. You say NO.

BECCA: Well I'm going sooo the rest of you can do whatever you want.

ABBY: Becca—seriously. You are not crashing Naomi's date.

Becca

Becca.

REBECCA

Muting the conversation won't stop me from killing you.

59

RILEY: Question. Will this murder be taking place at the Bella Luna? That'll be a double feature for me. Not that I want you to go to prison for murder. But if you have to, I'd like to be there. For support.

ABBY: Exsqueeze me? Do you think you're going to be spying on Naomi tonight?

RILEY: Ummmm ... yes?

ABBY: Ummmm ... no?

RILEY: Ummmm ... you get to go and I don't?

ABBY: If I go, it would only be to stop her from going.

RILEY: I'm not clear on why that means I don't get to go.

ABBY: If you show up, then I'm going to post that photo I took of you on our road trip to Quebec.

RILEY: ...

ABBY: Clear?

RILEY: As a Scientologist.

IT WASN'T UNTIL SHE WAS STANDING IN FRONT OF THE Bella Luna, disguised in large white Jackie O sunglasses and a wide-brimmed hat, that Abby was confident that she was going to crash her best friend's date.

Sliding her sunglasses down her nose, Abby peered at her reflection in the restaurant window and adjusted the brim of her dark blue hat. It was Riley who had mentioned to her that since she had recently accosted Will's boss, there was a good chance he would recognize her and a disguise might be in order. She knew the best way to avoid recognition was to spend the evening anywhere except the Bella Luna, but she also knew that that wasn't an option. Instead, she went with a big, floppy hat.

Pulling the brim down over her face, Abby checked the time on her phone. It was half past five, exactly as she had planned. Earlier in the day, she had decided that if Becca wanted to arrive a few minutes before Naomi, then she needed to arrive a few minutes before Becca, allowing her the upper hand, and the opportunity to pick the most discreet table. Inhaling the inviting scent coming from inside, Abigail pushed the door open and walked through.

Association to Freya aside, she was begrudgingly impressed with Will—or at least impressed with his taste in women and his choice in dining locations. The Bella Luna had always been one of her favorite city restaurants: a hole-in-the-wall tucked away on a busy street. Although not particularly noticeable on the outside, the its charm was in its warm and relaxing atmosphere, inspiring decorations, and of course, heavenly food.

"One?" the hostess asked.

"Uh, no. There will be two—but I'm a little early. If you wouldn't mind, I would like to sit over, um ..." Abby scanned the room for the most hidden, most out of the way, most inconspicuous table. Instead, her eyes fell on the auburn hair of a young woman sitting directly in the middle of the restaurant.

Instinctively, her fingers went to her temples as she tried to rub away the oncoming headache. "It seems my companion has arrived already."

She motioned toward Becca and then followed the hostess to the table. Rebecca, who had been tapping away at her phone, looked up at Abby.

Abby dropped her purse on the ground and settled into a seat, unsure whether to be furious or depressed. She decided to go with a little of both. "What are you doing here already?"

Becca let out a smug giggle. "I knew that if you were coming, you'd try to get here earlier. So, I came earlier than you."

"Uh-huh," Abby said. "That's great, Becca, but we're going."

"You're welcome to excuse yourself, but I'm staying."

"Oh my God. Then can we at least move? This spot is too out in the open."

"Of course, it is! It's perfect. We'll be able to see everything, no matter where they sit. You can move if you want, but I'm staying right here. That's a nice hat, by the way."

Abby's body shuddered like a shaken soda bottle about to explode, and Becca tilted her head, as if daring her sister to lose composure. Right then, the waitress stepped up to their table to take their drink order. Abby exhaled loudly and ordered a vodka tonic, knowing that it would be the first of many.

At a little past six and two drinks in, Becca flicked her eyes toward the door and grinned. "Is that our boy?"

Attempting to be subtle, Abby rotated her head a few degrees and looked out from under her hat. The familiar angular frame of Freya's associate producer was visible at the front. He was dressed in jeans and a pink button-down shirt, accented nicely with a thin gray tie. He spoke softly to the host, who gestured toward a table. As his eyes followed the host's direction, Abby whirled around and propped her elbow up on the table, using her hat to cover her face.

Becca sipped her water and watched him from over her glass. "It's him, huh? Not too bad! A little too plain Midwestern boy for my tastes, of course. I mean, jeans on a first date?" She clucked her tongue in disapproval. "But I'll give him extra points for pulling off pink."

"Okay, you've seen him now. Can we please go?" Abby whispered, keeping her head down and turned away.

"Go? Before I've even seen them together? Not a chance. Besides, I don't have anything to do until nine tonight. Brandon is going to give me a private showing of his gallery." Becca made a purring noise in her throat.

"I thought his name was Amos," Abby said, acutely aware that she had sunk to a place where talking about her sister's lovers was her preferred topic of conversation.

"Amos was last week. Keep up, Abigail!"

Annoyance rattled through her like a pinball bouncing between bumpers. "You've never known the names of any of my girlfriends."

"Says something about your girlfriends, then, doesn't it? Oh look! Here comes Naomi!" Rebecca said, making no attempt to keep her voice down.

Abby remained in position, facing away from the door, but she could hear the sound of Naomi's nervous voice,

63

followed by a soft chuckle from Will, then a follow-up giggle from Naomi. As they moved closer, Abby started to be able to make out what they were saying.

"... well she's not really a personal assistant, per se," Naomi was explaining, "She helps me with some of my—" Her sentence stopped abruptly.

Raising a corner of her hat like it was the lid of Pandora's box, Abby peered in the direction of the couple. Naomi stood a few tables away. She looked ravishing in the flowered maxi that Riley had picked out for her earlier that day, her dark curls tied back in a loose ponytail. She was staring directly at them.

Abby dropped her brim back down and pretended to fish for something in her purse. "She saw us already!"

"Of course she did!" Rebecca wiggling her fingers at Naomi. "Who wouldn't notice the woman wearing sunglasses and a ridiculous hat in the middle of the restaurant?"

Abby set her bag back on the floor and changed the subject. "What are they doing now? Did he see us too?"

"No, he's only got eyes for our Naomi. How cute. I think I like him. He's not my type at all, but he seems ... nice. Nice is good. For Naomi, anyway."

"Now you've seen them together, can we please get our check and get out of here?" Abby nodded toward the server, trying to get her attention.

Rebecca tapped her foot on the ground, considering Abby's request like a dictator weighing a subject's plea. "Mmm, I think not."

"You said—"

"I said I wanted to see them together."

"You have!"

"Yeah, but I don't feel like I've gotten the full experience yet. Come on, Abigail! Where's your sense of adventure? Where's your Joyeux Noelle?"

"My ... Merry Christmas?"

"No! God." Becca swung her eyes to the ceiling like an eye-rolling emoji. "Your joy of life. How is it that I know more French than my bookish sister?"

"I think you mean—"

"How's everything going over here?" their server asked, sashaying toward them.

*It's a nightmare*, Abby wanted to say. Instead, letting out a long breath, Abby nudged her glass toward the server and said in a low voice, "One more, please."

"I'll be right back with that!" the server chirped, scooping up the glass and heading back to the kitchen.

For the next hour, Abby focused on her vodka tonics while Rebecca focused on Will and Naomi.

"Oh, look at that!" Becca said, having taken it upon herself to provide Abby with a detailed blow-by-blow of the unfolding romance. "Their knees are touching under the table! Work it, Naomi!"

Occasionally, Becca would quiet down enough for Abby to be able to catch snippets of their conversation.

"—always wanted to be a detective as a kid," she heard Will say at one point. "I'd run around with a little notebook, trying to solve mysteries. On a small farm in Indiana, there aren't a lot of mysteries to be had. I think it was sometime in my late teens that I finally realized it wasn't mysteries I wanted, but people's stories. Who they are and where they've come from, and how they got there. Solving people is a lot more fascinating than solving crimes and usually involves a lot less danger. Well, sometimes. Anyway, that's when I decided I would—"

Becca's voice drowned out the rest of his sentence. "You should see the look on Naomi's face right now, Abigail. Come on, scoot over a little so you can see them."

"A boy and a girl," she heard Naomi say later. "Preferably the boy first. I never had any siblings, and I always thought it would be nice to have an older brother to look out for me."

"Don't be so sure." Will chuckled. "I never had any siblings either, but I had two younger girl cousins, whom I tormented endlessly. We're good friends now, but sometimes I still find myself apologizing to them for the hours of suffering I put them through."

"Oh yay! This keeps getting better and better," Rebecca said.

"Honestly, Becca, this can't be as fascinating as you're making it out to be." When her sister didn't respond, Abby raised her head enough to look across the table at her. Becca, however, wasn't looking at Naomi. Her eyes were trained on the entrance. Curious and concerned, Abby turned around to follow her gaze.

Standing at the door in a pair of bright orange Capri pants and a neon-green sleeveless shirt was ...

"Riley!" Abby said more loudly than she had intended.

Riley grinned at her and said something to the host. Checking their hair in the window reflection, they turned and began walking toward them.

"What a marvelous coincidence!" they exclaimed. "Of all the restaurants in all the world."

Abby stood, making sure to keep her back to Naomi and Will, and wrapped her hand around Riley's arm. "This isn't funny."

Riley's brown eyes sparkled with delight. "Of course it is!"

"Somehow, I think Naomi wouldn't agree."

This time, she received a dismissive wave. "Luckily, this isn't about her!"

"That's what I've been saying!" Becca inserted.

"Listen to your sister, Abigail. She knows what she's talking about."

"Since when do you think that?" Abby said with a screech to her voice that reminded her far too much of her mother.

"Since she started agreeing with me! Now be serious, Abby. These two have been on this date for ..." Riley glanced down at their watch. "One hour and two minutes. By now, they either like each other, or they don't. Therefore, I can stay."

Frustrated, Abby took the battering ram approach. "No, you can't!"

"You do realize that this argument and that hat are drawing more attention than anything else possibly could."

"Yes, I am quite aware of that." Abby tightened her grip on Riley's arm. "Which is why you have to leave. Now."

Abby gave a forceful tug on Riley's arm, noting ruefully that her hand failed to make the full circumference of their bicep. Carefully concealed in their lean frame was a surprisingly muscular build that could be useful. This was not one of them.

Unmoved, literally and figuratively, Riley raised an eyebrow. "Assault? Is that what you've resorted to now?"

"Not assault. Desperation. Now let's go!" Vaguely aware that her six-foot body—five-foot-nine in height plus an extra three inches in heels—barely cleared their shoulders, Abigail held tightly to Riley's arm and put all her weight into leaning backward.

It only took a tenth of a second for her to register that her foot was slipping out from underneath her, but in that nanosecond, she cursed Riley for their uncanny strength, wondered how painful her landing would be, imagined Will's reaction when he learned that the entire scene was directly related to him and, finally, offered a silent apology to Naomi. The only thought that didn't cross her mind was *who* she might land on. However, when she landed on something soft that let out a groan, it quickly did.

The cool marble floor was a welcome relief to the warmth creeping up her face. The whole reason she had come to this restaurant had been to prevent a scene exactly like the one she had just caused.

She looked up at Riley feebly, hoping they would say something to shatter the awkward moment, but Riley was watching whoever was behind and under her, a flipbook of emotions fluttering across their face. Amusement. Fear. Shock. What could they possibly be thinking?

Before she could ask, the host scurried over breathlessly. "Oh wow. Oh my gosh. Freya Jonsson. I'd recognize you anywhere. Are you okay?"

The same range of emotions she had seen on Riley's face

now crossed hers. "Freya ...?" She rotated her head slowly, like a dispensable character in a horror movie realizing the murderer was right behind them. A set of smoldering sapphire-blue eyes met hers.

"Abigail?" Freya peered inquisitively underneath Abby's hat. She seemed to make a positive identification because she snorted. "Of course it's you. Only you would be clumsy enough to pull off something like that." She calmly rose and brushed off her tailored pinstripe suit.

Abby pushed herself off the ground. The world around her began to fall away as her mind readied itself for the attack. This time, she wasn't going to need to throw a drink, because this time, she was ready. She squared her hat.

"Throwing a drink on me wasn't enough, I take it?" Freya asked.

"Apparently not," Abby said with a derisive snicker. "Since my intention was to make you go away, yet here you are. Again."

Freya lifted her brows. "I'm here to pick up Will. We're late for an interview. What exactly are you doing here?"

She smirked. "Me? I'm here to make sure Naomi is okay." That was partially the truth. The part that mattered in this argument, anyway.

Freya smirked too. "In a large hat and sunglasses? Looks to me like you're spying on them."

"Spying?" Abby repeated, mainly to buy herself time while she thought up a better way to frame the fact that she was, indeed, spying. "Spying!"

"Yes," Freya answered. Her face remained motionless, but it was impossible to miss a crackle of glee in her eyes.

Abby was cornered. "Okay, fine. Maybe I am ... spying!"

This battle was lost but the war would still be hers. "That's only because I'm worried about Naomi dating someone who is in league with evil itself. I wanted to make sure working for you hadn't turned him into a serial killer or something."

To her delight, a flash of irritation penetrated Freya's hardened expression. "Fifteen years later and you two are still running around like Laurel and Hardy."

"Laurel and Hardy? Are all your insults as outdated as your career?" Abby let her amusement dance across her lips as she saw another spark flare in Freya's eyes. She was back and on a roll. "And what about you? You bring Will to your reunion, you interrupt his dates. Do you get your inspiration from Darth Vader?"

"You may find this hard to understand, but sometimes we have to make sacrifices in our social life because the work that we do is important."

"You're right. Hurry, before someone grabs their phone and makes a TikTok about it."

Freya's lip twitched.

*Bull's-eye.* "It's no wonder you're always in a rush, given your entire industry is about to go the way of the dinosaur."

"This is about the award, isn't it?" Freya asked, her volume rising as her cool demeanor clearly started to melt. "You're jealous of me, like you've always been."

"Me? Jealous of you?" Abby exclaimed.

Freya tittered, sending prickles of fury down Abby's spine. "It's so obvious, Abby. It always has been."

"Obvious to who?" She swung her arm out and motioned around her, merely to make a point, but as she did, she became distinctly aware that Naomi, Will, Rebecca, Riley, and a large group of restaurant patrons had formed a wide circle around them. Her arm fell to her side. Freya had also noticed their audience and Abby didn't miss that the angry flush in her cheeks had softened to an embarrassed pink. As Abby considered what to say, Riley stepped forward and extended their hand to Freya.

"Ms. Jonsson, it's a real pleasure to meet you," they said. "I'm Riley Tahara. They/them pronouns. I've always been a fan of your work. Real hard-hitting. Have you ever considered doing a piece on up-and-coming designers? It can be a real roller coaster ride of emotions, you know. I think it would appeal to a wide audience. And if you're looking for someone, I happen to know a charming young person."

In an instant, Freya's scowl transformed into a warm smile, that pearly-white, dentist-poster grin that Abby especially loathed. Freya grasped Riley's hand and shook it warmly. "Thank you—Riley, was it? I'll certainly consider it."

Abby couldn't decide what made her more upset: the fact that Riley was drooling over Freya, or the fact that Freya had so easily shed her irritation from the last few minutes.

Freya released Riley's hand and turned to Will. "I came in here to let you know we're late."

Will looked startled. "It's past seven already?"

"7:09," she said, looking at her watch.

"Dammit—security won't let us in to see the prime minister if we're late. I'm sorry; I completely lost track of time. I'm ready to go, though."

Abby hoped Freya's reply would be as cruel as Gordon Ramsey critiquing a main course and reveal her true colors to Riley and Naomi. Instead, Freya clapped him jovially on the arm. "I've talked my way through tighter security teams before; I'm sure we'll be fine. I'll wait for you outside."

"I'll be there in thirty seconds."

Freya nodded and walked out the door, her needle-thin heels clicking on the floor.

"I'm sorry I can't stay longer, it's just—" Will turned to Naomi.

"The prime minister, I know." Naomi finished his sentence.

He whispered something in her ear and then kissed her on the cheek before darting out after Freya. Having known Naomi for most of her life, Abby could tell the smile on her friend's face was genuine pleasure and delight. Of all the boys in all the world ...

~

THE DOOR HISSED LOUDLY as it closed, sealing Abigail in the dimly lit, silent room. Her eyes flitted from friend to friend to host to patron, hoping to find the most forgiving expression but everyone seemed to be waiting for her to say something first. Abby pulled her hat from her head and grasped it to her chest pitifully, feeling like a naughty school child.

She glanced quickly at the door, wondering if grown women were allowed to make a break for it. She decided instead that even if she did bolt for the door, the combination of high heels, vodka and tonics, and a general lack of daily exercise wouldn't allow her to get very far.

Riley was the first to break the silence. They turned to

Naomi. "Sooo," they said, holding the *o* until they were nearly out of breath. "I should probably get going."

"Nice try," Naomi said. She pointed at a table. "You all get to sit down and tell me exactly what the hell just happened."

Abby hoped someone would tell her, too.

# Chapter 6
## *Freya*

FREYA PULLED UP IN FRONT OF A 1960'S-ERA BRICK apartment complex and put her car in park.

> FREYA: I'm here. Please don't take too long.

The message to Will was curter than she had intended and she followed up with a smiley emoji to soften it. She didn't mean to be annoyed with him. She also didn't want him to get the sense that she *was* annoyed with him, because then he might start asking questions and she would have to explain.

She didn't mind picking him up from a Rosh Hashanah dinner at Naomi's apartment so they could make their flight to Zagreb. Their job required this kind of swirl ice cream cone intermingling of personal and business. Without it, there would be little to no personal life at all. In the last few months alone, she'd brought him to a baptism, a dentist appointment, a haircut, and, of course, a high school reunion.

If he wanted to get in a little social time before a grueling travel and work stint, she was happy to help make that happen, but it was the reason that he needed her to pick him up that made her feel pricklier than a raspberry bush.

After the incident at the Bella Luna three months ago, she'd felt confident that the flicker of attraction between Will and Naomi had been snuffed out like a candle on a windy day. It hadn't been her plan to cause a scene when she'd walked into the restaurant to get him. Her plan had been to step inside, catch his eye ever-so-discreetly and give the tap-on-the-wrist signal, all the while staying carefully out of everyone's line of view, most especially Naomi's. No one needed to know that she was interrupting her colleague's date, least of all Naomi, who would most definitely take that back to Abby, who would revel in it and save it for future ammunition in her campaign against Freya.

Freya couldn't have foreseen that Abby would have already been there, lying in wait—but that was exactly where Abby was. She'd come out of nowhere, locked onto Freya with those empty eyes the color of grass burning on a hot summer day, and pounced like a hungry lion. The only thing that had departed was Abby's sense of style. Where was that snappy comeback when she actually needed it?

How could Will want to get involved with any of ... that? Once he knew that what had happened at the reunion wasn't some fluke, that Abby was one big drink in the face and that she was going to be wherever Naomi was, surely, he would see the oncoming storm and run far away.

But oh, no. He walked straight into the storm.

He was so in love with Naomi that his pupils had practically turned into cartoon hearts, and he was doing coupley things like helping her host Rosh Hashanah dinner in her home. That was bad enough, but, in the process, he was making Freya aid and abet him as his getaway driver for a relationship that put her straight in the path of Hurricane Abigail.

She couldn't say anything to Will. She didn't want to say anything to him. It wasn't his fault that he'd fallen in love with the best friend to the human equivalent of the word 'moist.' Naomi may have bad taste in friends, but as a person, she seemed as sweet now as she had in high school, and sweet was exactly what she wanted Will to have. He deserved a sweet life with a sweet love and 2.5 sweet babies and, of course, she would do whatever she could to make that happen.

But why did it have to be Naomi?

She looked at the clock in her car and pictured the long hours she was about to spend sitting on an airplane to Zagreb. Deciding that she might as well get a few extra minutes of full leg extension, she turned off the car and got out. She was dressed in airplane casual: a pair of colorful Versace leggings, a white satin shirt, and a cozy gray cashmere cardigan. The fall air held a chill, and she pulled her cardigan closed.

WILL: Be right down

Romantic relationships had never been a priority for Freya. After her parents had divorced during her freshman year of high school, she had been left with a tattered family life and a clear understanding of the consequences of falling in love. She didn't judge people for seeking out relationships, but she had chosen to keep things strategic when it came to romance, not using her needs or wants as a driver for any decision making. She'd dated through the years, a smattering of men that she'd kept at arm's length for short periods of time. While she appreciated the attention and the boost to her social status that came with being part of a couple, she'd never been interested in pursuing anything further for myriad reasons.

She couldn't imagine Will ever being strategic when it came to love. He seemed like the type that jumped into love like a high diver. She hadn't asked him very much about how things were going with Naomi, but it was evident that he was pumped full of endorphins, which suggested that things were going well. When she would ask about his evening or weekend or holiday, he would mention seeing Naomi from time to time, but generally she didn't follow up with questions. Depending on the day, it was either because of her desire to respect his privacy, or it was out of self-preservation. Mostly the latter. She needed to focus on her career. She didn't need to hear about dates that left her wondering about the possibility that he had spent time with Abby. Or wondering what Abby was saying about her. Or what stories she was inventing. Or what she was doing to warp his mind and turn him against her. She needed to be going through her stories with a fine-toothed comb, not dissecting Will's behavior to see if he was treating her any differently. Most importantly, she didn't need to expend any more thought or emotional energy on a piece of her past that held no bearing on her future.

This whole thing was absurd, she told herself. She was done with Abby. This wasn't high school anymore. She had left high school, and Abby, in the dust. She had created a life much more enviable than being popular in high school. That was the real win, not some petty verbal exchange.

Her phone dinged and she slipped it from her pocket. It was a text from her talent agent, Kiara. The woman had approached her at her book launch party a few years ago, handed Freya her business card, and, like some mysterious fortune teller at the beginning of a movie, told her that being a *New York Times* bestselling author was going to catapult her into a new level of popularity that would require a savvy gatekeeper. Like any main character who doesn't believe their fortune until it was too late, Freya had smiled politely and thrown Kiara's card away as soon as she was out of sight. Thankfully, she had a good memory, and was able to look Kiara up a few days later when she realized her prediction was spot on. Kiara seemed to continually have clairvoyant skills and was always on the forefront of trends, bookings, and opportunities.

> KIARA: Don't get too excited but...

> There's a rumor that Kent James is going to retire. Word has it they're going to be looking for a replacement. Nothing set in stone, but I'm going to make sure you're on the top of their mind when that time comes!

There wasn't a lot that gave Freya butterflies, but this text released the entire North American monarch migration into her stomach. This was the break she had been waiting for. Kent James *was* the news. His forty plus years as a journalist meant that "the world turns to Kent James for the news," a fact that billboards, TV commercials, and Spotify ads reminded her of regularly. She'd even heard her staff say it in passing on more than one occasion. While replacing James wouldn't automatically make the world turn to her for the news—she knew she would have to earn that trust from the public—it would give her the authority and validation she needed to achieve that place in people's homes or wherever they were watching. She typed a response.

> FREYA: Keep me posted

A reply from Kiara came quickly.

> KIARA: Not that you need reminding, but International News is a pretty buttoned up network so keep your nose clean.

Freya didn't need reminding. She knew the reputation of the television network where Kent had built his career. INN made her own network executives look like a tree-hugging drum circle in comparison. However, she was confident she'd pass any vetting process with flying colors and would be able to align herself with company values and expectations. She'd understood since high school that popularity meant being in the public eye and *that* meant following the rules at all costs, whether or not you necessarily agreed with them, thus ensuring a spotless reputation and along with it; a clear path to the top.

She was so caught up in the excitement of the moment that she almost didn't register the voices in front of the apartment building. It was only when the conversation started getting louder that her attention shifted and she looked up. It was a little after eight o'clock and the autumn sun had settled behind the horizon, but the twilight sky combined with the street lamps and the building lobby allowed her to see Naomi standing with her back to the apartment building entrance talking to someone. Instinctively, Freya sat down on the hood of her car and looked away. The absolute last thing she wanted was for Naomi to think she was crashing another date. When they got back from Zagreb, she would have to start making an effort to get to know Naomi enough to facilitate her coming by to get Will. This didn't seem like the right moment for that. In fact, it seemed like it was a moment that was getting worse.

"No!" The man barked so loudly that Freya's body twitched and she looked back at them. The entrance was close enough to the street that Freya was able to distinguish that Naomi had her arms wrapped tightly around her body. It was possible she was trying to keep warm, but Freya got the sense she wasn't protecting herself from the cold, but from the conversation.

"You can't even give me five minutes?" he said, still loud enough for Freya to hear.

Naomi inched backwards and said something softly.

Freya stiffened, trying to assess the situation. Was Naomi in trouble? Something was off, but was it off enough that she needed to step in and help? She stood, then sat back down on her car, anxiously indecisive.

"The hell?"

Freya's eyes followed the sound to see Abby standing a few feet away, her gaze squarely set on Naomi, and a bag of ice abandoned on the ground. Without hesitation, Abby stalked towards the entrance and inserted herself in between Naomi and the man. Although Freya couldn't make out most of what she was saying, her tone was unmistakably fierce.

Her arm flung out, her finger pointing away from the apartment building.

"Go. Now," she said, loud and clear.

The seconds dragged on and Freya began to wonder if he was going to refuse. Then, he took the slightest step back. Then another.

"I won't give up," he said, when at long last, he turned and started walking away.

Freya looked back at Naomi and Abby, who were silently watching him go. Once he was out of sight, Abby turned and wrapped Naomi in a hug. Freya wanted to get back into her car before they noticed her, but decided it was more than likely that any movement would draw their attention. As Abby released Naomi, Freya averted her eyes back to the ground and hoped they would head back into the building. Instead, they started talking. Quietly at first, but then loud enough for her to listen in.

"You haven't told him yet?" Abby shouted.

"If I tell him, then he's involved!" Naomi shouted back, sounding desperate.

"He's already involved!"

Their voices quieted and they continued talking for another minute. Out of the corner of her eye, Freya saw them come together in another embrace and then move towards the door. The tightness in her body relaxed. Whatever she had inadvertently witnessed seemed to have resolved and, thankfully, she had remained undetected for all of it.

Without warning, Abby turned towards the street. "You go ahead. I need to grab the ice."

She'd forgotten about the ice. Freya kept her eyes focused intently on the ground as Abby walked towards her and picked up the bag of ice. There was a rustling noise, followed by a squeak, and then an avalanche of ice cubes tumbled over the curb and onto Freya's boots.

Briefly, Freya contemplated if there was any chance that Abby wouldn't notice her, sitting on her car, feet covered in ice. She turned her head an inch and peeked up, hopeful that she wouldn't find Abby staring back at her. No such luck. Abby stood, holding a half empty, tattered, plastic ice bag, with her eyes planted firmly, sternly, on Freya.

The cool air was no match for the warmth that rushed through Freya's body. This was so much worse than if Naomi had seen her. The last time she had seen Abby, Freya had, with excessive glee, accused her of spying. She was going to have to let Abby think she was doing the same thing or, worse, explain herself in order to prove that she wasn't. Neither option was appealing. Both involved her being at the mercy of Abby's judgment.

She gave a small cough. "I'm picking up Will. He should be down any minute," she said, in an effort to drive the narrative before Abby got behind the wheel.

"How much of that you did you hear?" Abby asked, seemingly disinterested in Freya's narrative.

Her internal thermostat turned up ten more degrees. She had the sudden desire to ditch her cardigan and allow some natural air conditioning in. "Nothing. Well, a little, but I wasn't listening. I mean, I was listening but I wasn't ..." she trailed off as it became clear that the car was going off the road. Instead, she changed course. "I don't know what happened, but I've seen enough conflict to know that that wasn't a friendly gathering. Is Naomi okay?"

Abby heaved the ripped bag at her side upward and

attempted to cradle it in her arms, sending a waterfall of ice cubes to the curb. "She's fine." She made a grumbling sound and tried adjusting the bag again, losing more ice cubes in the process.

As Abby continued to struggle with the bag, Freya wondered what, if anything, she was supposed to do in this situation. Should she offer to help someone she disliked? Would someone who disliked her accept her help? She stayed, planted on her car, and watched, while more ice cubes cascaded to the ground.

Abby made another low, rumbling noise, but this time it didn't seem to be about the ice. "What should I do? If she was a client I'd have more tact." She continued to wrestle with the bag as she spoke. "But she's not my client, she's my best friend."

This unexpected glimpse into Abby's inner world caught Freya off guard. She had only ever seen Abby on the attack, her face as fierce as her words. It was a little startling to get a view of that same person, only gentler. Vulnerable, even. Freya remained silent.

Abby continued talking, venting her frustration into the losing battle with the bag of ice. "It's one thing to sit across from someone and listen to them tell you about choices that will impact a life you'll never see outside of your office. But Naomi is part of my life. I can't intellectualize it because I'm in it. I see it and I feel it. I want her to be happy and I suffer with her when she does. Except I can't fix things or make decisions for her and—" She looked up, almost as if she was realizing who she was talking to for the first time. "And why am I saying all this to you?"

The vulnerability that Freya had seen was gone, but the

fierceness wasn't there either. Abby wasn't on the attack, at least not yet. The Freya of only a few minutes ago would have taken advantage of this opportunity to catch Abby off guard, and a part of her brain was urging her to. Another part of her brain felt something she'd never felt for Abby before: sympathy. For the first time since they had crossed paths in high school, Abby wasn't making quips or judgements. She was struggling—with ice and with her worry about her friend. It made her seem almost ... sweet. That thought was oddly discomforting, and she brushed it away, reminding herself that she had promised she was done wasting any more time on someone that she had already bested. No attacks, no sympathy. Neutrality was the course she had laid out for herself, and the one she would stay on. "Frankly, I think you were talking to that ice."

Abby looked at the tattered remains of plastic in her arms. Only a handful of ice cubes were left at this point. She sighed, the pinching around her eyes giving way to a look of resignation. Whether that was resignation about the ice or about Naomi, Freya wasn't sure. Abby dumped the last of the ice onto the sidewalk. "I give up. Riley will have to make room temperature cocktails." She glanced towards the apartment. "Anyway, if I see Will, I'll remind him you're here."

Freya nodded, relieved that she had managed to navigate the situation without escalating it. As Abby turned, though, she realized that wasn't quite true. Her hand shot up. "Hey. You won't say anything about me overhearing all that. I don't want Will or Naomi to think I was—"

"Spying?" The left side of Abby's mouth lifted into an amused, almost playful, but entirely unwarranted smirk. Had Abby been thinking that the whole time?

"No," she corrected in a calm tone, hoping to give the impression that Abby's response, mostly that smirk, didn't put her on the defensive.

"Really? Because that's the word you used when I was —"

"At a restaurant in a giant hat, watching your friend's date?" The sudden tenseness in Freya's body made her words come out rapidly.

The smirk on Abby's face deflated. "Regardless," she said. "You don't have to worry. Your secret is safe with me."

That set her teeth on edge. The last thing she wanted was to feel like Abby was holding something, some *secret,* over her head. "It's not a secret," she said firmly. "I didn't want anyone to get the wrong impression, but don't do me any favors."

"I'm not doing you any favors." Abby shrugged nonchalantly. "Sure, I could take your lead and try to call you out in front of everyone, but unlike you, I choose to be the bigger person."

Freya crossed her arms. "Unlike me? You call throwing a drink on me being the bigger person?"

"I—" Abby opened her mouth. Closed it. Then opened it again. "Alright fine. Throwing a drink... was not ..." She cleared her throat. "I probably shouldn't have done that."

Freya couldn't stop her brow from lifting. *Probably shouldn't have done that* was the closest thing to an apology she'd ever heard from Abby.

"That was a momentary, slightly intoxicated, lapse in judgment." Abby held up a finger to indicate she had more to say on the subject. "However, while it may have been the low road, it was one you'd never have the chutzpah to take."

Freya's other eyebrow went up. "I beg your pardon?"

"Please, look at you." Abby visually scanned Freya from head to toe. "You swapped out your cheerleading uniform for designer clothes, but you haven't changed. The only thing you'll ever throw is insults from afar. You'd never be caught dead throwing a drink, or doing anything to ruin your perfect little image."

She didn't like how much that annoyed her. Abby's statement was laced with an ounce of truth. Freya had worked extremely hard to craft her image, but Abby was making it sound like that was a bad thing, like her efforts hadn't gotten her here, a successful journalist in a male-dominated industry, potentially in the running to be Kent James' replacement. She was absolutely capable of getting her hands dirty, even throwing something if the situation called for it. If she hadn't been at a reunion that night, in a gym full of people—former classmates, all armed with phones—and if Naomi hadn't swept Abby away seconds later, she just *might* have thrown something back. She wasn't afraid. She was calculating. In that moment, she had calculated that it was not in her best interest to do anything. This moment, though, alone on the street, with no one watching? If they had been here, it would have been different.

"Think whatever you like." Even as Freya said it, she knew didn't mean it. Is that what Abby had been talking about when she said she got to show everyone ... something? Did she think that she was showing everyone that Freya was too scared, too timid to hold her own?

Abby gave a short, amused huff and turned to leave. "Trust me, I will."

Freya's hand moved faster than her mind. Before she could stop herself, she'd scooped up a handful of ice.

"Ow! What the—" Abby turned back to look at her. "Did you just throw ice at me?"

She had. She had thrown ice at Abby, and it had felt *good*. She suddenly understood why Abby had let out a menacing laugh after tossing her drink because now a laugh of her own was bubbling up. She scooped up another handful of ice and hurled it at Abby—not hard enough to hurt but hard enough to get her point across. It was exhilarating.

Abby held her hands up protectively. "What are you—"

"You know, if I'm hiding behind a perfect image, you're hiding behind the image that you've got everything and everyone figured out. That somehow you're so above everyone because you know us better than we know ourselves." She sent more ice raining onto Abby. "You don't know the first thing about me or what I'm capable of. I think it drives you up an absolute wall. You're jealous of everything I've accomplished because you can't figure out who I am or how I'm doing it. You think you're the only one who can throw things? Think again."

As she gathered another round of ice, movement behind Abby caught her eye. The doors to the apartment building opened and Naomi shot out like she was crossing the finish line of an Olympic race with Will steps behind her. Behind them, two more people exited the apartment building. She recognized them as the same two people who were with Abby at the Bella Luna. Like Will and Naomi, they seemed interested in what was happening with her and Abby, but unlike Will and Naomi, they seemed to be more titillated than troubled.

"Freya." Will was at her side.

Behind him, Naomi was collecting Abby, the way she had since freshman year, with a measure of parental sternness and concern in her movements.

Her fingers tingled from the cold but she couldn't get the smile off her face. She wanted to explain to him, to everyone, that it wasn't what it looked like, except she wasn't sure to say. It wasn't what it looked like, but also, it kind of was. She said, "Ready to head out?"

"Sure," he said, hurriedly.

Without looking back, she returned to the driver's seat and unlocked her phone to pull up directions to the airport. Kiara's last message was still loaded on her screen:

Keep your nose clean.

She swiped it away. This was definitely the last time. She'd put Abby in her place, and she really was done.

# Chapter 7
## *Abby*

"OH MY GOD." ABBY'S EXCLAMATION WAS MUFFLED BY the popcorn in her mouth. "He did not just pick her!"

Riley reached for the bowl that sat between the two of them on Abby's sofa and clawed a generous helping. "The folks at this rose ceremony need hazmat suits, because it's getting toxic."

Abby glanced briefly at them before looking back at the television. "How long have you been saving that one?"

Riley tossed a piece of popcorn into their mouth. "Came up with it earlier this week. I'm pretty proud."

"You should be."

Her phone buzzed on the coffee table with a text message, and when she saw Naomi's name, she picked up the phone.

> NAOMI: Emergency! 📷

The fact that Naomi had time to add an emoji gave Abby the reassurance that this emergency did not involve imminent danger. She took another handful of popcorn and waited for the details.

> NAOMI: My dress ripped!

Abby's brain needed a few seconds to recalibrate from *The Bachelor* to real life. Naomi was somewhere ... she was ... right, at a fundraiser. Some fancy shindig downtown as Will's plus one for the evening. The kind of shindig where a ripped dress definitely qualified as an emergency, of the non-imminent-danger kind.

> NAOMI: The skirt caught on a doorknob and tore straight down. My ass is literally hanging out and I'm hiding in the bathroom. Please help me. Either by killing me so I never have to remember this moment or by bringing me another dress. Dealer's choice.

> ABBY: I'm on my way.

Then she added,

> ABBY: Can you let me know which way I'm going?

> NAOMI: Omg thank you. It's at the Cultural Center. Follow signs for the Chicago for Paws gala.

> ABBY: Which dress did you want? Not saying I won't kill you but I'll keep it a surprise until the end.

> NAOMI: The navy one with the black lace. It's hanging on my closet door. I was thinking about wearing it, but I changed my mind at the last second, which was a poor life choice apparently.

"We're going to have to put the drama on hold," Abby said. "Naomi's having a dress malfunction and needs us to bring her another one."

Riley brushed the popcorn particles from their hands and stood up. "There are few things that would pull me away from reality television and wine, but Naomi in dress distress is one of them."

Only a few minutes later, they were tucked into the back seat of a ride-share with Naomi's dress. The mid-November air was frosty and the two friends shivered under their winter coats as they settled in for the short ride downtown.

"Wow, this event has a red carpet and everything," Riley said, holding up their phone displaying the fundraiser's website. "I am not dressed for that!"

"I don't think there's going to be paparazzi outside taking pictures of you. The fundraiser started an hour ago. See?" She pointed to Riley's screen. "And regardless, we're not going to be walking any red carpet. We're dropping off a dress in the bathroom and leaving."

"I can't guarantee that the pull of the red carpet won't overtake me." Riley turned the screen back towards themself and resumed scrolling, reading aloud as they did. "The premier black-tie fundraiser for animal welfare in the Windy City. Set at the legendary Chicago Cultural Center, guests will indulge in a one-of-a-kind celebration, MC'd by our city's own beloved ... oh." Riley stopped mid-sentence.

"It's okay, I already know. Freya is the MC. Apparently, she's a well-known ... animal philanthropist or something."

"It's against my nature to advise against controversy, but this may not be the best place for you two to start throwing beverages in their various forms at each other."

She shot Riley a look. "I wasn't the problem last time. I was being perfectly polite."

Riley put their phone to their ear. "Hello? What's that? The bullshit detector is about to have a core meltdown? Hang on, I've located the source. Let me see if I can neutralize it." They set their phone down on their lap and smiled at Abby, who wrinkled her nose at them.

"I was being *almost* perfectly polite. I simply found it interesting that she was stalking Will outside our apartment when she'd been so ready to accuse me of spying—"

"You were spying."

"Of trying to avoid detection while attempting to prevent my sister from causing a scene—"

"Which you then caused."

"Oy gevalt, you're worse than her, Riley!" Abby crossed her arms, a half-smile, half-pout on her face. "Anyway, if by chance we run into each other, I won't say anything to cause *controversy*."

"It saddens me to hear it, even if it's the right thing to do."

Abby would never admit it, but she couldn't find it in herself to be mad that Freya threw those ice cubes at her. She wanted to be angry, but she was still so surprised. Even a little amazed. She'd made Freya ... lose the tiniest bit of control. The way Freya laughed, had talked about a side of herself that Abby didn't know, it was—clinically speaking—

fascinating. Turns out there was more to Freya than the uptight bully.

Abby's phone jingled the familiar *Little Mermaid* tune. She silenced the call. "There's zero chance my sister is up to anything I want to hear about on a Saturday night."

Riley snatched her phone before she could stop them. "Disagree. I need some alternative controversy to feed my appetite." They swiped to answer the call and put it on speaker phone. "Hello, darling."

"Riley? Is that you? Why are you—never mind. He ... knows ..." Becca's voice trembled as she said the last two words.

Abby looked at the phone and then back at Riley. It sounded like Becca was genuinely about to cry, or at least, it was the way that she remembered Becca sounding when she was little. She was positive she hadn't heard her sister do anything particularly genuine since she had hit puberty.

"Who knows what exactly?"

"It's not like I ever meant to hurt him," Becca said, her words interrupted by sniffling.

"Meant to hurt who?"

"Peter!" The sniffles gave way to sobs.

Riley's eyes widened to the size she imagined hers were.

"What happened?" they asked simultaneously, though Abby felt confident that they both knew what had happened, with the exception of a few small details.

"He knows. I don't know how he knows but he knows." Becca's explanation came in waves, a crest of words followed by a sob and jagged inhale. "He came home tonight and said he can't take it anymore and he's going away to think about what he wants and that I should do the same."

"I'm sorry, honey," Abby said, though sorry wasn't quite the right word. Although on most days she liked her sister as much as a swarm of mosquitos, she didn't like to see her hurting. She was also not sorry that Becca had been caught. Abby had never known how to handle herself around Peter, never known if it was her place to say anything about Becca's extracurricular activities.

"What do I do? Tell me how to fix it!"

Abby motioned at Riley, a 'feel free to step in any time here' gesture. All she got back was a slack jaw and a slow shake of the head.

"Becca," Abby took the phone back from Riley. "Help me understand. You've been cheating on the man for years."

A piercing cry emanated from the speaker. "Those other men didn't mean anything!"

Their car pulled up in front of the Cultural Center and Abby kept talking as they stepped out.

"Then why did you—"

"I don't know! You don't think I've asked myself that a thousand times already?"

"You're going to have to really ask yourself what you want," Abby said, as they reached the entrance.

"I want Peter," Becca said with a whimper.

"Then you're going to have to figure out what that looks like in a way that works for you. And Peter of course. Assuming he's even open to it." She opened the large door to the building and stepped inside. "While you think about that, we're going to run to help Naomi with a dress problem. I'll call you back later, okay?"

"I guess. I—"

Knowing that that was the closest she was going to get to

an agreement, she disconnected the call. "That was not on my bingo card for this year," she said to Riley as they followed a set of signs for the gala that pointed them up a grand, winding staircase to the second floor.

"I've never been so speechless," Riley said as they began their ascent.

Will was waiting for them at the top of the stairs. "I have a hard time imagining what could render you speechless." Behind Will was a short hallway that curved to the left and very clearly carried the sound of Freya's amplified voice. Abby only caught the tail end of it, but she must have made a joke, because the distinct sound of unified group laughter followed.

"How about Becca calling to say Peter left her for cheating and all she wants is to have him back?" Riley asked.

"Becca said that?" Will said, putting extra emphasis on Becca's name. "The same woman who came to brunch last week with her yoga teacher after spending the night with her contractor?"

"The same."

"That ... would ..."

"Exactly."

"Um, excuse me?" Abby heard Naomi's voice from somewhere down the hall.

"Sorry," Will said. "I'm so flabbergasted, I'm failing in my duty to direct you to Naomi. The bathroom is right around the bend there, on the left."

Abby nodded. "I'll bring her the dress and Riley can fill you in." Her directions were unnecessary. Riley already had a hand on Will's arm as they began to relay the entire conversation.

Abby could still hear Riley talking as she rounded the bend in the hallway. Ahead of her, the red carpet came into view. She was too far away to see into the room, but she could hear Freya more clearly now.

"Before we start dinner," Freya was saying, "I'd like to invite this year's board president up to speak on the—"

"Over here!"

Abby followed the sound until she spotted the bathroom, door cracked open, and an arm waving at her. Abby hurried over and handed the dress to Naomi.

"Oh my God, thank you, thank you, thank you." Naomi's arm disappeared and the door closed then opened again. "Wait, did I hear Riley say that Peter walked out on Becca?"

"Not only that, but she wanted me to tell her how to fix it."

"Fix it? Like she actually wants to be with Peter?"

"Apparently? I'm at a loss. She called on the way here and I told her I'd have to call her back, partially because I literally have no idea what to say to her."

"I don't know what to tell you. Being half naked in front of Chicago's elite is enough for me today. I can't handle any more this evening."

"I don't blame you. You focus on getting dressed."

As the door closed, Naomi called out, "Thanks again!"

The hallway went silent, except for what sounded like a symphony of silverware clinking against plates. "... Naomi isn't convinced." Will was talking in a hushed tone but the acoustics made it sound like he was next to her.

"You are though, right?" Riley replied.

"I feel like I shouldn't be. All evidence would suggest

otherwise. But for some reason, what you said makes sense. Maybe this really is just two people in love."

Her eyes returned to the red carpet. She had never been to a black-tie gala or, really, any gala that hadn't come by e-vite from Riley. Curious to get a glimpse, she continued walking down the hall.

"It is, and honestly, I'm furious at myself that it took me so long to see it."

"You think there's something *we* can do about it?"

"Will. You've been a part of our little cohort long enough to know that I am never wrong."

"I'm not sure I'd—"

As she neared the large set of double doors, she could see into the ornate ballroom where equally elaborately-styled guests were seated at large round tables decorated with eye-catching floral arrangements and sparkling china. She inched toward the wall, trying to stay out of sight, and craned her neck to get a better look.

She had barely gotten a peek before a movement at the door caught her eye. Actually, the first thing that caught her eye was the long, defined leg, exposed by the desperately high slit in the black sequined dress, then the curves that appeared to have been poured into the dress, then the neckline that plunged breathtakingly low. When she finally looked at the face of the person walking in her direction, her body seized up like she had been thrown into the frosty Lake Michigan waters. A small, gurgle-like noise escaped her lips.

"Abby?" Freya, sounding rightfully surprised, stopped in the middle of the hallway.

"It's Naomi," Abby said, shoving the flash of X-rated thoughts she had been having into a vault that would never be opened or so much as acknowledged ever, *ever* again. "She, um, her dress ripped. I brought her a new one. She's changing in the bathroom right now."

"Oh."

They stood in silence for a few seconds. Each passing moment, Abby became more accutely aware of the fact that she was at a gala, talking to Freya, in sweatpants and a sweatshirt, both of which were definitely covered in popcorn crumbs. "I'm leaving," she pointed towards the exit. "I wanted to look inside before I—aren't you supposed to be up there talking anyway?"

"Dinner started and I needed to get out of there." Freya glanced back at the room and said under her breath, "I hate speaking at these things."

"Isn't this what you do for a living?"

Freya looked back at her, and for the first time, Abby noticed that even the smokey eye makeup and thick false lashes weren't hiding the tight lines along her eyes. "In front of a camera, yes. Not live, in front of large groups of people like this." She squeezed her hands together tightly. "Anyway, I'm fine. I saw Naomi leave the bathroom just now so I'm going to ... you know ... go and try to remember how to breathe before I have to get back up there." She motioned behind Abby, getting paler by the second.

Abby stepped back to let Freya pass. "Have you tried tapping?" She nearly let out a scream. What in the Freudian Slip had made her offer professional advice to someone who hadn't asked for it? And who was also Freya Jonsson.

"Sorry, what?" Freya stopped again.

Abby wished her body would dissolve and melt into the floor. That would most certainly be less painful than this.

Having the expertise to help Freya, of all people, in a help-less moment should have made her feel powerful. Somehow, she had never felt so insecure. She reached for her necklace and traced the shape of the star with her finger. "Tapping." She repeated. Freya didn't say anything but she also didn't move, so Abby forced herself to continue. "It's an offshoot of EMDR, which is eye movement desensiti–never mind. It's a technique that's been proven to help when you're having severe anxiety. It kind of rewires the brain when it gets in a loop. It's really easy to do, and only takes a few seconds to start working. I don't know if you want me to show you or...." She trailed off.

Freya's eyes flicked towards the ballroom, then back to Abby. "Only a few seconds?"

"Pretty much. It's more effective the longer you do it, but it starts working pretty quickly."

Freya's hands flexed and unflexed nervously until finally, she said in a quiet voice, "Okay."

The color in Freya's face had gone even a shade paler and Abby wondered if she was nearing a panic attack. If she was, Abby needed to move quickly. "Alright," she said, mustering as much clinical detachment as she could. "I'll walk you through it one time so you know what it should feel like and can do it yourself. To begin, you put one hand on each shoulder and give yourself a hug."

Freya hesitated, but slowly lifted her arms up and wrapped them around her chest, grabbing an arm with each hand.

"It's more like..." Abby wavered before reaching out and using her fingertips to adjust Freya's hands so they were resting on her shoulders. She expected Freya to recoil or to laugh at her for falling for her trick, but when neither happened, she continued. "Next, pick a positive memory. Doesn't have to be the happiest moment of your life, only something that has happy associations. Once you've got that, you'll need to, well, close your eyes."

Freya studied her, and this time Abby was sure she was going to drop her arms and fire off an insult. She almost wished Freya *would* say something nasty. That would have felt safer and more normal than whatever this was.

Instead, she closed her eyes.

Abby forced herself to focus on the script. "Thinking about that memory, the sights and sounds and smells associated with it, start tapping your shoulders one at a time. Left, right, left, right." Freya began tapping in time with Abby's direction. "Perfect. Then I will count down from five and you take a deep breath with each count. When I get to one, you can open your eyes. Five..." As Freya inhaled and exhaled with each count, the color started to return to her face. Abby found herself wondering what kind of happy memory Freya might be calling up. The only happiness she had ever seen from her was the kind of villainous joy that came from delivering a cutting remark. Or, maybe, a cutting remark *was* the happy memory Freya was replaying. "One."

Freya opened her eyes and let her arms fall to her side.

Abby pursed her lips. "Okay well, that's it. Hopefully it helped." She didn't want to know if it had helped. Or rather, she didn't want to know if it *didn't* help and she'd spent the last minute of her life proving to Freya that she was a hack. "I'm going to head back now." She started walking towards the stairs, wishing she could break out into a run.

"Thank you. I feel ... better."

Abby paused, then looked over her shoulder at Freya's unreadable expression. She'd never heard Freya say thank you so maybe that was why she was unfamiliar with the expression of gratitude. "You're welcome. Good luck." She turned and continued walking. She tried not to walk too fast, but she wasn't in a hurry to get back to her friends either. Could she tell them what had just happened? What *had* just happened? Why had it left her with actual, trembling hands? She made herself follow her own advice and take a few deep breaths.

"If this doesn't work, Riley, it could do a lot of damage." Naomi's hushed voice from down the hall interrupted her thoughts.

"You've already made your reservations clear." Abby heard Riley. "But you know I'm right. We need to help them unleash their true feelings." Were they still talking about Becca?

"On the off chance that's somehow correct, how could we even do that?"

"Oh, I've got ideas. Plans. But we need to strike while the iron is hot. I think we could do something in the studio. Can you manage that, Will?"

"It might be possible."

"Of course, it's possible."

She rounded the bend, grateful that Riley was stirring up enough trouble to distract her. Will, Riley, and Naomi were huddled together at the top of the stairs. They looked up like startled deer.

"Where did you disappear to?" Naomi asked. "I came out of the bathroom and you were gone."

"I wanted a glimpse of the red carpet and I ran into—"

She waved her hand, deciding she was not ready to finish that sentence. "What are you cooking up for Becca, Riley?"

Riley touched an affronted hand to their chest. "Why am I the subject of your inquisition?"

"Call it women's intuition. Also, I heard you. You've got ideas, do you?"

"You know, we really should get back in there," Naomi said, taking hold of Will's arm. "Thanks again for saving the day."

As Will and Naomi walked hurriedly away, Abby followed suit, slipping her arm through Riley's as they started down the stairs. "I know you want to help Becca, but she's going to need to figure this one out on her own. No schemes, okay? This once?"

"This is only in reference to this specific situation with Becca, right? Not schemes in general."

"I would never suggest something so cruel."

"And that's why we're friends."

# Chapter 8
## *Freya*

FREYA STOOD UP FROM HER DESK AND STRETCHED HER arms over her head. The clock on her computer confirmed what her body was telling her: that she had been sitting for over two hours and she needed to move. It was after midnight and the stack of unread transcripts on her desk meant that the night was young, not that she particularly minded.

She walked the handful of steps to the other side of her office, a lounge area equipped with a love seat, small bar, several television screens, and, her favorite, an enormous window that offered a breathtaking panorama of the city skyline. Before she was Freya Jonsson, Senior Correspondent for *Nightly Global News,* with a corner office, and she was merely Freya Jonsson, Associate Producer for *Nightly Global News,* with a cubicle, she was able to *work*. She spent her days reading transcripts and cross-referencing lists and e-mailing sources and requesting files and really digging into a story. Now it seemed like most of her days were filled with meetings telling other people to do those things and more meetings convincing the executives to let her people do those things. By the time she sat down to do an actual interview, she'd already spent most of her time trying to navigate someone else's notes and the mountain of red tape from the higher ups.

Not that she wanted to be cubicle Freya Jonsson again, but she still liked to get her hands dirty sometimes. Nights were the only time she was able to do that. Working in the headquarters of a national television station meant things were never truly "quiet;" the building was always buzzing with people writing, filming, editing, broadcasting, and everything else required to produce content for dozens of channels, streaming services, and other programming. After *Nightly Global News* aired, though, her floor usually got *quieter*. On nights like this, Thanksgiving weekend, when everyone was on vacation, it got even more deliciously quiet. The meetings, calls, e-mails, demands ... they all stopped, and she was left with the work. The story. The puzzle. The truth. The part of her job she truly loved.

She lifted the stopper out of a crystal decanter, relishing the satisfying clink of glass against glass, and poured herself two fingers of bourbon. She opened the mini fridge, pulled out two ice cubes, plopped them into her glass, swirled, and then sipped as she let her gaze stretch across the night view. The frosty winter air revealed an inky black, starless sky. Twelve stories down, the parking lot was a work of modern art, a white canvas of snow patterned irregularly with circular dots from the streetlights, lines from tire tracks, and colorful rectangles of car roofs. From this height, she could still make out enough detail on the ground to recognize

Will's green Prius when it pulled up into the parking lot and four people got out.

With no one else around, she felt comfortable giving into her curiosity, and she pressed her forehead to the window, trying to get a better view. She recognized Will and Naomi easily enough. The other two, she wasn't sure. She couldn't make out much more than their heights: tall and taller. She wondered if it was the same pair she'd encountered twice before. Were they Will and Naomi's friends? She wondered what they were all doing here after midnight. She watched as Will and Naomi walked hand in hand into the building lobby, with the other two right behind.

She was taken aback by the sharp sensation in her chest. It wasn't a pain, it was a pang. She wasn't the type to go on midnight runs of any kind. Perhaps, more accurately, she wasn't the type to be invited on midnight runs of any kind. She hadn't wanted that, hadn't made room for it in her life. For as long as she could remember, she'd felt that she wasn't going to be anything less than the best and she couldn't waste her time on antics with friends. If life was a marathon, then friends were for cheering you on and handing you water from the sidelines, not for distracting you from the race.

She took a healthy sip of her drink, an attempt to replace the sting in her chest with the gentle burn of bourbon. It worked, for a few seconds, but as the sensation of the alcohol dissipated, the other feeling returned. Annoyed, she forcefully set her glass down on the bar and returned to her desk. Whatever this feeling was, it was no match for her ability to focus on the task at hand. She traced her finger down the page in front of her until she found where she had left off.

In the distance she heard the faint ding of the elevator.

She knew the door had opened because the silence was splintered by cacophonous laughter. She stared at the wall, as if she might develop x-ray vision and find out what was so funny. She and Will had had some good laughs over the years, but not like that. She'd never heard him laugh with so much abandon. It made her wonder if he was a different person at work than he was with his friends.

Her curiosity beckoned to her like a crooked finger. It lifted her out of her seat and brought her to her office door. She knew it was absurd. She knew she was too old to be pressing her ear to the door to try and listen in on conversations. Yet here she was, doing just that.

"… be nervous, you know what to do," Will said.

"Yeah, but I still don't believe any of it will work." Naomi. "I mean it's all speculation. We're not even sure that everyone is, you know, playing on the same team."

"Oh, you can doubt many things, but not that. I'm never wrong about that." Another voice, one she recognized. It was definitely the person she'd met at the restaurant when she'd gone to pick up Will.

"Even if that's true, that still leaves a lot of what-ifs."

"You mean like 'what if Riley is the most brilliant person I've ever met?'"

Or 'what if I have some fun?'" came a woman's voice she didn't recognize, most likely one of the two that had followed them into the building. "God knows, that's my motivation after the week I've had."

"How are things going with you and Peter?" Naomi asked.

"I don't even know. Abby somehow convinced both of us to go to therapy, but I don't see how it's going to help. I've never encountered a problem that can't be solved in the bedroom. Penis *is* therapy."

"Can confirm," Riley said.

"It's good that you're giving some, um, non-genitalia solutions a try first," Naomi said.

"On that note," Will said. "I see the light is on in Freya's office. Let's stop in and say hi."

Riley trilled, "Do you think she'd be interested in featuring me—"

Freya didn't hear the rest of that because she had shot back from the door like it had turned into an electrified fence. She scurried as quickly and quietly as possible to her desk, dropped into her chair, and propped her elbows on the table in her best I'm-deeply-engrossed-in-work-not-eavesdropping pose when there was a knock.

"Come in!" she said cheerfully, trying to mask that she was slightly out of breath.

The door opened and on the other side were four smiling faces.

"Hope you don't mind us dropping in," Will said. "We were out for drinks in the area, and I've been promising them a tour of the place, so I thought we'd stop by. I figured now would be a good time since the place is a holiday dead zone."

Freya waved them inside enthusiastically. "Come on in! Naomi, it's good to see you again!" She extended her arms and pulled Naomi into a hug. Maybe it was too much, but she was also genuinely happy that they had come to see her. In a small way, this made her part of the midnight antics too.

"It's good to see you, too." To her surprise, Naomi leaned into the hug and squeezed a little tighter.

"This is Becca," Will said, when they were done hugging. "And—"

Riley extended a hand. "Riley. We've met before. Although you may know me better as the Creative Director for the Fassi—"

Naomi coughed. "Not now, Riley. We don't want to keep you, Freya," she said. "We stopped in for a quick hi."

Freya closed the door to her office. "Come in for a minute." She motioned to the bar. "Can I get anybody a drink?"

Becca perked up. "Now we're talking."

Riley nodded. "While you're making drinks, maybe I could tell you about my idea—"

Naomi interrupted. "I think we're okay. We don't want to bother you."

Freya stretched her arms over her head. "It's a welcome break, honestly. I've been stuck in that chair all night."

"Do you have to work much longer?" Naomi asked.

Freya exhaled between pursed lips. "Two, three hours at least. A tour of the building sounds like a lot more fun right now." She looked at Will. "Are you going to take them to the observatory deck on forty-two?"

"Observatory deck?" Naomi asked, looking at Will.

"Yeah," Freya said. "The founder of the World News Organization was big into stargazing. Apparently when you're a billionaire, you can put a giant telescope on the top floor of a skyscraper if you want to." She smirked. "Although I've always suspected that he installed it for more ... romantic purposes. If you two want some one-on-one time with the stars, Riley and Becca can come enjoy the slightly less enchanting view here with me."

Riley's eyes lit up. "I would love to. In fact, perhaps we could—"

Naomi gave Riley a pat. "We should probably get going."

"You're right." Will appeared beside her. "Freya and I have to catch a flight tomorrow, and I don't want to be her excuse for being late. Again." He raised a threatening, if playful, eyebrow.

Freya smiled and gave a small wave. "All right then, you kids have fun." The four left and Freya headed back to her seat. The pang was still there, but the sensation had lessened. Seeing them, even for a few minutes, had been nice. Naomi had seemed genuinely happy to see her. It almost felt like Naomi was able to view her not as her best friend's foe, or her boyfriend's boss, or even as a public figure, but as simply Freya. She shook her head. She was definitely reading too much into one hug.

She looked back down at her papers. It was nose to the grindstone time.

One of the screens across her office flickered to life. It was the screen connected to the *Nightly Global News* studio feed. The empty anchor desk with the ambiguous skyline backdrop slowly came into focus. She stood up and walked over to the screen, picking up her drink from earlier as she passed the bar. The only reason the screen would be on was if the cameras were on. Why would the cameras be on?

She got her answer moments later.

"I hope I did that right. I don't exactly know how to work the control room." She heard Will's voice and then he appeared on screen. "I'm really not supposed to be touching anything but I figure I can turn the lights on in the studio for a few seconds so you can see where all the magic happens." He motioned to the anchor desk.

"Wow! Can you be star struck by an inanimate object?" Naomi appeared on screen.

"This lighting does wonders for me." Becca stepped underneath the bright lights, reached into her purse, and flipped open a compact, inspecting herself.

From somewhere behind the cameras, Riley cleared their throat. "Don't you mean it does wonders for me?"

"Oh right," Becca said, sounding less enthused. "I love the way it shows off your frame," she said.

"*Thank* you." Riley emerged from the darkness, carefully adjusting their shirt before walking over to Will. "Can anyone see us?"

"No, I didn't turn the cameras on," Will said.

"Oh yes you did," Freya said both amused and exasperated. She took a sip of her drink and kept watching.

"Excellent!" Riley spun on their heels and headed straight for the anchor desk. "Then she'll never know I was at her desk." They sat down in the chair behind the desk.

"Actually—"

Riley cleared their throat. "Good evening, ladies and gentlemen." They folded their hands on the desk. "On tonight's news, the world's sexiest human. And, oh look! Here I am!"

"Riley—"

Riley stood up and motioned across their body. "Six-foot-four, lucious skin that loves the camera, features that won't stop, and a sense of style that crosses city, state, national, and gender lines."

"That's not how you do it, Riley," Becca said, tossing her

purse to the ground. She walked to the front of the anchor's desk and hoisted herself up. Crossing her legs, she leaned back seductively. "It's more like this."

"That is not her desk," Will said, clearly annoyed. "And this is not an audition. Because no one can see you."

Freya smirked, wondering how they would feel if they found out they were, in fact, being watched.

Riley's face fell and their shoulders dropped. "Fine," they mumbled, walking around to the front of the desk, and stood next to Becca who was still striking poses. "It's fine. Because I wouldn't want to be Freya Jonsson for all the money in the world."

Freya's casual attention sharpened, and she leaned in a little closer.

She saw Will react too. His head whipped in Riley's direction. "What? Why not?"

"Why else?" Riley straightened and strode across the set until their entire face was nearly pressed up against the camera. "She has the most beautiful, most amazing woman madly in love with her, and she doesn't see it!"

Freya raised an eyebrow. Someone in Riley's cadre had developed feelings for her? They said she was oblivous. Did they know someone on her staff? That could make things awkward, though she was fairly certain she could still manage it. In her position, she was no stranger to people being attracted to her. Her agent, Kiara, helped manage her fan mail, but before Kiara she'd had to navigate the love letters, many of which crossed into disturbing territory. She had been happy to pass that task off to Kiara, although she did appreciate that she sent a few of the best letters to her for the occasional ego boost.

Will took a step towards them. "Who?"

Riley looked into the camera and for a moment, Freya thought they knew it was on. Then they began pulling at strands of their hair and she realized they were using the lens to see their reflection.

"Any day now, Riley," Will said.

Freya took another sip as she waited, curiously, to find out what they were going to say.

Finally, Riley whirled around and tossed their arm into the air. "Hello? Haven't you noticed? Abigail, obviously!"

The drink caught in Freya's throat. She managed to swallow before dissolving into a coughing fit. She ran over to the bar and poured herself a glass of water, trying desperately to listen in as she soothed her irritated throat.

By the time she could hear again, Will was standing in front of Riley, both hands on their arms. "—makes you say that?"

Riley peeled Will's hands off of them and brushed their sleeves before answering. "You think I would say something like this without being absolutely sure? I know her better than I know myself. That woman is smitten beyond belief. I'm not the only one who has noticed this—ask her best friend and her sister." Riley pointed to Naomi and then to Becca.

Becca was Abby's sister?

Becca, focused on her compact as she applied a layer of lip gloss, looked up. "Totally. Abby's been acting weird lately. Weirder than usual. For her. Not eating, not sleeping, looking like she belonged on the set of a post-apocalyptic movie."

"Sure," Will said. "That could be for a lot of reasons."

"True. Except Naomi and I asked her about it one night." Becca went back to applying lip gloss. After a few seconds, she looked at Naomi. "Didn't we, *Naomi?*"

Freya, Will, and Riley all turned towards Naomi. Naomi hugged herself, rubbing one hand up and down her arm. Freya had been in the business long enough to know that body language: Naomi had something to say but she didn't want to say it. Dear God, it was true.

"Yeah," Naomi finally said. "She confessed the whole thing. That she was madly in love with Freya and couldn't think of anyone else."

Riley pointed a finger at Will. "And there you have it! Naomi and Becca heard it themselves. Our Abigail Meyer is in love with Freya Jonsson."

Freya felt like she couldn't make sense of the information coming at her anymore. Abby? In love? She had so many questions and none of them were being answered. Why? When? *How?*

Will ran a hand through his hair, clearly overwhelmed with this news. "I can't believe it."

"It's true! She's wasting away and something needs to be done."

"Like what?"

Riley rested against the anchor's desk again and considered the question. "I think Abby should tell her," they said at last, giving a definitive nod of their head.

Will's eyes grew wide and he shook his head. "No! She can't do that!"

Riley appeared baffled at this answer. "No? Why not?"

"You've seen the way Freya acts around Abby. You know as well as I do what Freya thinks of her. While Freya has

113

many qualities, mercy isn't one of them," Will said. "If Abby told her, Freya would rip her heart to shreds."

This depiction made her cheeks tingle with heat. Was that how Will saw her? Merciless?

"What can we do for her then?" Naomi asked.

Riley gave a long exhale of defeat. "If what you say is true, Will, then there's only one thing we can do. We'll tell her she needs to get over Freya."

"I don't know if she can handle that," Naomi said. "As long as she has hope that Freya might love her too, she can keep going."

"Then we'll have to help her get over Freya in whatever way we can. I'm not going to let my dear friend suffer at Freya's expense."

"It's all so sad." Will sighed. "You're right, though, it's probably best if Abby never thinks about Freya again."

"Then we're agreed. We'll talk to her tomorrow." Riley clasped Will's shoulder. "There's no point in dwelling on it any longer! On with the tour!" They tossed an arm over their head and strolled off set.

"Okay then, I guess we're done in here," Will said with a laugh. "Why don't you join them; I'll turn things off."

The three walked off screen, but Freya continued after the cameras were turned off and the screen went black. She kept staring as she made herself another drink and sat down at her desk. Her thoughts looped like the menu on a DVD, replaying the conversation in her head. *Abby, in love with her?* It was impossible, but she'd heard them say it. It was impossible. But they'd said it. It was impossible....

# Chapter 9
## *Abby*

ABBY WALKED INTO HER OFFICE LOBBY TO REFILL THE hot water in her mug. As Riley liked to remind her, *lobby* was a generous word. It was a hallway that was barely wide enough to fit a loveseat and a water cooler inside. Last year, after nearly a decade of paying her dues, she had finally built up a big enough client base to afford a small—that being a generous word—office space of her very own. As she liked to remind Riley in turn, it was hers, and she could call the area whatever she wanted, and she wanted to call it a lobby.

The fresh infusion of water in her cup reinvigorated her gingerbread spice tea bag and filled her nostrils with the cozy scent of winter. She took a tentative sip of the steaming drink, careful not to burn her tongue, walked back to her office, and sat down in her chair. According to the clock strategically placed behind the sofa across from her, her next client was due in ten minutes, however with this particular client, she probably wouldn't show for another fifteen or twenty.

More out of habit than intention, she picked up her iPad

and began scrolling through her socials. First Twitter, then Instagram. She was about two minutes into her Facebook feed when she spotted it:

Will Quinn had added 4 new photos—with Naomi Hoffman, Freya Jonsson, and ten others. There were four photos of Will, Naomi, and Freya at—if she had to guess based on the office-beige walls and plastic cups—an NGN work event. Naomi and Will were going strong, and so she'd assumed that Freya was probably a part of Naomi's life, too. She'd done what her *Calm* meditations app had taught her to do with things she couldn't control: she'd packed that fact onto a little canoe and sent it down the river of her mind.

She'd done that a lot since Naomi had started dating Will. Like with the fact that Naomi still hadn't talked to Will about Simon. Abby had told Naomi, repeatedly, that she felt like she was making a mistake and putting their relationship at risk. Naomi had told her, repeatedly, that she was protecting Will and not letting her past define her future. Eventually, Abby had decided that she needed to let it go. It was out of her control. She hoped she was wrong. She liked Will. He had grown on her over the last few months. He had accomplished the near-impossible dating struggle of finding his place in a well-established group of friends, by adding a new and fun dynamic to their group while also knowing when he needed to sit out. Most importantly, Will had made it clear that he loved Naomi, and at the end of the day, that was really all that mattered anyway. So, every time she worried about Naomi's decision to keep Simon a secret, she put her concerns on a canoe and sent them on their way.

The problem was that the river of her mind seemed more like a lazy river than, say, the Mississippi. Instead of taking her thoughts far away and then dumping them into the vast and bottomless ocean, it seemed to go in one big, long circle that always brought her canoes right back to her.

Her thoughts about Freya had returned, docked, and disembarked. Freya and Naomi weren't crossing paths occasionally, as she'd assured herself. They were becoming *friends*. Facebook friends, but still.

She didn't want to know more, but she did. While she sat there explaining to herself why she should click away, her finger moved in and tapped Freya's name.

Her profile was almost completely locked down, dismissing the blossoming hope that it was a public profile run by some intern at *Nightly Global News*. There was only a profile picture of what appeared to be Freya accepting an award on stage —seriously, how pretentious—and a short bio:

*Mom to a Chou Chou named Amelie and a book named She Speaks*

There was so much to hate in those thirteen words—it was delectable and disgusting at the same time. Who touts their own book in a personal bio on Facebook? What kind of a title is *She Speaks*? It was probably some self-aggrandizing autobiography with a photo of Freya on the cover with her photoshopped face in her hands or her arms folded across her chest. Fueled by an addictive blend of self-righteousness and masochism, she didn't even bother to stop herself as she hate-Googled *She Speaks* and clicked on the Amazon listing.

*New York Times Best Seller*

*"Jonsson proves she is not simply a journalist, but an artist who can bring history out of the classroom and into our hearts."*—People

. . .

*WHEN WE SHARE OUR #MeToo stories, demand reproductive rights, and call for equal pay, we are not alone. Our words are carried on the voices of the millions of women who came before us.* She Speaks *explores the history of the feminine journey, the battles that have been fought to get us here today, and the critical role we play for the women who will come next.*

ABBY REACHED for her necklace and pulled at it, irritably. This was not exactly what she had been hoping for. If it had been written by anyone else, literally anyone, this would have sounded like a book she would have wanted to read. She put the thought that Freya might have written something good, something potentially meaningful, on a canoe, and gave it a good kick down the river.

"Knock, knock."

Abby looked up to see her client waving at the threshold of her office.

"Oh, hi Jeanine!" She motioned for Jeanine to come in.

As Jeanine walked toward the couch opposite her, Abby saw her glance at the iPad. "Oh my God," she said, taking a seat. "Have you read *She Speaks?*"

The question flustered Abby for a reason she couldn't pin down, and she focused on pulling up her Notekeeper app as she answered. "Ah, no. Went down one of those search rabbit holes, if you know what I mean. So, the last week," she said in the same breath, skimming her notes from her last session with Jeanine. "You were telling me about—"

"You really need to read it." Jeanine interrupted. "I know this sounds a little dramatic, but it was kind of life-changing for me. It shifted how I see myself. Remember when I broke up withBen last year?"

Abby nodded as she reached for her stylus and wrote down the date on Jeanine's file.

"Part of the reason was because I read that book. It made me see how I deserved to say what I want. We come from this legacy of women who have sacrificed to get us here, and they didn't fight so I could be with some guy that didn't think I was worth deleting his Tinder profile for. And I didn't want my legacy for women of the future to be one of not valuing myself and my worth. Seriously, you've got to read it."

Abby lifted the corners of her lips into a tepid smile. "I'll look into it."

"I even copied this one part down. Hang on." Jeanine patted the pockets of her jeans until she located her phone. After a few swipes, she nodded. "Here—'It was such a disappointment to grow up and realize that my parents hadn't been hiding the fact that I was secretly a princess, being hidden away until it was safe for me to take my rightful place as ruler of some far off country.

'If you feel that way too, you're not alone. It is one of the most pervasive narratives in our society—from *The Princess and the Pea* to *The Princess Diaries*, the story of the provincial girl who becomes queen is a tale as old as time. But why?

'I think it's because the story *is* true. We do come from royal stock. As women, we come from a line so powerful that since the very beginning of time, men have been trying to stop us, to hold us back, to own us, to blame us, to silence us, to burn us, to take away our names, our identities, our orgasms, our jobs—to do whatever they need to do to keep us from taking our place on the throne. The fairy tale is unfolding in your life right now. You know who you are. You are royalty. Put on your crown and fight for your kingdom.'" Jeanine clapped a hand over her heart. "I mean, oh my god. I cried my eyes out when I read that."

*Put on your crown and fight for your kingdom.*

Abby wrote the words down in her notes, her stylus barely touching the iPad. She didn't want Freya's words on her iPad but at the same time, it wasn't something she wanted to forget. At least not right away. She drew a single line under the quote.

"Anyway, you should check it out. But speaking of Ben," Jeanine said, putting her phone back into her pocket. "He called me yesterday."

Abby straightened in her chair and cleared her throat, doing her best to sweep any lingering thoughts of Freya from her mind. Luckily for her, at least in this instance, Jeanine was the kind of client who didn't need much prompting to talk, so most of the session, Abby nodded and took notes and, as she discovered after Janine left, also missed six calls and two texts from her sister.

BECCA: Peter and I went to see that therapist you recommended and then I found a wrinkle on my forehead afterward.

In a plot twist even Alfred Hitchcock would not have seen coming, her sister was not only fighting for her marriage but doing it in therapy. Abby didn't offer couples counseling in her own practice, but she had taken a semester of couples counseling in graduate school and none of her textbooks came close to covering a relationship like Becca and Peter's.

ABBY: You went? That's awesome!

BECCA: WRINKLE. Physical proof that therapy doesn't work

ABBY: You do understand that therapy isn't supposed to make you younger, right?

BECCA: Yeah but it's supposed to make you feel better. Not feel so stressed out that you age. Ergo, therapy doesn't work.

ABBY: I'm honestly impressed that you know the word ergo.

Becca replied with a gif of Chris Pratt winding up the middle finger in Guardians of the Galaxy.

ABBY: It'll get better, I promise.

BECCA: Or I can just think of something with less talking and more doing.

Abby waited, confident that her sister wouldn't be able to stop herself from finishing that sentence. It didn't take more than a few seconds.

BECCA: It. Doing it.

ABBY: Yep. I got you.

BECCA: Do you provide free Botox to all your clients or do they have to sign a waiver saying that you accept that you're going to make their collagen quit?

Abby did her own impression of Chris Pratt at her screen. Another message flashed on her screen, and she clicked it. This one from Naomi:

NAOMI: 🫘🫘🫘🫘

Jeanine was her last client of the day and she was due to meet Naomi at their favorite Mexican hole-in-the-wall.

ABBY: I'm leaving right now! I'm going to need an extra large margarita. Becca is blaming me for not fixing her marriage.

NAOMI: 😊😊😊😊

ABBY: Are you too hungry to communicate with words?

NAOMI: 💯 💯 💯 💯

Abby's stomach rumbled in agreement. Tacos sounded amazing. She turned off her office lights before returning to her lobby, where she began the long process of transforming into the Stay Puft Marshmallow Man: coat, scarf, earmuffs, boots. Then, a quick punch of the alarm code before putting on her gloves, and stepping out into the icy evening.

∼

ON A FRIDAY NIGHT, traffic into the city was always gridlocked as residents clocked out of work and immediately flocked downtown for shopping, drinking, and dancing. As her Lyft pulled up in front of the restaurant, Abby could see

Naomi waving at her from inside. She waved back as she got out of the car.

"You're not going to believe this," Naomi said to her in lieu of a greeting when she walked in. "It's a thirty-minute wait."

Abby looked around. The small waiting area was packed like a rush hour train, and she could barely hear Naomi over the din of hangry customers. "Apparently, it's not our secret spot anymore."

"I'm happy for them. They deserve the success."

"Yes, yes, obviously good for them," Abby halfheartedly agreed. "But in the meantime, I'm devastated for us. I don't mind waiting, but what are we going to do when we're drunk and desperately need the yummiest tacos in the city right away?"

"Wait, like the plebs we are."

Abby rammed her hands into her chest like she was driving a knife into herself. "My heart." She moaned. She expected to hear Naomi's laugh, but she only got a weak smile instead. "You okay?"

"Oh, yeah." Naomi gave a shake of her head and her smile got bigger. "What were you saying in your text? Why is Becca blaming you?"

Abby's eyes rolled so hard she took her entire head with her. "I guess she and Peter finally went to see that therapist I recommended to her," she said. "Which, don't get me wrong, gave me this funny feeling I've never felt before. Something akin to pride. I can't be sure. But then she needed to take time out of her day to tell me how terrible it was and make it sound like it was somehow my fault."

Naomi patted her pockets and nodded. "Uh huh, listen

could I borrow your phone for a second? Mine is almost dead and I forgot to check the, uh ..."

She was too far into her diatribe to stop so she kept rolling as she unlocked her phone and handed it to Naomi. "Which is this fun thing we've been doing since their whole marriage ... debacle, if you can even call it that. She asks me to help her. Not really asks, demands. Then hates whatever I suggest. Those two are an enigma, wrapped in a mystery, tangled inside of one giant ball of dysfunction. All I have to say is, be glad you are an only child."

Naomi, who, to Abby's annoyance, had been half listening and half scrolling, looked up with wide eyes when the sound of "Poor Unfortunate Souls" began playing. "Oh, hey," she stammered. "Looks like Becca is calling."

Abby considered the phone in Naomi's hand. "Oh good. Either a pocket dial or she's calling to register another complaint. I think I'll pass."

"No!" Naomi said it so loud it almost amounted to a shout. She gave a little cough and said, quieter, "No, um, it really sounds like she's going through a tough time right now. You literally just said you don't want to see her in pain."

Abby reluctantly took the phone. "You know, I don't feel it's proper best friend duty to throw my words back in my face and make me be a good person." She accepted the call. "Hello?"

She had to cover her ear but eventually she could hear what sounded like Becca in the middle of a conversation. "... borrow your handcuffs," she heard her say. "I tried to fix things Abby's way but now I want to try them my way."

"Hello?" Abby said again. She looked at Naomi. "Yep, pocket dial."

"My favorite kind of request on a Friday night," it was Riley. "Yes, let me grab them for you."

"What do you hear?" Naomi asked, inching closer.

"It sounds like Becca is at Riley's getting her version of a cup of sugar?"

"I'm glad you're here, I was just about to ask Riley something I'd love to get your thoughts on," came another voice.

"Oh my God," Abby laughed. "It's Will too."

"That's right. Will mentioned he might hang out with Riley tonight," Naomi said.

"Either way," Abby said, "I don't really need to listen to her talk about how she's going to use sex toys with Peter from the ass of her jeans." She lifted the phone from her ear.

"Wait," Naomi put a hand on her arm. "Aren't you curious to find out what Will and Riley are like when we're not around?"

Naomi made a compelling argument. She *was* extremely curious about that. In addition to the Will and Naomi romance, there appeared to have developed a full-fledged Will and Riley friendship. It tickled her, honestly. The only guys she'd known Riley to hang out with were ones whose name they'd forgotten in the morning, and she loved that Will had brought out this new side of them. She was dying to know what that side was. She wanted a peek into the locker room, so to speak, and Naomi was right—this was her chance. She rocked her head side to side, silently letting Naomi know she was open to this suggestion, and then pressed the phone more tightly to her ear.

"Here they are," Riley said, their voice getting louder. "Will, what is it you were about to ask me?"

"Yes, as I was saying to Becca, I need to get your advice,

but you have to promise you won't say anything." It was Will's voice.

"Alright, this might be worth it after all," Abby said to Naomi. "It sounds like Will is about to spill some tea." Is this what they did during their hang out time? Gossip?

They must have indicated their agreement because Will continued. "It's about Freya." Abby's mouth dropped open an inch. "She's in love." It unhinged further. "With Abby."

This time her mouth didn't drop open. The entire floor did, and she was swallowed up into quicksand. The noise of the restaurant was sucked into oblivion, and it was only her and the sounds in her ear remaining.

"I can *not* believe what you're telling me," Riley said. "How do you know?"

"She sat me down and told me," Will said.

"It makes sense to me," Becca said. "I've seen the way Freya looks at Abby."

"I am shocked. I am aghast. I am speechless except for this speech," Riley said. "Is there any chance you could have misunderstood? What were the exact words she used?"

There was a pause and the sound of some shuffling. She wanted to scream into the phone, "Yes, what were the *exact* words?" but she was afraid any sound might alert them to the fact that she was listening in.

"She said, um," Will faltered. "Help me, Will. I'm in love with Abby and ..."

"Yes? And what?" Riley prodded him.

"And ... it is a yearning so deep and ... passionate that I ..." There was another shuffling sound, and everything got muffled. She could hear talking, it sounded like Riley and Will, but she couldn't be sure. Maybe Becca was sitting on her phone or it had fallen into the couch cushions? She strained, pushing the phone against her ear with near brute force, desperation rising in her chest.

After another shuffling sound she heard Will clear as day. "Well, you get the point."

"Barely," Riley said.

"Enough to understand that she wanted my help. She wanted to know what to do about her feelings. She said she'd been able to live with them all these years but she keeps running into Abby, and it's too painful to see over and over how much Abby hates her."

"That poor woman. I can only imagine what she's suffered," Riley said. Abby heard a sound like two fingers snapping. "We have to tell Abby."

"Are you kidding?" Becca scoffed. "She'd have a field day with that information. She would become a heat seeking missile for Freya's heart."

"You make a good point." It was Riley again. "It's a high risk, high reward situation. If we tell her, she could decide to have mercy on Freya and maybe cut her some slack. On the other hand ..."

"Are you kidding?" Becca said. "She's like ... the Daenerys of relationships. She comes off all levelheaded and cool but she's really going to take her dragon and burn everything down. Freya is King's Landing, you guys, and Abby will legit destroy her if she can."

"That feels a little, um, over the top," Will spoke up. "I think what you're trying to say is, this thing between Abby and Freya has been going on so long, she might not be ready to believe us or Freya, and that could end up causing a lot more damage in the long run."

"Sure, or that."

"The other option," Riley said. "Would be to find a way to help Freya get over her feelings, and do our best to run interference, to make sure she doesn't run into Abby again."

"So which option do we go with?" Will asked.

"I vote don't tell her," Becca said.

"Although Becca got a little descriptive there, I think she might be right. To answer your question, I think it's safer for everyone involved if we keep this to ourselves."

"I guess it's decided then."

"Good, because that's my quota for talking about Abby for at least a week," Becca said. "And I've got some hand-cuffing to do."

"No offense Will," Riley said. "But hearing that kind of makes me sad about how my Friday night is going so far."

"Hey, the night is young." Becca said. "You never know how things might turn out."

"You can ask Naomi, I'm not that adventurous," Will responded. "Plus I'm taken."

"Right," Becca said. "That's a thing that comes naturally to you people. You need to send some of that monotony juju my way."

"Don't you mean monoga—"

"Tah tah!"

The sound of a door closing and then nothing but the clacking of heels and the rhythmic *shh-shh* of the phone brushing against Becca with each step. Abby waited for ... what? She wasn't sure. When it was clear that she wasn't going to hear anything else from Becca's call, she hung up.

"Hear anything good?" Naomi asked, startling Abby into recalling where she was and who she was with. Her brain felt like it had been flattened, turning her thoughts into a two-dimensional plane. What was she supposed to tell Naomi? She tried to navigate the conversation she'd overheard, but everything was shapeless and indistinguishable. None of it made sense.

If Freya was in love with her, then nothing she said to Abby could be taken at face value. Memories flashed across her mind, encounters and arguments being rewritten like a heist reveal at the end of a movie. Was she the oblivious bank manager happily guarding the front door while there was a tunnel being dug to the safe?

What would that even mean?

She didn't have an answer to any of it. She wasn't going to get any answers in this hot, noisy, restaurant with Naomi staring at her.

"I'm not feeling well all of a sudden," she heard herself say.

"Do you want to step outside? Get some fresh air?"

"I think I need to go home."

Naomi said something, but Abby was already turning to walk out the door.

# Chapter 10
## *Freya*

FEATHERS FLUTTERED AS THE BURLESQUE DANCER snaked the pink boa across her body to the beat of a smooth jazz tune. With each brush and tug, she invited the audience to imagine what could be. Her sequined garter band glittered from the stage lights as she teasingly lowered it down her thigh, her calf, then her toes, until she was spinning it on her index finger. As the music reached a crescendo, she winked and tossed it into the crowd.

The black material disappeared into the shadows of the dimly lit bar and Freya had no idea where it had gone, until it landed to the left of her feet.

"If you catch the bride's bouquet, it means you're getting married next," Will, seated across from her, said. "What does it mean if you catch the burlesque dancer's garter belt?"

Freya picked it up off the ground and smiled. At this very moment, everything felt good. Soft, hazy, and welcoming, the way it can only be in a dark bar after a few perfectly made cocktails. She tried to remember the last time she'd had this much fun, but she couldn't pull up a recent or even distantly recent memory. "I think it means I'm going to become a burlesque dancer." She dangled the garter belt at Naomi, who was seated between her and Will. "What do you think? Maybe Naomi and I could do a double act?"

"Me?" Naomi said with a laugh. "I don't think I—"

Freya didn't give her a chance to finish her protestation. She kicked her chair back as she stood up and in one graceful move, took Naomi's hand and pulled her to her feet. "Oh, come on, you know we'd be a sensational team. Here, just go like this." She did her best impression of a burlesque shimmy. Naomi giggled but then gave in and tried to copy her. "See? Look at us. Will would pay to see us dance, wouldn't you?"

The look on Will's face made her and Naomi burst out laughing.

"I think we broke him," Naomi said.

Dancing with her Associate Producer's girlfriend in a speakeasy some time well after midnight wasn't how she thought this night was going to go. She had thought she was going to be in her office, sifting through the ninety-seven e-mails that had accrued during her marathon of meetings that day.

Earlier that evening, she had begun the process of thinking about doing that. Her eyes were already blurry from the hours spent staring at video calls, and the idea of putting in another few hours staring at tiny words on a screen was about as appealing as attending a concert of nails on a chalkboard. Sitting at her desk, she had let out a breath, propped her chin onto her hand, and moved her cursor over the oldest e-mail, when a knock on the door saved her.

"Hey!" Will's silhouette framed her door.

"Hey, come on in," she'd said, straightening.

He stepped further into her office. "I don't need anything," Will preemptively reassured her. He pointed behind himself. "I'm heading out for the night. Wanted to make sure you were all good before I left."

"I'm good here," she'd said, lacking the energy to give that statement any enthusiasm. "I'm hoping not to be here much longer either. My inbox is a bit of a disaster so I'm going to slog through that for a bit. You doing anything fun on this exciting Thursday night?"

"Yeah, Naomi and I are heading to this speakeasy in River North. I saw something about it online and have been dying to check it out. It's located in the basement of another bar and apparently every hour there's a burlesque show."

The image of an underground bar and dances with fans covering just enough sounded so much better than e-mail, but she had ninety-seven reasons to stay where she was. "You'll have to tell me how it is," she said, curtailing herself.

Will had cocked his head to the side slightly. "Did you want to ... come with us?"

How could Will always pick up on what was simmering under the surface?

Of course, the answer was yes. She absolutely wanted to be holding a cocktail, not a mouse, and staring at alluring dancers, not her inbox, but she couldn't go. There were the e-mails, but there was something holding her back even more. It was the same thing that had held her back from spending unnecessary alone time with Will for the last few weeks. As evidenced once again by tonight, he always seemed to pick up on the little things, and she couldn't let him pick up on the fact that she had overheard him and his friends talking that night in the studio. She couldn't let him pick on the fact that learning about Abby's infatuation should have been the final, definitive, victory she had been looking for. Instead, each time she tried to fathom that Abby was in love with her, it felt like she was trying to imagine the sound of one hand clapping. It didn't make any sense, and it left her feeling exposed instead of fortified.

Spending time with Will was one thing, but it was something entirely different to spend time with Will *and* Naomi. Since that night, she'd seen Naomi in a distanced kind of way. A you're-close-to-someone-in-my-life-so-now-we-should-be-cordial kind of way. They'd done the social media thing, adding each other as friends. There had been a healthy exchange of small talk. Naomi had even watched her dog once when the sitter fell through at the last minute, but she'd never sat across from Naomi in an intimate space and talked. She'd never spoken with her while Will and Naomi were sitting there, unaware that she knew that they knew that Abigail Meyer was in love with her.

She'd waved Will, and those images, away. "Thank you, but I should really get through these e-mails."

Will was a bloodhound on the scent. He could sense she was waffling. "Come on, one drink. It's not far from here. Those e-mails aren't going anywhere."

She'd looked at her screen. "That's what I'm worried about."

"Did I mention they specialize in bourbon cocktails?"

That sounded heavenly. It had been a long day, and a long week, and she could really use a little down time. Could she actually relax around Will and Naomi?

She gave an internal shake of her head. This felt ridiculous. She couldn't keep avoiding Will like this. It seemed like

Naomi was going to be part of the equation going forward. She was going to have to get over it at some point. Somewhere her face would be obscured by her drink and the low lights seemed like the best place to do it. "Okay, one drink."

Will gave a celebratory fist pump. "Success."

"Easy, tiger," she said, a smile tickling the edges of her lips.

"Shut that laptop down and let's go to a bar I probably shouldn't take my boss to, and that we probably shouldn't tell HR about."

The smile won, but only for a few seconds. "You should check with Naomi first," she said.

She hadn't expected him to smirk in response.

"What?" she asked.

"I cleared it with her before I stopped by your office. I had a feeling you needed to blow off steam."

She opened her mouth, wanting to disagree, or at least find some way not to give him the satisfaction of being so completely right, but nothing came out.

"What can I say, I'm good at my job?" He'd grinned at her. "Naomi's really excited you're coming."

Something else she wasn't expecting. He was keeping her on her toes tonight. "She is?"

"She knows you're—" he hesitated over his words before finishing the sentence. "Important to me. She wants to get to know you better. I'd love for you to get to know her better too."

She wasn't sure what to say. Thank you? That's sweet? I feel awkward? I want to get to know her better too but it's not something I'm very good at? Are we not going to talk about the elephant in the room? Let's not talk about the elephant in the room, okay? Instead, she had shut her laptop with a flourish and said, "Let's get going, then." She held up a finger. "One drink."

After many more drinks, and hours, than she had planned, she walked with Will to the street to wait for her driver. "Thanks for inviting me out tonight." She held onto his arm for support, but given the way he was walking, she was pretty sure if she fell, he'd go down with her.

"I'm glad you came," he said, his words coming out a little more elongated and relaxed than normal.

"Me too." She stopped at the curb and checked her phone to confirm that her ride was nearly there. She looked back at Will. "Naomi is a great lady."

He gave her a full, happy dog grin. "I know. She's the most amazing person I've ever met," he said. He leaned in closer, as if to share a secret, and then said loudly, "I'm going to ask her to marry me!"

Maybe it was the sum of the cocktails, or the lingering enchantment from the evening in a secret bar, or maybe it was finally getting to spend time with Naomi, but Freya felt nothing but excitement at this news. "You are? When? What's your plan?"

"I don't know. I got the ring. I'm trying to figure out how to surprise her."

Freya's phone beeped just as a car pulled up. "Looks like my ride is here, but I'm so happy for you! Show me a picture of the ring tomorrow, alright?"

"You got it, boss." He paused and then laughed. "I got drunk with my boss."

"Night, Will." Freya got into the car and closed the door, enjoying the first silence she'd heard in several hours. As the car pulled out, she leaned her head back against the headrest.

Will had been right, about needing to blow off some steam, about getting to know Naomi better. She'd needed to get out of the office, out of her head, out of that night playing over and over in her mind. She'd needed to find herself again, to remember that it didn't matter if Abby loved her or hated her, because in the end, Abby was quite literally of no consequence to her. She'd needed to see the phones peeking in her direction as she danced, snapping pictures and videos, and to enjoy the hard-earned privilege of being in the public eye.

She also needed to drink water and take Aspirin before bed, but she hadn't done either yet.

~

"Oh, sweet lord, my head," she said to no one in particular as the elevator doors opened onto the *Nightly Global News* floor the next morning and her vulnerable pupils were attacked by fluorescent light.

"Next up, I'll be trying my hand at some new Easter Egg dyeing techniques with Rachel Rae!" Jane, the perky blonde host of *Wake Up! America*, spouted from the television mounted in the hallway. She turned to her co-host, Randy. "I didn't know you could improve on egg dyeing. Isn't it just dipping eggs into some food coloring?"

Randy chuckled into his *Wake Up!* mug. "Is the Easter Bunny even going to know what to hide? He's going to look into his basket and be like *what?*" This elicited a laugh from the studio audience.

Freya tried to walk as quickly as she could away from the

screens, but her legs weren't responding. She looked down at her feet and ordered them to pick up the pace.

"Looks like you could use some coffee." Will appeared in front of her. "I was about to make a run; can I get you anything?"

"The usual. Actually, let's go with a black coffee for right now, until I figure out if putting something in my body will revive me or kill me," she said. "Don't tell me you're not hungover."

"Oh, it feels like the running of the bulls inside my head right now."

"Can you act a little less chipper, then?" She rubbed her temples.

"Freya!" Brian waved at her from the other end of the hallway.

"Of course, this is what I need," she said, keeping her voice quiet enough that only Will could hear her. She straightened her shoulders and yanked her cheeks up until she felt like she was smiling. "Hey, Brian!"

"We missed you at the executive golf retreat last weekend," Brian said, slowing down for his approach. His rotund cheeks were sun-kissed, a rare sight in the frosty Chicago spring.

She gave the most apologetic shrug she could muster. "I hate to miss it, but I've got a lot on my plate right now. And golf's not really my thing, so ..."

"Not your thing, huh? I guess we should do a manicure and brunch retreat next time so you'll come." Brian was the only one who laughed at his own joke.

Maybe she didn't need coffee, just a dab of patriarchy in the morning to get her brain up and running again. "I prefer firearms. I'm a pretty mean shot. Let me know if you ever want to join me at the range."

Brian made a little hemming noise. "Anyway, I wanted to talk to you about the McCallister story you pitched in the meeting yesterday. We're going to have to table that for now. It's too controversial."

Frustration roiled in her already upset stomach. It had been a long shot pitching a story about a young man's experience at conversion therapy camp, but like the Light Brigade, she'd decided to charge forward—and like those brave soldiers, she was met with her inevitable fate.

"As I mentioned on the call, studies show that these programs aren—"

"This is network television, not cable. We need stories that are family-friendly."

She knew what "family-friendly" was code for. The network didn't have problems showing limbs peeking out from rubble in war-torn areas or substance users passed out with needles in their arms. She also knew that there was no point in arguing. The network was never going to change.

"That means, obviously, we'll need you to come up with a new story to fill that slot," Brian continued.

She looked at Will. "Can you pull up that other story we were looking at last night and send it over?"

"You got it, boss." The phrase tickled her memory, bringing up images from the night before.

*Show me a picture of the ring tomorrow, okay?*

*You got it, boss.*

"Hang on, Brian." She held up her hand, a genuine smile emerging. "If you're looking for family-friendly, I've got one idea."

# Chapter 11
## *Abby*

ABBY ARRIVED IN HER LIVING ROOM WITH TWO BOTTLES of wine tucked under her arm, a large glass in each hand, and a bottle opener hanging from her back pocket. "Here we are!"

Riley lay sprawled on her couch, studying themself in their phone camera. "Riley, what are you doing? Can I have a little help here?"

Riley's phone locked with a click. "It's been all day, and you haven't said a single word about my hair. In fact, no one has."

"Let's see," Abby said as she handed them the glasses. "First off, I think maybe the launch of your own clothing line has possibly overshadowed your new bouffant."

"It's not my own clothing line. It's a few pieces under the Fassi label that are bastardized versions of my original designs."

Abby set the bottles down on the table. "And second, I did say something about it. In fact, we had an entire conversation, if I recall. It went something like—I like the new look,

139

Riley. The single green stripe down the middle reminds me of that faux hawk you had a few months ago, only without any spikey part. It's like a faux-faux hawk. And then you said," she put a hand on her hip and adopted her best Riley affectation, "I'm calling it a no-hawk, darling. And it's not green, it's moss. Spring has sprung after all. I'm invoking the new season."

She looked at them, waiting for a sliver of recognition.

Riley reached over and tugged the wine opener from her pocket. "That's all pleasantries. Like saying 'how are you' to someone when you don't really want the answer."

Abby raised two fingers to her temple and closed her eyes. "Hmmm," she said. "My spidey senses are telling me that somebody may be transferring their feelings about other things to their hair."

"Yes, are your senses also telling you that I haven't slept, eaten, or seen a naked man in several months?" Riley asked as the first bottle of wine opened with a satiating *pop*.

Abby flopped onto the couch. "I think I would feel worse for you if you hadn't, I don't know, taken your career to a whole new level today?"

Riley poured a liberal helping of wine into a glass and handed it to Abby. "I wouldn't call it a new level. This is the first time I've been the creative lead on an entire line. It's like a stepping stone. A time-consuming, soul-eating, stepping stone."

"Here's to landing on the stone with some of your soul intact." Abby lifted her glass and clinked it against Riley's.

Riley took a large gulp and then collapsed back into the cushions. "I have literally been counting down to this moment." They rolled the stem of the glass between their fingertips, watching the wine slosh around the glass.

"What about the big launch party yesterday? I thought you were looking forward to that."

"You know what they don't tell you in school?" Riley mused. "They don't tell you that when you finally do strike it big, you're going to be too busy to enjoy a roomful of beautiful people and the steady flow of alcohol. I was being pulled in so many directions at the launch trying to get ready for the runway show, I hardly had a moment to bask in my own glory. And then I was too exhausted to relish the after-party."

"Oh, you poor thing," Abby said in a baby voice. "It must be hard being so fabul—"

Knocking interrupted her.

"It's me, open up!" Naomi said from the other side of the door.

"Okay, see? See how she knocks even though technically she has keys?" Abby said, giving Riley side eye as she got off the couch.

"I'm not sure I understand what you're getting at," Riley said.

Abby opened the door, and before she could say hello, Naomi burst in, shouting, "Turn on the TV, turn on the TV!"

They both watched with raised eyebrows as Naomi scrambled across the living room, dove for the remote, and began stabbing at the buttons.

"What? What is it?" Abby said anxiously, until she saw the grin plastered on Naomi's face and knew that whatever it was, it wasn't bad news. She carefully slipped the remote from Naomi's grip. "Here, I've got it."

"You look like you could use this more than me," Riley remarked, handing her their glass of wine. They sat up and pulled Naomi down to the couch with them.

Abby turned on the television. "What channel?"

"Nine. Channel nine," Naomi said, gripping the wine glass with both hands.

Abby pressed nine on the remote control. "Channel nine ..." she said, her brow creasing. "Isn't that the WNO?"

Riley gasped in what Abby assumed was an overdramatic response to her question until she heard them say, "Oh my God, is that a *ring*?"

Abby turned to look at Naomi, but stopped when she realized she was already looking at Naomi ... on the television.

A *Nightly Global News* anchor flirted with the camera as a picture of Naomi and Will floated in a small box above her head.

"—bit of excitement right here at Nightly Global News. Will Quinn, an associate producer who has been with NGN for almost three years, invited his girlfriend to join him on the job for what he told her was going to be a routine interview taping with Freya Jonsson. What she didn't know was that he and the rest of the crew were ready to give her the surprise of a lifetime."

"What?" Riley shrieked.

Naomi pointed at the TV. "Keep watching!"

The image cut to a shaky shot of Freya, in a dark wool coat, being handed a microphone. Behind her, a frosty Lake Michigan churned and tumbled against the backdrop of a cloudless blue sky. Freya held the microphone close to her mouth. "How's that sounding? It's pretty windy out here," she remarked, glancing up at the camera which quickly zoomed in and out from her face several times. "Good? Okay."

The camera steadied, the image focusing and refocusing until Freya was perfectly in view, her azure eyes the same color as the lake behind her.

As her eyes fell on Freya, Abby's skin begin to burn as memories of Riley's pocket dial bubbled to the surface of her mind.

*"It's about Freya. She's in love. With Abby."*

She barely remembered leaving the restaurant after that call. She'd managed to mutter an excuse, but her body was on autopilot while her mind swirled like a tornado.

*"Now that she keeps running into Abby again, it's too painful to see how much Abby hates her over and over again."*

Freya? In love with *her*? Freya didn't like women; she was straight. She'd only dated men in high school. More importantly, Freya didn't like Abby. Freya *couldn't* be in love with Abby, because she hated Abby.

She had walked aimlessly for a few miles, her mind hopelessly churning, until she found herself turning onto her mother's street and realized she hadn't been walking aimlessly at all.

"You look tired," her mom had commented in a worried tone, going into Jewish Mom mode and bringing out food to resolve the issue.

"Not tired," Abby had said, sinking into a chair at her mom's kitchen table. "Just have a lot on my mind lately." Her fingernails tapped on the kitchen table like Morse code as the call continued to echo in her brain.

*"She's like ... the Daenerys of relationships. She comes off*

*all level headed and cool but she's really going to take her dragon and burn everything down."*

Abby had looked up at her mom who took a seat across from her. "Do you ... I mean, do I ... what do you do when the rules change?"

Her mom gave a little chuckle that reminded Abby of Becca. "In what way?"

"I don't know." She rested her head in her hands. "In the way where you haven't changed, but the other person has, and it confuses everything."

"Honey," her mother said, bringing more food from the refrigerator. "All you can do is take care of yourself and do what's right for you. When your father changed into a cheating putz, I went ahead and changed too. Every lock on our house."

While perhaps not the most appropriate anecdote, it had served to bring some clarity to Abby. Riding in a cab home later that night, Abby decided there was nothing she could do about the call, and even if there was, the little stock of energy she had left at the end of the day would not be spent on Freya, of all people. She needed to take care of herself and do what was right for her. As the cab pulled up to her apartment, she put the entire incident in a canoe and locked the canoe in a vault and tossed the vault into the river where she imagined it sinking to the bottom. Forever. Lazy river or Mississippi, it didn't matter, the river of her mind was never bringing that canoe back.

And it didn't.

Until she watched Freya, on her television, look at someone off-camera and say, "Would you mind standing here? I want to get a sense of the framing." She beckoned with her fingers and nodded encouragingly. "Come on—just for a second."

Abby thought that she had already had the wind knocked out of her, until she saw Naomi shuffle onto the screen and realized she still had a little bit in reserve.

She wore the same pair of flared jeans and hooded DePaul University sweatshirt that she had on now. Thoughts of Freya were superseded by the realization that this must have been footage from earlier this afternoon. Why was Naomi on national news?

TV Naomi glanced nervously at the camera and then planted her eyes on the ground, her lips stretching into a part grimace, part smile.

Riley clapped their hands excitedly. "Oh my God, you're on TV!"

"There we go," Freya slipped the microphone into her coat pocket and then reached forward, placing two leather-gloved hands on Naomi's arms, positioning Naomi across from her. She reached for the mic again. "Bet Will forgot to mention that we were going to put you to work when he invited you to come along today."

Both Naomis giggled, and Abby cut her eyes to the Naomi in her living room who was watching the television intently, eyes and mouth wide with delight. Abby turned back to the TV.

"—a little to your left. See! You're a natural at this!" Freya was saying. "Right, okay—so how's this looking?" She took in the full view around her, then lifted the microphone up. "Okay, then I'm talking to you and—" She held the microphone toward Naomi, giving a slight hum of disapproval and took a small step backward. "Much better. Good, so let's see. Now then I'm interviewing you and I say something like—So how are you today, Naomi?"

The microphone tipped toward Naomi. She looked at Freya and then stammered, "I ... I'm great, thank you." Then she added, with a sniffle, "A little cold."

"I see. And tell me, Naomi," Freya said, bringing the microphone back to herself, "Have you decided whether or not to accept Will's proposal of marriage?"

Naomi gave a confused laugh. "His what?"

Before she could say any more, a hand emerged from behind her and tapped her gently on the shoulder. The camera pulled back to reveal Will, lowering to one knee and holding out a small black box. Naomi's hands flew up to her mouth, and she gasped.

"Naomi Hoffman," he said, looking up at her. "From the moment we met, you have changed my life for the better. You make me happy in ways that I never even thought were possible, and I want the opportunity to spend the rest of my life making sure I make you just as happy. If you'll let me." He inhaled and opened the box to reveal a shimmering three-stone ring. "Will you do me the honor of becoming my wife?"

Still holding her hands over her mouth, Naomi's head rocked up and down. Finally, her hands dropped from her face, revealing tear-stained cheeks. "Yes, of course!"

Will leapt up, wrapped his arms around her, and kissed her while the crew clapped and cheered. He pulled away long enough to slip the ring on her finger before he was kissing her again.

The image of Will and Naomi entwined against the backdrop of the majestic lake froze and shrank until it was positioned above the shoulder of the news anchor who gave the camera another seductive glance.

"Congratulations to Will and Naomi. We'll be—"

Abby had heard enough. She hit the power button and the television went dark.

"Oh, you missed the announcement!" Naomi put the glass down on the coffee table, a bronze glow in her cheeks.

"There's more?" Riley asked.

"Oh, it gets even wilder! Abby, are you listening? You'd better sit down for this."

Abby lowered herself beside Naomi, exchanging the briefest of glances with Riley. Their eyes flashed the same concern she was feeling, and she pursed her lips, wondering how they were able to sound so gleeful despite glaring issues.

Lost in her excitement, Naomi missed their furtive glances and squealed. "Nightly Global News didn't only let Will propose to me on the news, they decided to do a whole wedding special. You know, like the kind they do on talk shows sometimes? They've decided they want to have NGN follow us over the next month as we prepare for the wedding, and they're going to pay for everything!"

"Month?" Abby repeated in a hoarse whisper. "*One* month?"

Naomi nodded. "I know, can you believe it?"

Abby gulped, trying to choose her next words carefully. No, she couldn't believe it, but not for the reasons Naomi was asking. There were so many reasons that this was a terrible idea, but she knew this was not the moment for pragmatic or negative thinking. Still, she wanted to leave the door open for the discussion about the practicalities of getting married to someone Naomi had known for a little under a

year in an incredibly public forum that could draw the attention of some unwanted people such as a stalker ex-husband.
In a month. Maybe something that expressed jubilance but
was tempered with a small amount of concern.

She gave Naomi her most enthusiastic smile. "You can't
be serious." She raised a hand. "No, wait, that is not what I
meant to say. What I meant to say was … was … okay, that's
exactly what I meant to say. You can't be serious!"

Out of the corner of her eye, she could see Riley vigorously shaking their head. The reversal of roles was not lost on
Abby, and for a millisecond, she tried to remember the last
time Riley had been the one trying to enforce good behavior.

Naomi looked crestfallen. "What do you mean? You're
not happy for me?"

"No, sweetie. I am. I'm happy for you." Abby leaned
forward and gave her friend a quick squeeze. "But do you
really think this a good idea?"

"Why? You don't think I should marry him?"

"It's not that. It's that it hasn't even been a year since you
started dating each other. He's a great guy, don't get me
wrong. And it's obvious he loves you very much. I mean,
wow, look at that rock. But, well, a month. Is that enough
time to convert to Judaism?"

"Oh." Naomi gave a small smile. "He's not going to
convert. But he's fine with having a Jewish wedding and
raising our kids Jewish."

"You always said that was really important to you, and
now you're throwing that away for someone you hardly
know?" Abby couldn't care less if Will converted. But she'd
seen enough of Naomi giving away parts of herself to fit the
relationship and she was done with it.

Naomi's brows dipped down. "It was important to me when I was twenty-two and marrying Simon, but I've changed."

"Speak of the literal devil. Have you even told him about Simon yet?"

Naomi didn't respond but from the look on her face, Abby knew the answer was no.

"This is what I mean, Naomi!" Abby said, her voice reaching soprano. "How can you build a future with a man that you won't let into your past?"

Naomi stood. "I've already told you; Simon has nothing to do with me and Will."

Abby stood, too, and looked in Naomi's eyes as they began to shimmer with tears. "How can you say that an entire part of your life has nothing to do with you? You loved that man, you married him, you wanted to have children with him. You can't act like he didn't happen!"

"When I'm with Will, he didn't!" Naomi said, a few volume clicks away from a shout. "Don't you understand? I can finally let go of all that baggage!"

Abby smacked her hands against her legs, partly for emphasis and partly to release the deep-seated frustration that had once again been let loose and was dancing through her veins. "This is not the baggage claim at the airport, Naomi! You can't pick up someone else's suitcase and hope nobody notices!"

"You think I don't know that?" Naomi snapped back at her. "I have to live with that for the rest of my life! But Will doesn't! I don't want to make him suffer because of my mistakes!"

"Sweetie, that's part of what marriage is! You don't get to

149

pick and choose the parts of you that he gets to marry!"

Naomi exhaled, a combination of a sigh and a growl. "Even if I wanted to tell him, Abby, you think I could now? What am I supposed to say?"

"I don't know—how about 'hey, Will, I think you should know that I was married once before and I'm sorry I didn't tell you earlier?'"

"You're acting like it's so simple!"

"Because it is! You say the words and then you go on to have a happy, healthy marriage!"

"No, because then he's going to think I was lying to him!"

"You are lying to him!"

"I'm protecting him!"

Riley materialized behind Naomi. "For God's sake, ladies, what is happening here? Why are we yelling, why are we standing, and most importantly, someone explain to me *why* we are not all drinking? Both of you—sit down now and imbibe." They pointed a stern finger at the couch, and Abby found herself sitting meekly next to Naomi.

Riley thrust a wine glass into Abby's hand, filling it to the brim, and then did the same for Naomi. "You two have put me in a very uncomfortable situation here. I make it my personal mission not to have to be the mature one in the room, but clearly this is an emergency situation that calls for extreme measures. And so, as the interim mature one, I would first off like to say to Naomi that I forgive you for stealing my limelight today. Sure, this is a defining moment in my career and tonight was supposed to be about cele-brating me and my accomplishments and you managed to outdo me in a way that completely ties my hands from bringing it up or attempting to put any of the attention back on me, but I totally understand and will not hold it against you."

Naomi tilted her head and looked from Riley to Abby, seeking some sort of translation.

"Riley's clothing line launched yesterday," Abby said.

Naomi gave a little gasp of embarrassment. "Oh, it totally slipped my mind in all this commotion. Congratulations, Riley!"

"Yes, well, we can talk more about that later," Riley said, knitting their eyebrows together in a show of steely authority she had never seen before. "I need my two moms to stop fighting. So, let's start with you, Abigail. Abby, tell Naomi that you're sorry for being an extra verse in Alanis Morissette's *Ironic* and that you can't wait to help her with her saffron and tea-green wedding that will bring out the luscious amber of her skin tone."

Abby couldn't decide what rankled her more: being called out by Riley, being told to apologize for something that she knew she was right about, or knowing deep down that Riley was probably even more right than she was. She went with the first two. "I'll apologize right after you tell her that if she wants to protect her boyfriend—sorry, fiancé—then maybe she should think about the repercussions of getting married on national television where her stalker ex-husband might very well see her. Oh, and you might also want to mention to her that flaunting her love story in front of a man with a history of unpredictable and violent behavior seems very unsafe."

Naomi stood again, still holding her wine glass. She scowled at Abby and then said to Riley, "You tell Abigail that I'm not the girl I was when I married Simon and that she can stop trying to control my every move!" She stomped toward the door and pulled it open. "And tell her if she really loves me, she'll stop trying to fix me, and she'll tell me that she's happy for me and that she'll be my maid of honor because that's what best friends are supposed to do!"

The door slammed and Naomi was gone.

Abby stared unblinking at the door until Riley's voice brought her back. "That went well. Remind me again what you do for a living?"

Abby turned her head to meet Riley's gaze. "What just happened?"

Riley lifted their eyebrows "How can I put this gently?" They cleared their throat. "You channeled your sister."

Abby winced. "That was gentle?"

"You're right. That was cruel. But she does have a knack for making any situation about her, and you managed to do that to your best friend."

"I wasn't making it about me! I was making it about her! You can't pretend I'm not right. I mean, the whole thing is—"

"Of course it is! Everything you said was spot on. That girl is heaping loads of trouble onto herself."

Abby threw her arms into the air. "Why didn't you back me up?"

Riley crossed their legs and adopted a professorial expression. "Abby, when you threw a martini on an award-winning journalist, what did Naomi do?"

Her face flushed at the mention of that incident, to her chagrin. "That is totally different, and you know it!"

"That's not what I asked. What did she do?"

Abby thought for a moment. "She told you, is what she

did. First, she made me leave, then she told you. Then you two made fun of me."

Riley gave a slight nod. "Exactly! And what about that time in sophomore year of college when you decided to try a certain illegal substance and then you ended up falling and spraining your ankle? What did Naomi do?"

"She ... drove me to the emergency room," Abby recalled, a smirk yanking at the corner of her lip as she remembered that long night at the hospital. "Then she called you. And you two made fun of me for months."

"Mm-hmm," Riley confirmed. "And what about that time you pretended to like camping so you could impress that girlfriend that we all hated—"

"Jasmine," Abby said in the vocal equivalent of an eye roll.

"Yes, Jasmine! That's it. And she broke up with you and left you stranded in the middle of Wisconsin? What did Naomi do?"

"She drove up to get me and then she told—" She tossed her head back. "Okay, I get it. What's your point, Riley?"

"My point is that we are not like ... this." They motioned around the room, conjuring up the last few minutes. "That's what I love about us. Our little group— we're a safe place to do the stupid things that all of us need to do to find our way. Lord knows we've all made some unfortunate decisions in the past. Remember when I thought I could effectively pull off parachute pants? Good God that was a mistake. But what matters is that we have each other to lend support and bring a little levity to the situation. Naomi doesn't need you to tell her what to do. She doesn't need you to rescue her. She's never needed that.

She needs her best friend to give her a hug, then you call me, so we can make fun of her."

"Oh my God," Abby said, as impacted by Riley's point as she was by the fact that it was Riley making the point. "You're right."

Riley blew out a long breath. "For the love of all that is holy, can you please go make things right so I can stop being so serious? I can feel it affecting my elasticity as we speak. Besides, Naomi has my wine, and I am not going to let this evening spoil all my celebration plans."

Abby didn't bother to answer. Instead, she leapt off the couch and hurried down the hallway to Naomi's door. She raised her hand to knock, but the door swung open before her knuckles could make contact.

"Naomi—"

"No, let me go first," Naomi said. "I was coming back over. I hate that we keep fighting. We never fight, Abby! I know you're looking out for me and I'm sorry for getting so angry."

"No, I'm sorry." Abby reached out and clasped her hands around Naomi's arms. "I don't know what keeps coming over me, but I promise it will never happen again. From here on out, you shall see hide nor hair of the Bridemaidzilla you met back in my apartment."

Naomi gave a little laugh. "So, you'll do it, then? You'll be my maid of honor ... again?"

"Are you kidding? Of course, I will! Besides," Abby added. "I have a feeling this network-sponsored event is going to be a little different from your last wedding."

"Oh God, yes!" Naomi exclaimed. "I was so poor! Do you remember how we handmade all the invitations?"

"To this day I can't look at a glue gun without breaking out into a cold sweat." Abby and Naomi both chuckled and fell silent.

"I'm so glad you're here, Abby," Naomi said finally, her voice soft. "I couldn't do this without you."

"You're my best friend, Naomi. I'll always be here for you."

"Oh, I love you, Abs," Naomi said, throwing her arms around Abby.

"I love you too, Naomi."

"Hallelujah!" The girls both jumped and released their hug, startled at the sound of Riley's voice beside them. "Just like in the ancient text, the Red Sea was parted, but by my hand, it was united again."

Naomi and Abby looked at each other and smiled. "I think the Red Sea parting was a good thing," Abby said, turning around to look at Riley "But I get your point."

Riley clicked their tongue. "Oh, just because you're Jewish doesn't mean you get to lecture me about the finer points of Biblical history. I saw the movie, or at least parts of it. Definitely the part where Adam—"

"Moses," Abby said.

"—parted the waters. But don't forget, my love, after he parted them, he brought them back together again. At a crucial moment, I might add. Why does no one talk about that key incident of the story? Without the waters coming back together when they did, the Romans—"

"Egyptians," Abby corrected.

"—would have wiped everybody out anyway."

"You've been coming over for Passover for nearly a decade and that's what you've taken from it?"

"What I've taken from it is that it's as much about the parting as it is about the coming together. Without Naomi and Abby coming together, I would have been forced to carry the heavy burden of serious, wrinkle-inducing conversation. But my powers of persuasion prevailed, and I can add mediation to my list of natural skills." A door creaked open and Mrs. Pachenkis appeared, stroking a long-haired cat and eyeing them under her drooping brow.

"I think we'd better head inside," Abby said.

"Excellent idea. I believe there's a glass of wine waiting for me in Naomi's apartment, anyway." Riley breezed into the unit with the gait of someone who was quite satisfied with themself. They called out, "And we can continue the party in here. You do have liquor at your place, right, Naomi?"

Naomi ushered Abby into her apartment, closing the door behind her. "I think I have something in the pantry," she said to them. "And I want to hear more about the launch party last night."

"Right after you ask me about my hair," Riley said, dropping to the couch with a flourish.

Abby sat beside Riley and gave their leg a friendly pat. "I think what they mean is, right after you tell us more about this wedding. One month?"

"Yeah." Naomi blew out a breath of air, ruffling the hair around her face.

"And they're paying for ... everything?" Riley spotted their wine glass sitting on the windowsill and stood to retrieve it.

Naomi took a seat in the overstuffed chair opposite the couch. "Pretty much," she said. "They think it'll be good publicity for the show. Something about the softer side of the news."

"I thought you hated being in front of a camera. I think the last picture I have of you is from our college graduation, and I had to take it when you weren't looking," Abby said.

"I do," Naomi replied. "But I've had a little acting practice lately." Naomi exchanged an unreadable look with Riley.

"What kind of practice?" Abby said, suspicious. "What's going on with you two?"

Riley gave a sharp laugh that bordered on a holler. "Do you think they've got your engagement video on YouTube yet? I want to watch it again!" They snatched Naomi's laptop from the coffee table, nearly spilling their wine. "And will someone please tell me that they like my hair?"

# Chapter 12
## *Freya*

"Knock knock," Freya said, not actually knocking on Will's door, which was wide open.

Will was standing at his desk, bent over his computer, fingers flying over the keyboard. He looked up briefly. "Hey, just give me one second. I'm trying to get this FOIA request in before I head out." He mumbled out the words on his screen, double checking what he had typed, then nodded, and gave a confident click of the mouse. He straightened and smiled at her. "There! Sorry, It seems like I only get seconds to do my actual job these days."

Freya still wasn't quite sure how, but what had started as an idea to get the NGN executive producers to give them a little breathing room had blossomed into something a lot bigger. Less than one day later, the story of Will and Naomi's engagement had gone viral. With each new segment shown at the end of *Nightly Global News*, Will and Naomi's popularity grew. People around the globe were tuning in, streaming, downloading, sharing, memeing, recapping, and all around loving their story. In a sudden and unexpected reversal of roles, Freya found herself acting as Will's Associate Producer, helping him manage a schedule that now involved podcast, radio, magazine, and television interviews. They'd even gotten their own couple name, dubbed by the internet as #Wilomi.

She had never confessed this to Will, but for the first few days, a part of her was entirely flummoxed. Not that she didn't think Will and Naomi were wonderful and deserved all the attention, but why had a five-minute wedding segment with, if she had to be honest, fairly-low production value, captured the attention of the entire planet? She'd spent a few nights on her office couch, scrolling through posts, videos, and comments before she found an answer. In a world where the twenty-four-hour news cycle exists because there is always something dark and depressing to report on, a story about two ordinary people finding love amidst chaos was, as most people commented, refreshing. The next most common words were "heartwarming," "uplifting," and then "comforting." It seemed like Will and Naomi had become a worldwide chaser to all of life's troubles. If two ordinary people living ordinary lives, not stars or influencers or politicians or one percenters, could find a happily ever after in the middle of all of the endless pandemonium, then maybe everyone else could too.

That, at least, made sense to her, even if she was a little jealous that the secret was out. It was that ordinariness that had allowed her to open up to Will, to see him as not only an Associate Producer, but a friend. Will had goals and aspirations for himself and his career, but unlike most people in their industry, he wasn't willing to compromise on who he was to achieve them. Somehow, amazingly, he'd managed to find his counterpart in Naomi. Spending time with the two of them was, yes, refreshing. It was one of the only times she didn't feel like she had to be anyone but herself. That had remained true even after these past few weeks. Despite all the attention, they were still the same down-to-earth people.

Naturally, the executive producers didn't care what it was about Will and Naomi that people liked. Importantly, advertisers liked paying to be seen alongside what viewers responded to. Each day, the network budgeted more time, more money, and more resources to the wedding special, eager to ride the wave and cash in on it as much as possible. She'd never seen them so excited, which irked her more than she wanted to admit. Maybe the award-winning, truth-exposing, hard-hitting work that she'd done wasn't quite as sexy as a viral wedding segment, but—scratch that. It was sexier. This was reality TV and, sure, it was a good idea, but journalism wasn't only about money and views. At least it shouldn't be. At least they could pretend it wasn't.

"Aren't you supposed to be at your fitting?"

The daily wedding specials highlighted the latest in the countdown to the Hoffman/Quinn marriage. In two weeks, Will and Naomi had picked flowers and invitations, tasted cakes and sampled dinner menus, auditioned bands, selected their first dance, and made a laundry list of other decisions, all on camera. Heading into week three, it was time to dress the groom and his groomsmen, who would be introduced to the audience for the first time.

"I'm waiting on my wedding party. They should be here any minute and then we'll head over. The crew is supposed to meet us there." Will snapped his laptop closed.

"Heard anything from Naomi? How's her fitting going?"

Somewhere on the other side of the city, Naomi was supposed to be trying on wedding dresses.

"I haven't heard a peep, but I'm guessing they're pretty busy over there. Seems like a lot more work to pick out dresses than to stand there while someone measures your inseam."

"Who did she decide on for her wedding party? Does she have any siblings?"

"No siblings or cousins or anything. She went with her chosen family." His pause was almost imperceptible but it was just long enough that she knew what was coming next. "Abby, as her maid of honor, and her sister, Becca, as her bridesmaid."

Freya held her face still, hoping the lack of reaction would assure him that there was nothing for him to worry about. Ever since that night at the speakeasy, she had left Abby where she belonged: in high school. She was pleased to note that she felt nothing at the mention of Abby's name. "I think that's wonderful," she said, and meant it.

The slight pull around Will's eyes relaxed. "Yeah. I'm a little envious that she has friends that are so close to be honest."

"Who did you end up picking?" The decisions for the wedding party had been between Will and the executive producers, who had gone from "sure, you do that," to micromanaging every aspect of the event. Will had been pulled out of a meeting two days ago to go over his picks and get them started on the vetting process.

"Lucas, my cousin, as my best man. We're not super close, but we spent a lot of time together when I was growing up. He got married right out of college and I was his best man, so it felt right. And Riley. You probably remember them. Tall, impeccably dressed, hair always a different color."

"That's a rather bland description of me, but I'll take it."

Freya turned around to see a tall, impeccably dressed person, with silver hair. She recognized them, most notably from when she'd watched them from her office screen, as they declared that Abby was in love with her. The memory flickered in her mind's eye, before she blinked it away.

"Riley." She extended a hand. "Good to see you again."

They returned the handshake, adding a slight curtsy. "The pleasure's mine."

"Riley!" Will stepped out from his desk to give Riley a welcoming hug. "Love the new hair."

"It was entirely out of necessity. Waiting to find out if you were going to pick me to stand in your wedding caused me so much distress that I actually found," they cupped a hand around his mouth and whispered, "a gray hair." Riley raised their hands and spoke louder. "I don't know what happened then. I panicked like I was some kind of rookie murderer trying to get rid of the evidence. I blacked out, and the next thing I knew, I was standing in front of the mirror, my hair covered in bleach, and a box of silver dye on the counter."

Will put a hand on Riley's shoulder, his smile belying his condolences. "I wish I could have told you sooner. I wasn't allowed to say anything until they told me I could."

Riley put a hand over Will's. "All I ask is that you remember my sacrifice."

"We'll put it on your gravestone." Will took his hand from Riley's shoulder and stretched it out in front of him, as if he was reading from a headstone. "Here lies Riley, who laid down their hair for a friend."

Riley clucked their tongue. "Not that I appreciate you discussing my death so flippantly, but to be clear, my place of rest will be a sight to behold. We're talking Studio 54 for dead people. No sad little gravestone with some one-liner about my selflessness."

"Wait, is the Studio 54 for people who are dead? Or for the people visiting the dead people?"

Riley let out an exasperated breath but the smile in their eyes gave them away. "I'll tell you what, with an attitude like that, you won't be invited to the party either way."

Will laughed. "I have an attitude because I ask questions?"

"Yes! It's rude!" Riley said, the smile spreading from their eyes to their lips. "Speaking of, don't tell me I wasn't fashionably late enough that I'm the first one here."

"I guess so. I'm surprised Lucas is late." He walked over to his desk, picked up his phone and checked the screen. "I would have heard if his flight was delayed or something. Let me see what's going on." He unlocked his screen and started tapping.

"Excited for your television debut?" Freya asked Riley, filling the silence while Will's attention was on his phone.

Riley patted the hair on the side of their head. "I have to admit, it's thrown me for a little bit of a loop. First the hair thing, then the tuxedos. I'd never pictured that my breakout role would be in a cookie cutter tuxedo. I asked the producers if I could at least do a Billy Porter at the Oscars and wear a tuxedo dress, but they flat out denied me."

*Let me guess, it wasn't family friendly*, she wanted to say.

Instead, she nodded sympathetically. "Television likes to play it pretty safe and uniform when it comes to these kinds of things."

"Well," they said, attending to the other side of their head. "I hope they'll at least let me add a pocket square and cufflinks that have some personality. If I'm stuck dressed in all black like the Wicked Witch of the West, I might actually melt like her too."

"That's weird," Will spoke up. "Lucas says he's not in the wedding anymore."

"What?" Freya asked.

Will typed something on his phone and then held out the phone for her to take. "Look."

She took the phone and angled it so that Riley could see.

> WILL: Hey, almost here?

> LUCAS: What do you mean? I thought I wasn't in the wedding anymore.

> WILL: What?

> LUCAS: Yeah, somebody from the studio called me this morning and said there was a last minute change of plans. I figured you knew.

> WILL: I have no idea what you're talking about. Let me find out what's going on.

Freya skimmed the conversation and then gave the phone back to Will. "Last minute change of plans? What are they talking about?"

Will gave a frustrated toss of his hands. "This is the first I'm hearing of it."

More micromanaging from up top, no doubt. "Let's see if we can get some answers." She walked over to Will's desk phone and, without having to look at the keypad, turned on the speaker phone and dialed Brian's extension.

"Brian Green's office," his assistant answered.

"Dylan, it's Freya." She sat down on the edge of the desk. "Is Brian in?"

"Hey Freya, one second."

There was a click, silence, and then, "Yello."

"Brian, hey, it's Freya and I've got Will here."

"Hey, Brian," Will said, taking a step towards the phone.

"My two favorite people! What can I do you for?"

"Yeah, hoping you can help us out here. Will's groomsman Lucas said that someone called him this morning and said there's a last-minute change of plans and he's out of the wedding?"

"That's right," Brian said.

"Okay," Freya said, making a 'speed it up' motion with her hand towards the speaker. "What's the change? We're all in the dark down here."

"Don't tell me no one talked to you."

"No one talked to anyone except Lucas, apparently."

"Dammit. Someone was supposed to come down and talk to you both this morning."

Freya dropped her head backward and glared at the ceiling in an attempt to channel her annoyance. "No one did, so can you fill us in?"

"Oh, well sure. The long and short of it is, it's you."

"You, who?"

"You, Freya."

"I ..." She stretched the word out, trying to encourage him to finish the sentence.

"You are replacing Lucas. We'd like you to be the best man—well, er, woman. We still need to talk to legal about what to call you."

Freya's head snapped back to center and she met Will's eyes. "Wait, what?"

"Our polling suggests that it will land really well with the viewers. They didn't seem particularly interested in meeting the wedding party since they don't know anyone, but they know you, and as it turns out, they want to get to know the softer side of Freya; the friend." When neither Freya nor Will said anything, Brian added, "I assume that won't be a problem?"

"Umm," Freya stammered. She didn't know if it was a problem yet. It was the last thing that she'd been expecting to hear, and she couldn't translate Will's expression. "It's ... okay with me, if it's okay with Will."

"Uh, yes," Will said, giving his head a little shake like he was trying to bring his thoughts into focus. "Yes, absolutely, it's great. In fact, it'd be an honor to have you stand for me."

"Excellent," Brian said, sounding eager to finish the call. "Glad we got that taken care of."

"So," Freya said, her brain scrambling to put the pieces together. "I'm going to the fitting with Will today?"

"You got it. The tux shop is expecting you, and wardrobe sent over your measurements this morning, or at least they were supposed to. It seems like no one is interested in doing their job. I assume that you don't have any issues wearing a tuxedo?"

She didn't, but Brian's assumptions were really starting to irk her. "No, I suppose I don't."

"Good. Any other questions?"

"Uh, nope, that'll do it," Freya said. "Thanks Brian."

"You betcha," he said.

Freya lifted the receiver and put it back down, disconnecting the call. "Listen," she said to Will. "This is all about the numbers to them, but it's your wedding, so you should have whoever you want standing up with you. I can still go talk to them ..."

"No, no," Will said, taking a seat next to her on the desk. "Don't misinterpret my surprise. I think this is fantastic."

She had expected "fine," maybe "okay," but "fantastic?" "You do?"

"Yeah," he said. "If I'm being honest, I'm actually ... closer to you than I am to Lucas. I'd considered asking you, but then I talked myself out of it. I figured you wouldn't want to be part of this hoopla, doing confession cam interviews and stuff. Plus, you're so busy, especially with me dealing with all this wedding stuff."

Freya breathed in deeply, taken aback by the feeling of elation that flooded her chest. She *was* busy and she *didn't* want to be part of the hoopla, but she *did* want to be part of this special moment in her friend's life. Apparently, he wanted her there too. It seemed this friendship had deeper roots than she'd realized.

"In that case, I'd love to be your best man, um, woman. Person."

"Sweet!" Will opened his arms like he was going for a hug, but seemed to have second thoughts about halfway in. Freya wasn't sure what the etiquette was for professional, friend, wedding party hugs, but leaned toward him, giving him an even more awkward pat on the back.

They'd have to work on that part of the friendship.

"Oh, come on," Riley appeared beside them and threw their large wingspan around the two of them, bringing them into a tight squeeze. "There is no tighter bond than between a man and his wedding party."

"Thanks, Riley," Will said in a muffled voice from somewhere under Riley's arm.

Riley released them and stepped back. "I think we're not recognizing the magnitude of what's happening here. No offense to your cousin Lucas, Will, but he doesn't hold a candle to Freya. Your wedding party now consists of, hands down, the two most beautiful people in the city, nay, the country, possibly—if I may be so bold—the world?"

Will smirked at Riley. "It's only a bold statement once you get to the entire world?"

Riley raised a single 'talk to the hand' palm and continued talking. "What I'm saying is that this is the beginning of something special," they turned to look at Will, an unreadable expression on their face, "Something, *explosive*."

"Alright," Will stood up quickly and shuffled Riley towards the door like a petulant child late for school. "We're late, we need to get going."

It took Freya a moment to remember that she was part of the "we" in that sentence. She technically wasn't ready to be on camera but, thankfully, she was always fairly prepared. Her lipstick might need a refresh, but the rest of her, from her stiletto heels to her deceptively casual beachy wave curls, were in perfect form. "Lead the way."

She spent the short car ride on her phone, canceling

meetings and distributing a few assignments. Google told her that the average tux fitting took fifteen to twenty minutes, but between set up, interviews, and whatever extra Riley might bring, she was expecting to be gone for a few hours.

When they arrived, the camera crew was already there.

A thin, gangly man with a mop of brown hair that hung over a headset walked up to her. He was one of the associate producers on *Nightly Global News*. "Hi, Freya!"

"Hey, Max!"

"I'm the AP du jour," he said. The associate producers had been taking turns directing the shoots for the Wedding Special each day. Freya had been worried that they would be resentful of the task, having to give their co-worker special treatment and taking on the extra workload of reality TV production, something that wasn't in their job description. As far as she could tell, though, much like the viewing public, they seemed to be enjoying the refreshing change of pace from the news. "What brings you here?"

"I'm glad I'm not the only one they forgot to tell," she said, more to herself than to him. "There's been a change in the wedding party."

Max looked at Riley and Will, then to her, then to the clipboard in his hand. "I've got Will, obviously, and then Riley and Lucas?"

"Not anymore," she said. "Lucas is out. I'm in."

"Oh," Max said. Then again, more forcefully, "Oh!"

"Yeah," she said. "I found out about twenty minutes ago. You're looking at the new best woman, title pending legal approval."

Max scribbled something on his clipboard, suddenly seeming a little more nervous. He was a newer addition to the *Nightly Global News* team and hadn't worked with Freya one-on-one yet.

"It'll be fine. Treat me like one of the crew—or I guess cast." She playfully nudged her elbow towards his ribs.

His laugh was too anxious to be genuine. He wrote something on his clipboard and then cleared his throat. "We were planning to do a CCI—oh a, um, a confession cam interview in case you weren't familiar—with Lucas first. So..."

She held out her arms, indicating her flexibility. "Tell me where you need me."

He pointed at a sofa at one end of the shop, where soft box lights and a camera on a tripod were already set up. "Take a seat and we'll be right over."

She walked to the sofa, making slight adjustments to her crepe silk blouse before she settled on the cushion in front of the camera. Out of the corner of her eye, she could see Max talking to Pete, one of the seasoned camera operators. After a short and hushed exchange, Pete gave him a reassuring clap on the back and the two of them walked over to her.

"The best woman, huh?" Pete said to her by way of a greeting. "I didn't know the execs had it in 'em to be so progressive."

"I think we can chalk this one up to accidental progressivism," she said, with a laugh. "They were only thinking about the money."

"Aren't they always," Pete replied, setting himself up at the camera.

Max leaned over her and attempted to attach a lavalier mic to her collar. "Oh, sorry," he muttered as his fingers danced uncomfortably around her shirt.

"I've got it, Max," she said, as kindly as she could, taking the mic from him and clipping it to her blouse.

"Oh, thank you," he said, more a sigh of relief than a sentence. He stepped outside of the camera's line of vision and waited until Pete gave him the thumbs up that they were ready. "Let's get started then."

"Fire away." There was something oddly comforting about being in front of a camera. That glassy black circle, sucking in your every movement like a black hole, gave most people anxiety, or at least a little pause, but to Freya, it almost felt like a second home. It was perhaps the only place where she could feel seen, not necessarily for who she was, but for whom she wanted to be. When the camera turned on, everything else fell away and it was only her, the best part of her, that was on display. She shifted her shoulders, giving the camera her best angle, and smiled.

Max smiled. "Okay, well, um, as you probably already know, I'll ask you some questions, but they're designed to get you started. You can answer however you want and feel free to add on whatever you'd like." She nodded at him, and he continued, looking at his clipboard like it was a lifeboat on the *Titanic*. "I'll give you a softball question to get us going. How do you feel about being asked to be in the wedding?"

She turned her smile up a notch. "I can honestly say it was a surprise, but an incredible one. I've had the pleasure of working beside Will for years now. We've traversed the globe together and have had some pretty incredible, and sometimes even frightening, adventures. Working that closely creates a bond, for sure, but it's based on more than just proximity. Will is a good guy, one I'm grateful to call my friend, and it's been a real privilege to have been able to witness his beautiful love story with Naomi. She's the perfect match for him and I couldn't be more thrilled to be part of celebrating their special day."

"Great, thanks," Max said. He looked to Pete for confirmation and got a nod. He looked back at the clipboard. "Oh, you probably haven't thought about this yet since you only found out a bit ago but, um, it's typical for the best man or, er, the person in your position and the maid of honor to give a speech at the wedding. Any ideas what you're going to talk about? Or do you have anything planned with the maid of honor?"

She gave an on camera sized laugh. "No, we haven't—" She stopped mid-sentence as her entire body locked up like a seized engine.

"Freya?" Max asked after several seconds had passed.

She didn't look at Max, she looked at the camera. She looked in the lens, her place of comfort, as if it could give her answers. "Oh my God, the maid of honor is ..." Warmth traveled up her neck. It was not the creeping kind of flush, but a roaring bonfire that threatened to melt the layers of setting powder right off.

Being in the wedding party meant that Abby wasn't someone inconsequential in her past. It meant she was someone Freya would be walking up the aisle within two weeks.

*She confessed the whole thing. That she was madly in love with Freya and couldn't think of anyone else.*

The words that she'd tried so hard to forget were back, twirling through her mind like an evil witch on her broomstick, and with it, the questions. There were so many questions. It changed everything, but ... did it? It didn't change that Abby was still the same controlling, self-righteous, know-it-all that she had been since freshman year of high school. It didn't change the things that Abby had said and done to her. Did it? If all those things had been said and done not out of hate but out of ... love? Love? No. It couldn't be. Could it?

"We can skip that question ..." Max said. He looked at his clipboard again, flipping through pages, as if there were responses to her behavior in there.

His voice brought her back. She looked back at the lens, back to center. She couldn't do this now, not on camera of all places. She took a centering breath and reapplied her smile as best she could. "Apologies. Let's try that one again, shall we?"

# Chapter 13
## *Abby*

"WHAT I CAN'T UNDERSTAND IS WHY SOMEONE WON'T blindly spend that much money on me after meeting me for one day. This show makes me hate myself."

Riley's voice resonated so loudly on speakerphone that Abby's cell rattled on the coffee table and sent small ripples through the glass of wine resting next to it. Abby rescued the glass, snatching it from the table and topping it off with the last of the bottle she'd opened at the start of her *90 Day Fiancé* marathon date with Riley. Cramming a year's worth of wedding planning into four weeks had left very little time for their reality TV and wine nights. This evening, Naomi and Will were selecting wedding rings, which meant that the wedding party had the night off. She and Riley had put it to good use by catching up on one of their favorite shows.

It was strange watching a reality show since she was in the middle of her own. Knowing what the behind-the-scenes were really like had dulled some of the shine, if she was being honest with herself. In between the *90 Day Fiancé* episodes, she and Riley had stopped to watch tonight's

Wedding Special, which was the recap of wardrobe shopping from the day before. Out of the several hours spent—and a few especially good one-liners that Abby had been sure would make the cut—Abby's only screen time was her repeatedly trying, and failing, to bustle Naomi's dress. The tiny buttons and loops were not only invisible on the cascade of fabric, but when she was able to find them, they were inhumanely small.

"You're going to be late for your reception because I'll be spending two hours trying to get these buttoned," Abby had said, unflatteringly sprawled on the floor, tongue poking out from her lips as she tried for the tenth time to replicate what the bridal attendant had shown her.

"Here is my fool proof way to ensure you'll be ready on the wedding day," the attendant said.

"I'm listening," Abby replied.

"The night before the wedding, get some drinks in your system. When everything gets a bit fuzzy, practice. Then drink a little more, and practice some more. The muscle memory will be fresh for the next day, and you'll be prepared to do it a little tipsy."

Naomi looked over her shoulder. "Sounds like we have a plan for the night before the wedding, Abby. Drinking and bustling."

"God help me," Abby had replied.

This is what *Nightly Global News* had decided to highlight, which, she told herself, was definitely better than if they had chosen her reaction when she found out that Freya was the best woman. She had let out what she could only assume sounded like a death rattle upon envisioning what it would mean to walk arm-in-arm up the aisle with Freya at the wedding, while having to act like she hadn't overheard that Freya was madly in love with her and had been since high school. Luckily, her friends had no clue that she knew, and they likely assumed that her reaction was pre-pocket dial. Pre-pocket dial Abby would have reacted strongly to having to be Freya's wedding counterpart, but for different reasons than post-pocket dial Abby. Post-pocket dial Abby, despite her best efforts to keep all the thoughts vaulted at the bottom of the river, couldn't stop playing every interaction between her and Freya over and over in her mind. She couldn't stop picking apart their conversations—if they could be called that—looking for clues, and answers. What did it mean? What did it change? What was going to happen when they spent time together? How was she supposed to act now? Pre-pocket dial Abby knew exactly how to behave around Freya, but the thought made post-pocket dial Abby's insides feel like they were being vacuum sealed, which was probably what caused that horrible sound to come out of her mouth.

Naomi had checked on her privately, once the cameras were pointed away, to make sure that she understood that this was something the studio had done, not her or Will. She'd been grateful when the wedding attendant pulled her away to try on another dress, forcing a change of subject, as it gave Abby time to regain her composure. Thankfully, no one, including *Nightly Global News*, had taken it any further, leaving her to deal with it in an entirely untherapeutic way of coping which involved copious amounts of wine and trashy reality TV.

"You must have finished your bottle of wine too," she said to Riley as she petted Lancelot, who was nuzzled, fast asleep, in her lap. "You've moved on to the self-loathing phase of your drunkenness."

Riley exhaled noisily. "You're right, and it makes me hate myself even more."

"That means it's time for you to go to bed. We're out of episodes anyway."

"True," they agreed. "Or..." they drew out the word.

"No or."

"*Or* we could select one of the other ten thousand reality shows available to us on demand, keep drinking, and push *through* the self-loathing phase into the giddy phase," they said.

"That sounds like a terrible idea on a school night," Abby said as she stared at the empty bottle of wine that perched on her coffee table.

Riley stretched. "It's only midnight. Besides, you can't tell me there's going to be a big difference in the hangover created now versus the one created by a martini. Or two."

"I look forward to hearing how tomorrow Riley feels about that statement."

"You can tell tomorrow Riley to suck a dick."

"I feel confident that tomorrow Riley would love to do that, so as insults go, it's not a very strong one."

"Fair point."

"What you're saying is that the grownup thing to do is go to sleep," Abby said.

"That is what I'm saying, yes."

"Well now I hate me *and* you."

"Goodnight, Riley."

"Goodnight."

Heeding her own advice, Abby gave Lancelot the heave-ho and then shoved herself off the sofa. She eyed the remains of the evening: three Chinese takeout boxes, a fortune that read *If certainty were truth, we would never be wrong,* a plate, silverware, napkin, and one, accusing, empty bottle of wine.

As tempting as it was to follow in Riley's footsteps and leave the problem for Tomorrow Abby, she was confident that—unlike Tomorrow Riley—her future self would most definitely not want to suck a dick. She gave her own noisy sigh and then scooped up the leftovers, carried them into the kitchen, and hastily shoved the items in their appropriate receptacles. Once she felt that the kitchen was decent enough to leave for her future self, she returned to the living room where her nearly full glass of wine was waiting for her. Her phone sat beside it, the screen glowing with a new notification.

*Five unread e-mails*

Five e-mails in the few minutes it had taken her to clean up? What the ever-loving hell was going on at this hour?

As she snatched her phone, every *Buzzfeed, Vox, Mind Body Green* self-help article (or perhaps more accurately, headline) that she'd ever read about the importance of not checking your phone right before bed tapped on her shoulder. Whatever it was, it couldn't be an emergency. She'd get a text or a phone call if it was an emergency. It could probably wait. She should put the phone down, walk away, and check it in the—

*Freya Jonsson Subject: Bachelor/Bachelorette Party (5)*

While her id and ego had been battling it out, her face had unlocked her phone. Seeing Freya's name on her screen

—not only on her screen, but in her inbox—felt like a half dozen shots of espresso in her veins.

Too late now. She had to click and see what it said.

It was also addressed to Riley and Becca, which soothed her nerves a little. Whatever it was, it wasn't specifically to her.

*Subject: Bachelor/Bachelorette Party*

*Hi all,*

*Hope you're doing well.*

*I know I've met everyone at some point or another but since joining the wedding party, I haven't had time to connect with all of you. So, let me start off by saying I'm looking forward to celebrating our friends' big day with you!*

*The studio would like the wedding party to plan a joint bachelor/bachelorette party for our soon-to-be-wed friends. I've been asked to get the ball rolling by emailing you all with the budget and event expectations (attached). They want us to host the party two days before the wedding, so that means we've got less than a week to pull this off!*

*Please take a look when you have a moment and let me know your thoughts!*

*Freya*

*Freya Jonsson*

*Senior Correspondent*
*Nightly Global News*
*She/Her*

*1 Attachment: WillseyBachelorSpecs.pdf*

As HER EYES reached the signature line, Abby realized that she had barely read the e-mail. She sank into the couch, picked up her wine, and, after a comforting sip, read it a second time.

It was an incredibly benign message. Polite and professional, but friendly. What had she been expecting to have gotten her so worked up that her cheeks were still toasty warm?

Rather than answer that question, she downed a little more wine and scrolled to the next message, which, according to the time stamp, had arrived one minute after Freya's e-mail. It was from Becca.

*Yesss! If there's anyone equipped to pull off a last-minute bachelor/bachelorette party it's me.*

*Okay so I've looked through the doc. Now, when they say no strippers ... do they mean like no full nudity? They can't mean just NO strippers.*

*Becca*

Riley's response came immediately after.

*Yes, and when they say "budget," do they mean "suggested budget"? Because for this amount of money, we can have a nice party in my Grandma's basement.*

*-R*

Becca's reply was next. Abby wondered if she'd even get a chance to provide input.

*I know some dancers who can give us a good deal. I'll take care of that part of the party.*

*Becca*

And there was one more.

*Okay, I know it says "Chicago venue" but what do we think about going to Vegas?*

*-R*

That had gotten out of hand fast.

She took another swig of wine.

Surely Will or Naomi had warned Freya about the Riley and Becca Effect. Someone must have told her that those two can't simply be set loose in an echo chamber like an e-mail chain with a directive as open ended as "plan a party." Frankly, she was impressed that it took—she checked the time stamps—seven minutes for them to end up with strippers in Vegas. Maybe they were slowing down in their old age.

Her finger hovered over the Reply All button. She probably needed to say something. But what?

Another e-mail rolled in from Becca, relieving her of any immediate decisions.

*Yaaaas! Vegas! Even better for strippers.*
*You think we can get a private jet?*

*Becca*

Abby laughed into her wine glass. She should have seen that one coming.

Her phone chimed with an incoming message. Then a second.

The banner across the top of her screen flashed *UNKNOWN NUMBER*. She hesitated, knowing that she was going to read it, of course, but was giving herself a moment to run through a few thousand scenarios in her mind. What was waiting for her was outside the scope of her likely scenarios.

> UNKNOWN NUMBER: Hi

> It's Freya.

There were bubbles. More messages were coming. She waited.

> UNKNOWN NUMBER: This is a little weird but I have everyone's contact information from the studio and … well, I was wondering if you could give me some insight into how to … proceed. I don't want to get off on the wrong foot with everyone by shutting down all their ideas, but we're not going to have strippers or go to Vegas. Is there a friendly way to let them down?

There was a surprising vulnerability in the messages that caught Abby off guard. While she wasn't expecting to get a text from Freya Jonsson, she definitely wasn't expecting to get a text message from Freya Jonsson asking how to play it cool with *her* friends.

Was it at all possible that what she'd overheard was true? Did Freya truly have...

It was impossible.

And yet.

She read the messages again.

Abby caught her lip between her teeth and chewed. She couldn't ignore them. What's more, she wasn't entirely sure she wanted to. Curiosity, if nothing else, demanded that she engage. She would have to exercise extreme caution. She didn't want to tip her hand, letting on that she knew how Freya maybe, possibly, potentially felt.

She needed to be cool. And aloof. Yes.

> ABBY: I apologize on their behalf. When the two of them get started it can be a little much. I'll handle them.

She swiped over to her e-mail and typed out a message.

*No strippers or jets. The budget and rules, unlike Becca's morality, are not flexible.*

*Abby*

She nodded, feeling pleased that her witty reply was both cool and aloof.

A reply came back almost immediately from Becca.

*The wet blanket has entered the chat.*

And then another, from Riley.

*So what you're saying is, it's better to ask for forgiveness than permission.*

So much for "handling them." Abby's ears tingled with embarrassment.

UNKNOWN NUMBER: 😂

What did that even mean? Was Freya laughing at her? Was she laughing at the situation? Did Abby care either way?

E-mails continued to roll in.

*That's my philosophy for all of life. So. How about the Bellagio?*

*Becca*

*I'm on board. Can you do that thing where you call and pretend to be someone's assistant to get us in?*

*- R*

*I texted my person and he's got some connections in Vegas. Let's see what he comes through with. If not, I will happily impersonate anyone to get us an in at the Bellagio.*

*Becca*

> UNKNOWN NUMBER: Would it be helpful to have a direction to point them in?

> ABBY: I think so. Is there something in particular you think we should do for this party?

It was an odd feeling, working *with* Freya on something. Is that what they were doing? Working together?

> UNKNOWN NUMBER: Something local and benign.

> ABBY: So the opposite of strippers in Vegas?

*Your* person?

*- R*

> UNKNOWN NUMBER: Yes. Something like...bowling, or axe throwing.

ABBY: You've seen how Riley and Becca are. You sure you want to give them alcohol and then have them throw heavy objects?

UNKNOWN NUMBER: Touché

*I don't know what you'd call him. Someone of the male persuasion who removes his clothing for money and with whom I am acquainted in a very intimate way.*

*Becca*

UNKNOWN NUMBER: What about renting a yacht?

ABBY: If the studio wants footage of me throwing up over the side of the boat the entire time, then yes.

She paused, then added,

ABBY: Don't you remember what happened at senior prom?

*Talking about a stripper you've had an affair with makes you shockingly verbose.*

*- R*

UNKNOWN NUMBER: OMG you were the girl that threw up on Lewis?

Abby instantly regretted bringing it up. For a second, perhaps with the help of her wine, she'd almost forgotten who she was talking to. *Of course* Freya Jonsson would eat that fodder up like the rice cakes she probably subsisted on. She pouted at her phone and typed back defensively,

> ABBY: Yep 🤢. I learned that I get seasick that day.

Cue a million laughing emojis. Or a doubled-over laughing gif. Or maybe the classic all caps "HAHAHAHAHAHA"

*What can I say? Naked men bring out the best in me.*

*Becca*

> UNKNOWN NUMBER: Maybe we need to use this party as an excuse to throw you another prom so you can have the experience you deserved. What if we make the bachelor/bachelorette party prom themed? We could do like…a Love Boat theme. That's almost like prom on a yacht, but with less seasickness.

She read the message. And then read it again. And then one more time. Each time, it made her skin hum from something she couldn't quite name.

Tenderness?

No.

> UNKNOWN NUMBER: Or…something else. We can do that too. Forget that idea, it was stupid.

Okay, she might go so far as to call that somewhat adorable. There was that hum again. Yes, it was definitely tenderness.

> ABBY: No, it sounds…great. Really great.

> UNKNOWN NUMBER: Yeah?

> ABBY: Yeah

*This decision to have a martini has definitely not brought the best out in me though. Je regret. Abby, if you're reading this, you can keep your 'I told you so's' to yourself.*

*- R*

She wasn't reading the e-mails anymore. Not really. She was thinking about her prom.

> ABBY: Although I'm not sure kids these days know what the Love Boat is. I think that prom theme ship has sailed (no pun intended).

> UNKNOWN NUMBER: What?! I loved that show when I was growing up. I wanted to be the cruise director, Julie McCoy.

> ABBY: I always felt so bad for her—the one woman on the entire staff. And like an old school, decently misogynistic, I'm gonna call you honey and sweetie, staff.

> UNKNOWN NUMBER: That's what made her awesome. She was a trail blazer.

*This is probably a good stopping point anyway. I've been sitting here in my lingerie this entire time. Peter is probably very confused about where I am. Goodnight loves.*

*Becca*

> ABBY: True. And she had excellent hair

> UNKNOWN: Fun fact, I got a third degree burn on my ear from stealing my Mom's curling iron and trying to give myself a "McCoy." The scar is still there to this day.

Dammit. Adorable. Again.

> ABBY: You were a true McCoysian. McCoyer? McCoyite.

*Have fun you crazy kids.*

*Goodnight.*

*- R*

The three dots appeared. She waited, as the dots

demanded, for the message that would follow. They danced across her screen for nearly a minute, giving her ample time to wonder what Freya might have to say that would be so lengthy.

They disappeared.

Then reappeared.

Her text screen promptly switched to an incoming call.

*SECURISAFE*

It was the alarm company for her office. There were zero good reasons they could be calling at this hour.

She frowned and swiped.

"Hello?"

"Yes, hello, this is Brandon with Securisafe. May I speak to Abigail Meyer please?"

"This is she."

"Can I have your pin number?"

Wine brain made it hard for her to recall her pin. Eventually she remembered it was the birth days of Becca, Naomi, and Riley in order of ascending height (so, Naomi, Becca, Riley).

"Ms. Meyer, there has been a break-in at your office."

"What!" She leapt to her semi-unsteady feet.

"The police have been dispatched. Are you able to come to the building?"

"Yes, of course." She scooped up a hoodie that was hanging on the armrest of her sofa and then her purse. "I'm about twenty minutes away."

"Excellent. I will let the officers know to expect your arrival."

She ordered a Lyft and then did what any self-respecting woman in her thirties would do in this situation:

she called her best friend and told her what was happening.

"Be careful, Abby!" Naomi pleaded as the Lyft pulled up in front of her office building. She spotted the police car right away. It was empty but the piercing blue and red lights still swung atop the car, casting an eerie shadow puppet show on the building's façade.

"The police are here. The burglar either isn't there anymore or he's in custody," she replied, opening the door to the office complex. Acting brave for Naomi helped her feel brave. The wine also helped.

"I know. But still, be careful. And call me back as soon as you know more."

"I will." She disconnected and dropped her phone into her pocket as she walked up the flight of stairs to her floor. The heavy metal door at the top of the stairs creaked loudly as she opened it. When she stepped into the hallway, an officer was already walking in her direction.

"Ms. Meyer?" The officer, a tall man who looked to be in his fifties, approached her, notebook in hand.

"Yep." Her nerves and the drive over had almost sobered her up, however, the almost part of almost sober meant that she could feel her body ever so slightly swaying from left to right as she tried to look up and focus on him.

"We've conducted a search of your office and, despite the alarm showing that the it had been opened, there doesn't seem to be any sign of a break in. The door and lock appear undamaged, and there are no obvious items missing."

"Okay," she said, unsure what that meant. The door was opened but by "no one" who did "nothing?" "That sounds ... good." The gauge on her anxiety lowered.

"Potentially. Since you are in the mental health field, it is possible that someone was trying to access the files on your computer."

Up again. "Oh God, that didn't even occur to me."

"We're going to need you to look through your office and let us know if anything physical was taken, but you should also check to see if there has been any tampering on your computer."

"Can't you, like, dust it for prints?"

His facial expression didn't change, but the corner of his eye twitched just enough to tell her she wasn't the first person to try and *Law and Order* the situation. "No ma'am," he said. "We typically don't bring in a crime scene investigation team when there has been no actual indication of a break-in."

They probably wouldn't bring in a team even if there was an "indication." She could only assume that the postage stamp office of a broke counselor was not a Ocean's 8 situation. "Alright," she said, with all the amiability she could muster, which wasn't very much.

She followed the cop into her office where his partner was waiting and together, they walked through the space. They weren't kidding, there were *no* signs of a break-in. There were no signs that anyone had been there since she'd left six hours ago. Not even a picture frame lay askew. Her laptop and iPad both seemed untouched, as far as she could tell, but then, if somehow someone did have her passwords and did log in to her computer to download patient files, she wasn't entirely sure how she'd know.

Seeing her office looking so normal, so not-broken-into brought her anxiety back down further. With a manageable amount of stress and two officers watching her, she realized what she was wearing: Hello Kitty sweatpants, a ten-year-old Pink sweatshirt that was covered in a sheen of Lancelot's fur, and oh good God her hair—she could only imagine how many directions it was sticking out from a ponytail that had endured an evening watching reality TV on the sofa. As she combed her office, she tried to subtly brush herself with her hands in a much too late attempt to tame her hair and remove the cat fur. She could do nothing but regret still having Hello Kitty pajamas. The two officers, by choice or indifference—it was merciful either way—seemed not to mind her appearance.

After fifteen minutes of working through her office, she had to spend another fifteen on the phone with the security company while she, and the police, confirmed that there did not appear to be anything stolen.

"It's entirely possible that whoever entered the premises fled as soon as they heard the alarm," the Securisafe specialist told her.

"Sure," she responded, her words and eyelids growing heavy. Her clock said it was past 1:00 a.m.

"I'm glad that Securisafe was able to do its job, then," the specialist continued.

"Is there anything else you need from myself or the officers?" she asked, eager to hang up.

"Not at this time. The officers will need to file their report and then we'll follow up with you directly if there's anything else. Other than that, we're set. Have a safe night."

"Yeah, you too." She disconnected the call and thanked the officers for their assistance. They followed her out and waited while she got in a Lyft to go home. As the car drove off, she let out a long breath, slumped into the seat, and prayed the driver wouldn't be one of those five stars for "good conversation" drivers. She was on the other side of a cortisol rush and her whole body felt limp with exhaustion.

Her phone buzzed and she pulled it out of her purse. It was a text from Naomi. One of six.

> NAOMI: Everything okay?

> Let me know

> Literally a thumbs up so I know you weren't murdered

> Okay send me a thumbs down if you're being murdered

> I was being silly before but now I'm regretting making jokes about you being murdered when I think maybe it is real now.

The last one that had come in said—

> NAOMI: Will is telling me to relax and go to bed. You know what always helps a woman relax? Having a man tell her to relax.

Abby smiled to herself and wrote back a quick message.

> ABBY: I'm okay. It doesn't seem like anything was taken. Or even touched. Go to sleep now. I'll tell you about it tomorrow.

The bubbles popped up immediately.

> NAOMI: OMG I'm so relieved. Okay, sleep well.

Her finger stretched up to lock her phone when she noticed the (1) in the upper left-hand corner. She tapped the arrow back to her messages. There was one unread message.

> UNKNOWN: Let me ask you a question...

She'd forgotten. Freya had been typing something when she got the call. She must have missed the text in her rush to get to the office. She had to scroll back to remember what they'd even been talking about. Freya's fascination with Julie McCoy from the Love Boat. That's right—Freya. Freya, saying kind and adorable things. Freya, bringing out feelings of tenderness. Like her entire evening, that was not something she had expected.

She immediately questioned if she had made it up and had misread a courteous conversation for something else. She typed back:

> ABBY: Sorry, something came up all of a sudden. What's your question?

The reply came right away.

> UNKNOWN NUMBER: Oh, nothing important. Let's touch base tomorrow about the party. Goodnight!

She locked her phone, but continued looking at the dark screen.

The pin prick of disappointment surprised her. What had she been expecting Freya to say? Nothing at all.

She unlocked her phone.

Had she misread? Was that all it was? She scrolled through their entire conversation and tried to figure out what to make of it.

She locked her phone.

Another wave of exhaustion crashed over her, the riptide of sleep pulling her eyelids downward. That was a question that needed to be answered, but Tomorrow Abby would be in charge of that.

She unlocked her phone. Tomorrow was another day of wedding prep. She couldn't let anyone see these texts. There was a 100% probability that one of her friends would be on her phone before the day was over. Either way, that meant there was a very good chance that one of them would stumble upon these texts. She needed to delete them.

She locked her phone.

Or should she wait until she'd had a chance to read through them when she wasn't drunk on lack of sleep and possibly still on wine?

She unlocked her phone.

No, she needed to delete them. She couldn't risk it. Her friends would be *all* over this. Whatever *this* was. She was having enough trouble making sense of it herself, and she didn't want them jumping in.

She opened her messages. Her finger angled towards the delete button when another thought occurred to her.

If Freya were to text her again for some reason ... and an unknown number text came in ... someone might get curious.

She didn't need to give anyone an excuse to look at her phone or ask questions.

Her finger moved in a different direction.

New Contact.

She pursed her lips together. She couldn't put Freya Jonsson as the name, obviously. She needed a name that no one would think twice about. An average name no one would know.

The only synapse still working in her brain fired.

NAME: Julie McCoy

Save.

She went back to her texts and deleted the conversation.

She locked her phone.

# Chapter 14
## *Freya*

*Subject: Wiliomi bachelor/bachelorette location confirmed*

*Hi all,*

*I've received word that we were able to reserve the Beach Club restaurant for the party! I'm ccing Debbie, our set designer. She can help us with, or at least point us in the right direction for, decorations. I'm going to be slammed over the next few days, so won't be able to assist too much.*

*Thanks,*

*Freya Jonsson*
*Senior Correspondent, Nightly Global News*
*She/Her*

*Say no more! I will take it from here. I've never pulled off a party of this size in a few days, but then again, I'd never slept*

with twins until this weekend, so I know that I am truly
capable of anything.

Riley

*Thanks for the help, Debbie! I see Riley is coming in hot
today. Sorry.*

Abby

*Ha! I don't mind a little spice in my inbox first thing in the
morning. Nice to meet you all. Riley, should I be working
directly with you?*

Debbie Lynn
Set Design, Nightly Global News
She/Her

*Decorations aren't really my thing, but if you want spice in
your inbox, I'm your girl.*

Becca

*I can already tell we're going to get along perfectly, Debbie.
How about we grab coffee this afternoon and start planning?*

Riley

Debbie,

*Thanks for helping with this! In the week and change I've gotten to know Riley, I think they'll do a fantastic job with the decor. If they try to make things too, well, spicy, feel free to loop me in.*

*One special request between us: I'd love to have something like this included in the decor (see attached image).*

*Thanks!*

*Freya*

*Attached: LB_1024563.jpg*

*Cute! We can definitely incorporate this. Don't worry about a thing. We've got this. The party will look fantastic. And not too spicy. :)*

*Debbie*

*Thank you! I'm heading to North Carolina tonight but will be available in the evenings. Don't hesitate to reach out.*

*Freya*

FREYA GAVE HERSELF ONE FINAL CHECK IN HER CAR'S visor mirror. She took out the soft, cherry red lipstick from her clutch and dabbed on a little more color, not that she needed the touch up so much as she needed a few seconds to herself. Although her car was in park, her internal organs still felt like they were being jostled on a bumpy road.

She had tried to convince herself otherwise, but there

were simply no two ways about it. She was nervous. She was allowed to be nervous, she told herself. She had good reason to be.

The last three days had been a sleep-deprived blur of planes, trains, and automobiles in a race to interview a prisoner that she had been granted permission to speak to as part of her series on justice reform. The interview, one with a death row inmate who had lost his final appeal, had been painful and demoralizing. It would have been hard under any circumstances, but having to navigate the frantic sprint of travel, the red tape of the prison system, and the heartbreak of the broken justice system, with a different associate producer, had left her even more drained. In the final days leading up to his wedding, Will's popularity had reached "Kardashian" level, and Will had been put on full time wedding duty. When he and Naomi weren't shooting segments or promos for the wedding special, they were being primped, prepped, and prodded by *Nightly Global News* staff for interviews, cameos, autograph signings, and even the occasional TikTok dance challenge.

Freya had arrived back in Chicago on a redeye flight only that morning, feeling more like she'd been tossed out of a wheelbarrow than had walked out of first class. Thankfully, Mimi in makeup had been able to work wonders on the dark circles under her eyes, including employing her secret of using an explosively red lipstick as a way to draw people's attention away from other areas of the face.

It hadn't really hit her until she was parked in front of the Beach Club restaurant, applying and reapplying layers of lipstick, that she didn't know what was going to happen when she walked through the doors of the restaurant. That made her extremely uncomfortable. She didn't like the unknown.

It wasn't only that she didn't know how the party was going to go, or even look, although those were both large circles in the Venn diagram of her anxiety. If she was being completely honest with herself, the biggest unknown ... was Abby. She hadn't communicated with her, except by way of group e-mail, since the night that they had texted. That night left her with the distinct sensation of walking on a tightrope in high heels. Obfuscated by contradictions and confusion, the truth seemed like a wobbling balance board that she couldn't keep her balance on.

She had devoted her career to the pursuit of truth, and if there was one thing she knew, it was that Abby hated her and she hated Abby. It wasn't theory. It was a reality, like the sun rising in the east. It was plain, it was simple, it was fact, until she overheard something that called it all into question. Until she was up late texting Abby about high school memories and missed proms and Julie McCoy hairstyles. Until Abby was writing things that made her smile. Until she was starting to wonder if Abby was, really, truly, in love with her, and all those years, all those fights, were about something completely different. Until she found herself staring at her phone wondering "what if?"

Let me ask you something ...

She didn't know which question to ask, but she had wanted to ask anything that would bring her back to solid ground.

Do you ever wonder what would have happened if we had gotten off on the right foot in high school?

Do you think it's possible we misunderstood each other all these years?

Do you want to start over right now, from this conversation?

Do you really love me?

The more Abby's silence dragged on, the more she told herself that whatever she had read into Abby's messages was nothing more than a trick of the light. By the time Abby responded, she had put her phone and her questions away.

*Never mind.*

But it wasn't as simple as *never mind*. Since that night, their conversation had bobbed in her thoughts like driftwood on the ocean. Each time Abby appeared, uninvited, in her mind, she felt an overwhelming desire to push the thoughts away, and an equally strong desire to explore them further. She yearned to slam the door shut and go back to the safety of a world she knew, or more importantly, a world in which she knew that she could come out as the victor. Something urged her to push the door open a little further and take a peek inside. It was scintillating and infuriating to be so flummoxed by a single person.

A tap at her window startled her and her hand that was holding the lipstick slipped, nearly giving her a Joker makeover. When she saw Will's exuberant face, she rolled down the window.

"Didn't mean to startle you," he said.

"You didn't. I'm a bit groggy from the trip." She gave him a smile.

He let out a breath of frustration. "Yeah, I bet. I can't

believe I couldn't come with you. We've been trying to talk to this guy for how many years?"

"Many," she said.

He leaned an arm on her window. "How did it go?"

"About as well as you might expect it would go sitting across from someone who knows they're helping to fight for something they'll never get to see. The courts have basically said that at this point even DNA evidence wouldn't exonerate him because it wouldn't eliminate him from the crime scene. It's utterly incomprehensible. But," she gave a weary smile, "for a few hours, at least, let's not talk about work, and enjoy your bachelor party, shall we?"

"Fine, but I want to hear more right after," Will said. "I can't believe that's the end of the road. I just can't."

"Yes, later." She capped her lipstick like a form of punctuation and then returned it to her clutch. "Are you heading in?"

"Yes, Naomi stopped to ... do something with her dress. I'm not entirely sure."

Freya gave an "oh, men" shake of her head as she rolled up her window, turned the car off, and opened the door. As she stepped out of the car, the silver and black sequined folds of her dress cascaded out with her. The backless mermaid dress was the only thing in her closet that looked remotely like the images that came up when she'd Googled "prom dress" a few hours earlier.

Will's mouth rounded into an "oh," but he seemed to catch himself. "You look very nice," he said, instead.

That's when she noticed. He was wearing a blue tuxedo, complete with thick white ruffles that looked like someone had sprayed a can of Cool Whip down his chest.

"Hi Frey—oh wow!" Freya saw the puffy pink sleeves of Naomi's dress before she saw Naomi.

"Oh, *prom*," she said mostly to herself as she looked from Will to Naomi and back. She hoped that Mimi's red lipstick trick would keep either of them from seeing the blush of embarrassment creeping up along her neck. Leave it to her to bring a cocktail dress to a costume party. "I assumed ..."

"That's my fault," Will said, holding up a guilty hand. "I knew you were busy, and I should have made sure you saw the e-mail about attire."

"I can head back to the studio," she said, feeling blindly for the car door handle somewhere behind her. "I'm sure a wardrobe department on some floor has a, you know, vintage prom dress I can use."

"Don't go," Naomi said. The metallic layers of her dress rustled as she stepped closer to Freya and put a hand on her arm. "You look so stunning, they'll be too overcome to even notice."

It was the small gesture of familiarity and fondness that calmed Freya more than the flattery. "You're sure?"

Naomi gave a fervent nod. "Absolutely, this is all in good fun anyway." She motioned towards the restaurant. "C'mon, let's head in."

"I know we said no work talk," Will said, as they walked through the parking lot, "But did you hear that Kent James announced that he's retiring?"

She had heard even before the announcement had gone live. Kiara had texted her sometime after midnight with an all-caps message that "it was happening" and that Freya was under strict instructions to say nothing and to continue keeping her nose clean while Kiara continued to work her magic.

"End of an era," she said, as noncommittally as possible.

The entrance to the Beach Club buzzed like a beehive, with staff and crew flying in and out of the door at a frenetic pace. As the three stepped inside, Naomi let out a squeak of delight. The simple white and driftwood paneled restaurant reminded her of the restaurants that she had eaten at in Cape Cod, and it had been transformed into a kitschy, prom-themed cruise ship. A red carpet led them through a giant life-ring-shaped gate that read "S.S. Wilomi" and into a sparkling, balloon-filled, flower-drenched room.

When she heard the "test, one, two" she realized that there was a stage, a band, and a banner that said, "Set Sail For Love." She barely had time to take it in before she spotted it at the back of the room, the most important part of any prom. The photo backdrop. An eye-popping set that looked like the deck of a cruise ship, including a long railing that led up to an actual winding staircase.

"Yoo hoo!"

She turned to find Riley relaxing on a poolside lounge chair, one of many sprinkled throughout the room, one hand holding a bright pink cocktail in a hurricane glass and the other waving in their direction.

As they walked, several cameras followed them. Naomi and Will seemed to have become so accustomed to their Kardashian lifestyle that they took no apparent notice.

"Welcome aboard!" Riley exclaimed when they were close enough. They were dressed in a floor length, navy-blue ballgown accented with gold embroidery, suggestive of a captain's uniform.

Naomi clasped her hand. "Riley this is incredible! Way better than—" she paused, awkwardly, and then said, "My actual prom."

Riley took a pull from their straw. "I'm pretty pleased with how it turned out. Especially since I basically had to do it by myself."

"Dirty, lies, Riley. I helped." Though they had only met a handful of times, Freya had come to recognize Becca's very distinctive purr. She was covered, if that word was even appropriate, by a floor-length, sheer dress, with a minimal amount of strategically placed rhinestones. It seemed that she wasn't the only one who hadn't gotten the prom theme attire memo.

"You put me in touch with some strippers."

Becca took a seat on the edge of Riley's lounge chair. "It's not my fault the studio refused to listen to reason! If no one is going to get naked, can you even call this a bachelorette party?" She placed both hands behind her and leaned back. "Speaking of getting naked—"

"That didn't take long," Will interjected.

"—has anyone seen Peter?"

"Peter?" Will, Naomi, and Riley said in unison as if this was part of a comedy sketch Freya hadn't been given the script to.

"The last I heard ..." Naomi started to say and then trailed off, glancing uncomfortably at Freya and then back to Becca.

"It's fine, honey," Becca said to Naomi. She looked at Freya. "My husband and I were having a little, you know, trouble. My Dumpter Fire of a sister had us going to couples counseling and group therapy and obviously, none of that helped. Then I figured out what the answer was. See, I was looking to other people for something Peter could give me all along. The excitement and variety I was looking for? All we needed to do was role play. Well, and the occasional three-some, but mostly roleplay!" She leaned back a little further, locking onto the nearest camera and giving it a seductive wink and kiss.

The rest of the group remained silent, so Freya decided to follow suit.

Becca, more interested in talking to the camera than her friends, continued. "So tonight, we're running with the prom theme. I'm the prom queen, obviously, and he's going to be a nerdy kid who always had a crush on me, and I'm going to pop his c-h-e-r-r-y."

"Out of everything, that's the word you feel you need to spell out?" Will looked at everyone except Becca as he asked the question, suggesting he knew he wasn't going to get an answer.

"We rented a room at a seedy motel," Becca said. "I tried to get the same motel I used for my *actual* prom but it's gone, tragically."

"Well, mazel," Naomi said, interlacing her fingers in front of her lips. "I'm so happy that you and Peter found something that works for you. I knew you two would figure it out."

"Yes, congratulations on your ..." Will's voice rose to an uncomfortable falsetto as he finished his sentence, "role ... playing?"

"Rediscovering marital bliss, while certainly a feat, is no excuse for abandoning me," Riley said with a petulant shake of their head. "As I was saying, I basically did this by myself."

"I'm not even going to try and argue with that," Freya said. "I've been completely checked out for the last three days, so thank you, Riley, for taking on the lion's share of the work, and doing such a fantastic job."

A server walked by carrying a plate of hors d'oeuvre. "Mango shrimp in endive leaves," he told them, holding the plate out in the middle of their circle.

"What about Abby?" Naomi asked, accepting an hors d'oeuvre and unceremoniously popping it into her mouth. "Oh my God, this is fantastic."

"Wait until you try the coconut and pineapple spring rolls," Riley told her. "And Abby? Well, she—oh here she is, right on cue."

Freya's heart thumped so hard that she was sure everyone around her could hear it. She forced herself to inhale, slowly, and lifted the corners of her lips into a friendly, but distant, smile, and turned around. Behind her, Abby shuffled towards them in a shiny purple pencil skirt with matching peplum top that looked like it came fresh out of a time machine from the '90s. Of course, she had paid attention and dressed up. The sequins on Freya's dress were starting to feel like spotlights, making her stand out in the worst way possible.

"Sorry!" Abby's matching purple heels clacked as she took her place between Will and Naomi. She stopped, bent over, hung onto Naomi's arm, and fanned herself with her hand as she tried to catch her breath. The one thing she didn't do was look at Freya.

One point for camp Abby hates Freya.

"You okay there?" Naomi asked, patting her friend on the back.

Abby stood up and put a hand on her hip, letting out a long breath. "Yes, sorry. I really thought that I could get here in time to help set up. I tried to explain to the police that it was a false alarm and that I had a party to get to, but they still made me go through the entire process."

"Your alarm went off again?" Naomi asked, sounding concerned.

Abby must have noticed, because she brushed her hand down Naomi's arm in gentle reassurance. "I didn't want to bother you while you were getting ready for your party. But yes. Again."

"What is that, the second time this month?" Will asked.

"Fourth time in less than two weeks."

"That's so scary!" Naomi said, her concern ratcheting up a notch.

"At this point it's annoying A-F. No one has any idea what's going on. The alarm keeps showing that the door is open, but it's not, and nothing is missing. The alarm company thinks it's an electrical short. The building super thinks it's a mouse."

Riley sucked in a breath sharply. "Now that *is* scary!"

"I know! Can you imagine if it showed up while I was in my office?" Abby gave a little shudder of disgust.

"Why don't you bring Lancelot to your office?" Riley suggested. "Let him live up to his name a little and save a damsel in distress."

Everyone emitted a unified chortle of polite amusement, so Freya did, too, despite not following most of the conversation.

"This is the last straw for me," Abby said. "The alarm

company keeps promising me that they've solved the problem and it won't happen again. Then it does, and it's a huge waste of my time ,because I have to go all the way down to my office each time, talk to the police, inspect the place, and confirm to them and the alarm company that nothing has been stolen or destroyed. It's more than an hour out of my day each time. I've decided if it happens again, I'm ripping the panel out of my wall and setting it on fire while I dance over its melting body."

Will tapped a finger to his chin. "You'd need like some kind of blowtorch to light—"

Naomi squeezed his arm and gave him her loving *not now* smile.

"How are things going here?" Abby said, accepting a pineapple chicken appetizer from a server. "And also, *what* is going on here? Explain to me what kind of prom you three are dressed for?" She jutted her chin towards Becca, Riley, and finally Freya. She lingered, for a moment, on Freya, and her eyes seemed to ever so slightly trace the curve of her dress.

So then ... one point Abby loves Freya?

"Oh, this old thing?" Riley rustled the thick fabric of their skirt. "Just a little something I whipped up for the occasion. I couldn't find anything on theme that complimented my nearly invisible waist while making the rest of me as visible as possible, so I had to take matters into my own hands and alter a dress to my liking."

"I wanted to be as visible as possible too," Becca said, eyes flicking down to her sheer dress.

"I, er, missed the memo and tried to find something I owned that looked like what the kids are wearing today,"

Freya said, willing herself not to shrink as she admitted her mistake.

Abby gave a harsh laugh. "I don't know what's worse, the fact that you have something like that in your closet ready to go, or that that's what kids are wearing today."

One point, Abby hates Freya. That brought the score to two to one for hate.

"Hi everyone." Freya turned again, this time to see Max, with a headset and clipboard in place, standing beside her. "Since you're all here, let's get started. I've met some of you, but for those of you I haven't, I'm Max, and I'll be the producer for this evening's event.

"We've got about fifteen minutes before the other guests start to arrive, so, we'd love to get our CCI's in while we have some time. Who wants to go—"

"Me!" Becca's hand shot up so vigorously that Freya was certain the paper-thin dress was going to rip. "I love me some Confession Cam. Besides, I want to make sure there's nothing to interrupt me and Peter once we get, you know, started."

Max didn't bat an eye. Freya wasn't sure if that meant he didn't get it, or he'd been prepped for Becca. She hoped, for his sake, it was the latter. He gestured for her and the two cameras that had been circling them to follow him, and walked off, with Becca slinking behind.

"It's honestly a wonder that they can use any of the footage from Becca's interviews," Abby said. Becca wasn't quite out of earshot, but apparently Abby didn't care.

"From what I've heard, they pretty much can't," Will said, sounding amused.

No one picked up the conversational ball, and the group

fell into silence. Freya's eyes skipped around the semi-circle, in the age-old tradition of looking to see if someone else would start talking. When she reached Abby, who was tugging uncomfortably at her necklace and inspecting something on the ceiling, she found herself drawn to her hazel eyes. She'd never noticed the kaleidoscope of rich gold, chocolatey brown, and emerald green, and she watched, mesmerized, as the colors seemed to shift in hue as she moved her head.

Perhaps sensing Freya's stare, Abby looked down, and the hazel irises were replaced by pupils, staring directly at her. And an almost imperceptible smile. It was faint, but it was definitely there.

Another point for Abby loves Freya, bringing them to 2-2.

Freya felt her cheeks flush, and she quickly looked at Naomi and Will, feeling desperate to move things along. "Only a couple more days until you walk down the aisle, you two. Are you ready?"

Naomi opened her mouth to speak, but Riley was first out of the gate. "I would be a lot more ready if we weren't having this wedding at noon. On a *Monday*," Riley stressed the word Monday, adding venom to each syllable. They plucked the cocktail parasol from their drink and jabbed it in Freya's direction. "Can you explain to me how that is a thing that is happening? Who gets married on a *Monday* afternoon?"

Freya, grateful for Riley turning the attention on themself, chose to ignore the umbrella being stabbed at her. Instead, she did a check of her left and right, to confirm that there were no cameras near them when she revealed the studio's secret sauce. "People who care about ratings do. These two have the biggest following with stay-at-home moms and viewers in Europe," Freya explained. "Twelve p.m. central is lunchtime here and end of the day over there. Ratings are king."

Riley gave their head a shake. "That explains a lot. The patriarchy is once again doing us in. If ratings were queen, I think we'd be approaching this differently. Ooh, queens!" They hoisted their tiny umbrella over their shoulder and rolled it between their fingers. "That gives me an idea. Naomi, let's replace your wedding guests with drag queens, and that could be a spin-off show: Drag Queenzilla, where a bunch of drag queens crash your wedding and—is this making sense, or have these Pink Bikini cocktails finally caught up with me?" Riley downed the last of their drink and tossed the umbrella into the empty glass. "Maybe time to switch to the punch. Anyone else? You know what? Never mind; you're all getting one. Don't worry, it's a true prom and the punch is spiked."

Riley leapt from their reclined position like they were pulled up by marionette strings and, after adjusting their skirt, made their way towards the drink table.

"Hoo boy, Riley is going to keep us on our toes tonight," Abby said. Even though her words came off as exasperated, Freya could see that Abby's face was alight with enjoyment and adoration as she watched Riley head towards the bar. "Has anyone ever *un*spiked punch before? Because we might want to."

Naomi laughed before turning slightly to look at Abby and Freya. "We thanked Riley already, but I wanted to thank both of you for helping put this together. It's phenomenal, and the party hasn't even started."

Freya gave an appreciative nod and added, "I wasn't kidding when I said Riley put this together. They are a good friend."

"We—" Abby seemed to trip on that word, and she started again. "I think, well, my only contribution was helping to come up with the theme." It appeared that Abby didn't want to be associated with Freya after all.

Three to two, Abby hates Freya.

"I loved it as soon as you told me. What sparked the idea?" Naomi asked.

"Some late-night reminiscing over wine," Abby replied before giving a furtive, possibly even playful, glance at Freya.

Three to three, back to a tie.

"Okay, who's next?" Max was back.

"That was fast," Naomi said.

"Becca got, um, distracted."

"Sounds about right," Abby said.

"I can go," Will told Max.

Max inspected Will, then Naomi, before pointing two fingers at them. "Great. Let's have you two do this one together first and then I'll have you each go separately."

The moment they were alone, Abby made it clear that she was eager to get away, "I'm going to ..." she said, not even bothering to finish that sentence before she turned to leave.

Four to three, with a pretty definitive win for Abby despising Freya's very presence.

She didn't have time to consider how she felt about that before the *tap tap* of Abby's heels walking away from her slowed and then stopped. She heard a soft gasp and then an even softer laugh, and turned to see Abby looking at the photo backdrop at the other end of the restaurant. At first, Freya thought Abby was looking at Will and Naomi, who were starting their CCI in front of the backdrop, then she realized what had caught Abby's eye.

Freya had forgotten until that moment about the special request that she had sent to Debbie. From here, she could see it plainly. On the bow of the photo backdrop ship in tall letters was the name of the Love Boat: "PACIFIC PRINCESS." Freya wished she could melt into the cracks of the wooden floorboards. It had been a momentary lapse of judgment. No, of madness. With a sprinkle of masochism. It had been an idea that had popped into her head and ended up in an e-mail just as quickly. For reasons that she couldn't even recall, she'd thought it would be cute to include a nod to the hidden Love Boat theme tucked inside the prom theme, and all it had done was expose her, but when Abby swiveled to look at her, she saw that Abby was smiling. It wasn't a biting smile or a sarcastic smile or a menacing smile. It was a genuine ... smile. Something about the joy on her face, the way her eyes sparkled and her cheekbones plumped up like juicy apples, caught Freya's breath in a way she could never have expected. Freya tried to recall if she had ever actually seen Abby happy before.

Abby said something to her, but her voice was muffled by the sound of glasses clinking somewhere on the other side of the room. Freya walked the handful of steps to close the gap between them.

"Sorry, what?" she asked.

"You didn't," Abby said. "Did you?"

Freya forced herself to take in some air. "It wouldn't have

been a Love Boat prom without the Pacific Princess, would it?"

The smile upgraded to a grin. "If I'd known, I would have busted out my curling iron." She looked from the boat to Freya, then said in a tone that made the score four to four, "I love it."

A tie again.

Freya wondered what a tie meant, if anything, as she watched Abby walk away.

# Chapter 15
## *Abby*

Abby sat in a makeup room tucked away on the thirty-first floor of the WNO building, where a makeup artist was putting the finishing touches on her. She had been at the studio since 4:30 that morning. Without her phone, much less any windows nearby, time had begun to lose all meaning. After several more hours of sitting motionless in a chair while studio stylists transformed her, the adrenaline that had gotten her up and moving had long since faded to exhaustion. All she could think about was coffee. When she first arrived, a perky PA with a clipboard had offered to bring her some, but she and the rest of the wedding party had been whisked off to a small green room where someone in charge of something shook their hands, gave them a little pep talk, and ordered a different, but eerily similar, PA to "get these people some coffee."

Before the coffee was delivered, they were moved to the chapel for a walk-through. There, she was once again escorted to a new location before anyone could bring her any caffeine. She did eventually get some, but only after she was strapped down to the makeup chair and unable to move an inch. The liquid had long since stopped steaming, but, at that point, Abby didn't care.

The door to the makeup room opened, and another identical PA in a headset stepped in. "Twenty minutes, people." Abby wondered if they were cloning PAs in the back somewhere.

"We've still got to get your dress on. Exciting!" Mimi, the incredibly beautiful and impossibly tall makeup artist, did a little jig, making Abby wonder if she had been drinking all the undelivered coffee. "I'm on the home stretch here. Hang on."

She tugged at a drawer ,which opened like a magical pop-up book, revealing a hundred different lipstick colors. After a few swipes, dabs and adjustments, Mimi dropped the lipstick brush onto the counter and inspected her work. "There!" she said, flipping her bangs out of her eyes. "As much as I'd like to have you admire my art, we need to get you to wardrobe! Chop chop!"

With impressive dexterity, she swept Abby out of her chair and into the adjacent room where Naomi and Rebecca were being dressed.

"There you are!" Becca, in nothing but a pair of lace panties and a bra, planted a hand on her hip.

A PA clone tapped Abby on the shoulder. "Would you like anything to drink? Water? Coffee?"

"Please, yes, for the love of God, a cup of coffee," Abby begged the replica.

"No cups!" Mimi barked. "Only things you can drink of out a straw."

"I don't care anymore," Abby said weakly. "Anything caffeinated. I'll snort it if I have to."

"Strip!" the wardrobe attendant ordered, snapping her fingers at Abby.

Abby started to unbutton her dress, casting a glance at her sister. "I didn't realize we were modeling for Victoria's Secret," Abby mumbled, letting her dress fall to the floor and revealing a pair of comfortable black panties and a black cotton bra. In the pre-wedding bustle of the last week, laundry had dropped to the bottom of the priority list, and as she groped through her drawers at 4:00 a.m. , she had realized that she'd reached the bargain bin leftovers of her clean undergarments.

Rebecca's wardrobe attendant crouched down and held out her dress, allowing Rebecca to step carefully into it. "I'm prepared for this evening," Becca said. "Peter's going to pretend like he's crashing the wedding and trying to pick up bridesmaids. I figure we can do it in the bathroom during the reception."

Abby went to smack her own face in exasperation, but Mimi grabbed her hand. "No touching!" she ordered with a surprisingly gruff voice.

In lieu of a literal facepalm, Abby gave herself a satisfying moment to imagine a mental one before she addressed Naomi. "How are you doing over there?"

Her best friend was in a corner, her back to the group, as several members of the wardrobe team buttoned up the long dress. "Good!" she called out over her shoulder. "Do you look amazing?"

"I haven't seen myself yet," Abby admitted as her dress

was zipped up and a flurry of hands tucked, folded, poked, and prodded.

"I'm sure you look spectacular."

"Are you nervous?"

"Incredibly," Naomi said. "Not about marrying Will. I'm okay with that."

"Well, I would hope so."

"It's all the people. They said they're expecting like thirty million people to tune in. I really wish that they hadn't told me that. I feel like I'm going to throw up."

"Try not to, you know, think about that," Abby said, but her stomach was starting to churn haphazardly like the tired old washing machine in her building's laundry room. Up until now, she'd been so busy worrying about Naomi that she hadn't had time to worry about herself, but all she could think about was tripping her way down the aisle in front of *thirty million people*.

She swallowed, her throat making the nervous gulping noise she thought was only a sound effect in cartoons.

The door to the wardrobe room swung open and a nonde-script, petite woman with a headset entered. She looked like she couldn't be a day over twenty-five. "Time's up, people! Show starts in five minutes." When no one responded, she walked farther into the room and started swinging her arms toward the exit. "Let's go!" Twenty-five or not, she had the boss vibe down.

Someone tossed Abby her satin heels, which now seemed absurdly high. She slipped them on, recalling the length of the aisle and wondering why she had thought those shoes would be a good idea. *Thirty million people.*

"Good luck!" Mimi called out to them, waving.

"We're on our way," the woman said into her headset as she escorted the three women down the long, brightly lit corridors of the WNO studios. "I'm Lexi, by the way," she said to them.

"Nice to meet you, Lexi," Abby nearly had to yell to be heard over the sound of three pairs of clicking heels echoing in the hallway. She noticed Lexi was in a pair of very silent, very flat, very comfy looking Converse high tops.

She smiled at them. "You know what you're supposed to do?"

"Don't trip," Abby said.

"Don't throw up," Naomi said.

"Don't behave," Rebecca purred. "No one wants to sleep with the goody two-shoes bridesmaid, after all."

Abby looked at Naomi apologetically. "It's not too late to throw her out of the wedding party, you know. I bet Lexi would be happy to do it for you, wouldn't you, Lexi?"

"You'll all be fine," she replied noncommittally.

"You do lots of these national wedding ... things?" Abby asked Lexi in a desperate attempt to give her mind a toy to play with besides the number *thirty million*.

"Nope." Lexi shook her head. "First one for me. I work for the WNO morning news program, so they tagged me to help with this."

"Is it safe to be walking out in the open? Will isn't going to see me, right?" Naomi asked breathlessly.

"You're safe. He's already in the chapel. Don't worry, we're a superstitious bunch here." She grinned broadly at them, then stopped in front of a pair of double doors and pressed a button on his headset. "We're in place." She released the button. "We've got about three minutes." Lexi pointed at a TV mounted from the ceiling where Randy and Jane, the hosts of *Wake Up! America* were laughing in their leather chairs.

"We're getting the signal that it's about that time," Randy said, and Abby watched enviously as he sipped a large mug of what she could only assume to be coffee.

"It literally cannot come fast enough," Jane said, crossing her legs. "I'm so excited. The wedding of the year!"

"Year? Try decade! People from all over the world are tuning in to this special right now to watch America's favorite couple tie the knot."

"Okay, well, before we join everyone in the chapel, let's take a quick look at the Wilomi story."

Their image faded to a snapshot of Naomi and Will arm-in-arm in front of Lake Michigan and a voice began speaking. "This enchanted love story started the way any love story should—with an unexpected meeting across a crowded room."

"Want to take a look?" Lexi asked in a hushed voice.

She tugged the door open an inch and the three of them squeezed together to peer inside.

"I don't know if they told you this when they gave you the walk-through, but this chapel is a permanent addition to the building. We use it for all the soap opera weddings," Lexi said to them as they watched the last few rows of family and friends file into their seats. Abby saw her mom already at her place near the front, fanning herself with the program and chatting away with the couple next to her. "You watch *Live Another Day* or *Until Forever*?"

Abby and Naomi shook their heads, but of course Becca squeaked with delight. "I knew it looked familiar! Oh my

God, Naomi, you're going to get married where all the soap opera greats took their vows! Or at least tried to take their vows."

Abby could see the skin around Naomi's mouth tighten. "Tried?"

"Well, you know how it is—there's always something! A lover or a twin or an axe murderer ..."

"An axe—"

A slight commotion from at the back of the room interrupted Naomi. A door had opened, and Will emerged. As he walked to his spot beneath the floral chuppa, he kept his hands clasped in front of him and his eyes darted around the room at a pace somewhere between excitement and anxiety. Immediately behind him, in fitted black tuxedos accented with light green pocket squares, were Freya and Riley.

Unlike Will's frenetic stare, Freya was still and calm as she scanned the room. When her gaze reached the back of the chapel and landed on Abby, the corners of her eyes and lips lifted into a smile that was so small that Abby knew it was only for her. Abby gasped involuntarily, a mix of surprise and embarrassment at the unexpected intimacy of the smile, followed by surprise and embarrassment at her reaction, then ducked behind Naomi before the chain of surprise and embarrassment could continue any further.

"Are you okay, Abby?" Naomi asked.

She patted herself on the cheeks, encouraging the rush of warmth to subside and grateful that Mimi wasn't around to stop her. "Fine!" she said. Rather than explain herself, she forced herself to look over Naomi's shoulder, deliberately skimming over Freya to Riley, who was apprehensively caressing their hair.

The studio execs hadn't been particularly comfortable with Riley's avant-garde look and had, at the last minute, cut their hair short and dyed it a color Abby had never seen: their natural chestnut brown. At about nine in the morning, they had passed each other in the hallway on the way to makeup, and Abby had done her best to console them during their fleeting moments together.

"Consider this your most radical look yet!" was the best she could come up with in the few seconds she had.

"Okay, we're about to go live," Lexi said. "Take your places."

"I don't know about you, Randy," Jane was saying on the screen above them, "but I can't wait another second. Let's head over to the Wilomi wedding!"

The scene changed to a live image of the chapel.

"There's the groom!" Jane's voice said over the image. "Doesn't he look handsome? I could eat him up!"

Randy laughed. "You and about a million other people. Sorry, this man is officially taken."

Jane let out a long, disappointed sigh before revving up again. "They're seating the last of the guests now and then the ceremony will begin. I can't wait to see the bride!"

"What?" Lexi said, holding her hand to her headset. She looked up at the screen and Abby followed her gaze. A young-ish man in a suit was standing near the front of the church.

"Mr. Quinn!" He waved his hand, trying to attract Will's attention. "Patrick from NBS."

"Dammit, we've got a creeper," Lexi said. She pressed another button on her headset. "Somebody get in there and remove him."

"A creeper?" Abby repeated, her already thumping heart picking up the pace in her chest.

"Oh, it's nothing." Although she spoke indifferently, Abby noticed that he kept his eyes on the television. "Just a reporter from a rival station. They like to try and get in on the action instead of going to find their own stories. He must have used an alias somehow to get on the guest list."

"Uh-oh!" Jane said. "Looks like we've got an uninvited guest!"

"Is it my uncle Robert?" Randy snorted with laughter.

"Mr. Quinn!" the man said again, not failing to miss the two large men inching toward him. "What is your reaction to the allegations that Naomi is having an affair with her ex-husband?"

The chapel fell silent.

"What?" Will asked, his face draining of color.

"The story broke seconds ago on NBS," the reporter said. He pulled out a small tablet and held it up. "Naomi was photographed in the arms of her ex-husband last night."

Security had worked their way through the row of guests and were taking hold of the rogue reporter.

"Wait," Will commanded. They loosened their grip on the man, but didn't let him go. "What do you mean, Naomi's ... ex-husband?"

"Oh my God," Naomi said, staggering against Abby.

"Take a look for yourself." The reporter tried to hand the tablet to Will, but the burly men at his side held him back, so he tossed it. It landed with a *thump* on the altar stairs. Will hesitated, then bent down and picked it up.

"How the hell—no, sir, I was in the control room all

morning," Lexi was saying into her headset. "Yes—yes sir. Of course, sir."

It wasn't until Abby saw Naomi racing down the aisle on the monitor that she realized that her friend had slipped away.

"Turn it off!" Abby snapped at Lexi. "Cut the feed! Whatever!" Lexi was too focused on whatever was happening in her ear to pay any attention to Abby. Abby tore the door to the chapel open and ran inside after her friend.

"It's not me!" Naomi was wrenching the tablet from Will's grasp and staring at the screen. "I wasn't with Simon last night, I swear, Will!"

"Simon?" Will said, his voice hoarse. "You know this man?"

Abby skidded to a halt in the middle of the aisle as an overpowering sensation of dread locked up every joint in her body. Her worst fear, the thing she had fought so hard to prevent, was materializing before her eyes.

Naomi looked down at the ground, her body shrinking into her dress. When she looked up again, her face was streaked with tears. "He's ... he's my ex-husband," she managed to say.

Will's inhale was ragged. "You were married before?"

"I'm sorry I didn't tell you sooner. I'm so sorry," Naomi cried. "But I swear, that's not me in the picture. I would never ..."

Forcing herself to move, Abby bounded the rest of the way down the aisle and took the tablet from Naomi's hand. There, on the screen, was a picture of Simon holding hands with ... with ...

"This isn't Naomi," she said, zooming in as close as she

could. It was pretty grainy, taken from far away and at night, but Abby instantly recognized the location because she could see their apartment in the background. It was across the street from their building.

The woman in the photo was the same petite height and build as Naomi, with Naomi's long, curly hair, and wearing the DePaul University sweatshirt that Naomi had, but she couldn't see the woman's face. None of the pictures showed her face. Abby looked at the reporter, wishing she could burn a hole through him with her eyes. "Where did you get this?"

Her anger only seemed to embolden the young reporter. "Those photos were sent to us last night from an anonymous source. There's more, too, if you keep going. We analyzed the photos and were able to confirm these photos aren't photoshopped and the newspaper on the bench confirms the date."

Abby scrolled through the photos—Simon holding her hand, Simon holding her waist, Simon kissing her.

She heard Riley beside her. "It can't be her." They took the tablet from Abby's hands and looked through the photos. "There's no way. Besides, you were with her, right. That was the plan, you were going to spend the evening practicing the bustle?"

The question filled her with sudden, prickling terror. "It was. We did ... except ..." she said, her stomach turning to lead as she tried to speak, "The alarm at my office went off again. I was there, talking to the police for over an hour."

The air was sucked out of the room as the entire room gave a little gasp.

"Where ... where were you last night while Abby was gone, Naomi?" Will asked, his voice trembling.

Naomi's body was wracked with sobs as she tried to

answer. "In my apartment. I swear. It isn't me!"

She reached for Will's hand, but he wrenched it away from her. "How can I believe you? You've been lying to me this whole time." His eyes filled with tears. "How can I believe anything you've ever said to me?"

"No! Please!" Naomi pleaded desperately. "It isn't me!"

"I can't ..." His voice cracked. "I can't do this."

"No!" Naomi shrieked as Will turned and walked toward the exit. When he didn't stop, she picked up the hem of her dress and ran out of the chapel, following him. Every free-standing camera available chased after them, capturing as many angles as possible as she pushed through the doors shouting, "Please, Will! Please!"

The room remained motionless long after the door had swung shut. Abby stared out at the crowd, looking at the stunned faces that expressed everything from confusion, to anger, to disbelief—all the feelings she was experiencing. They stared back at her as if looking to her for direction. In an instant, everything had gone topsy-turvy and what was up was now down, what was north was now south and what was impossible, like her best friend cheating on her fiancée with her ex-husband, was now possible.

The one thing that she knew was that she needed to find Naomi. Kicking off her heels, she jumped off the altar and sprinted out the door. The hallway was empty, except for Lexi who hadn't moved an inch, hand still pressed to her headset. From where she was standing, the hallway went left, right, and straight, and she had no idea which way Naomi had gone.

"Which way did they go?" she shouted.

Lexi didn't even look at her as she responded to the voice

on the other end of her headset, "I will, sir. Right away."

She growled in Lexi's general direction before picking up her skirt and heading straight. After a short sprint, she came to another intersection and found herself having to decide which way to go again. By the fourth turn, she knew she was lost, and nowhere near Naomi.

Desperately, she made one last turn and stopped cold when she saw Freya. She was a few paces in front of Abby, her finger pointed squarely in the face of a middle-aged man in a suit.

"—don't know what kind of amateur hour you are running here!" Freya was yelling as she inched closer to the man. Her bowtie hung loosely around her neck and her hair was uncharacteristically disheveled. "I will make sure that you never—"

It didn't really matter what Freya was saying. Abby couldn't hear a word of it. All she knew was that every ounce of shock, fear, hurt, anger, and disgust she was feeling had found its target.

Her shoulders hunched, Abby stalked toward Freya. "You!" she roared.

Freya looked up, startled, and the middle-aged man took the opportunity to scurry away.

"You asshole!" she bellowed at her, her fists clenching. "This is all your fault. None of this would have happened if you hadn't tried to make a few dollars off Naomi!"

Freya flinched. "Abby, I didn't—"

She jabbed a finger toward Freya. "The hell you didn't! Because of you, I had to stand by while some scum-sucking asshole reporter tried to get his fifteen minutes of fame by humiliating and degrading my best friend in front of the entire world." She could hear her voice shaking as her throat started to burn. "Because of you, I had to watch, completely helpless, while my best friend had her heart ripped out of her chest at her own wedding. Over what? Some stupid photo of the back of someone's head?"

She expected Freya to fight back, to shout at her with the same force that she was shouting. Instead, she answered her softly, "Abby, I never wanted this to happen. I don't know how to—"

"Don't tell me you don't know. Don't tell me..." Her hand fell to her side and her body began to crumple as she dissolved into tears.

She felt Freya's touch on her arm, tender but firm enough that she felt herself leaning into the unexpected but much needed comfort, the support, the...

It took several seconds for Abby's brain to register what was happening: not only was Freya Jonsson kissing her, but she was kissing Freya Jonsson back. In fact, she found herself having to grip the fabric of Freya's shirt to keep her knees from buckling under her. Freya's hand slipped around her waist, pressing Abby's body tightly up against her chest and sending such a powerful ripple of pyrotechnics through Abby that she yanked herself away. Gasping for air, she wiped a hand across her lips and scrambled to reclaim what little sense of reality she had left.

"What—" She let that old familiar sense of hatred for Freya wash away any lingering sensations her kisses had brought on. "Are you out of your mind?"

Freya opened her mouth to respond, but the sound of footsteps down the hall seemed to distract her. "Not here," she said, pointing to a small door marked *Green Room*. Freya hurriedly opened the door and stepped inside. Abby followed her like a hungry dog, furious and ready for a fight. As soon as they were both inside, Abby slammed the door shut and whipped around to face her. "How dare you! Who the hell do you think you are?"

At least, that's what she had wanted to yell. Instead, she wrapped her arms around Freya and kissed her. Freya met her lips with the same veracity, slipping both arms tightly around Abby and stepping forward until Abby's back was pressed against the door. Abby leaned gratefully against the support and let her leg wrap around Freya while her hands moved to Freya's jacket, tearing it off her before returning frantically to the buttons of her blouse. It was more than frantic. It was desperate, like running out of air underwater and kicking furiously to make it to the surface in time. She needed to feel Freya's skin against hers, she needed to taste every inch of Freya, she needed to make Freya moan with surrender.

Freya's hands were desperate too, like a starving animal ravenous for any morsel. They moved from Abby's back to her breasts, urgently tugging at the thin fabric of her dress before sliding down to her waist, down to her hips, down to her thigh ...

It was only when Freya's hand slid under her dress, her slender fingers working their way up Abby's leg, that Abby remembered her comfortably sized granny panties. Instinctively, her hand shot out.

"Wait!" she said with a gasp. "Hang on ... wait a second. Shouldn't we be thinking about ... um ..."

Freya pulled back, her chest heaving, her lips swollen with Abby's kisses. "Naomi and Will?" Freya said, her eyes taking Abby in so greedily, she could almost feel the touch of Freya's glance. Abby had to suppress a shudder of pleasure.

"Right. Them." Abby pressed her palms against the door and took a few deep breaths to try and calm her rapid heart-beat. "This, whatever this is, it needs to wait a second. That's a lot more important."

Seemingly undeterred, Freya traced her finger up Abby's leg. "True, but this is something that can be solved a lot quicker than that."

Feeling the little resolve she had quickly drain out of her, Abby bit down on the inside of her mouth to create some distraction. "This," she said, concentrating, "is about how your producer abandoned my best friend in front of the whole world."

At that, Freya looked up, her forehead lifting just enough to suggest that she hadn't expected Abby to say that. "You mean, how your best friend cheated on her fiancé the night before the wedding?"

That was the splash of cold water Abby needed. "I beg your pardon?" she said, straightening up and feeling the sexual fog lift from her vision. "That wasn't Naomi in those photos."

"It sure looked like her."

"You can't see her face!" Freya still had Abby pinned to the door, which was beginning to feel less seductive and more stifling by the second. "Doesn't that seem suspicious to you?"

"No. It *seems* like she was too busy making out with her ex to allow the photographer to get a good shot of her."

Abby tucked her hands under her arms to prevent herself from pushing Freya away from her. "This is unbelievable!

First, you kiss me. Then, you tell me my best friend is a liar and a cheater?"

Freya's hand went to her head, and she ran her fingers through her hair. "My kissing you and my assessment of the situation with Naomi and Will are totally unrelated."

"That's not true!" Abby slid out from under Freya's arms and began pacing the length of the tiny room, each step reminding her that her legs were not totally freed from the wobbly effects of desire.

Freya turned and rested against the door, hands in her pockets. Her shirt was still half unbuttoned, and Abby had to clamp her teeth down harder on the inside of her cheek to keep her gaze from wandering. "Well, if that's the case— what about you?" Freya asked.

Abby stopped pacing and stood to face her. "What about me?"

"You kissed me too, you know."

"So?"

"So, by your logic, shouldn't you have to consider the possibility that Will may have been the one who was wronged in this whole thing?"

Abby pursed her lips tightly together as she considered how to respond. She didn't for a second believe that Naomi was having an affair with Simon, but, aside from gut instinct, she didn't have a lot to back that fact up. She knew that if Naomi hadn't lied about being divorced, that scene might have played out differently, but she wasn't ready to admit all that to Freya yet.

"How about this," Freya said. She took a step forward and pulled Abby close. "I think we can both agree that there are some unanswered questions that need to be addressed."

As she spoke, Freya's fingers strummed a tune on Abby's back that made her body hum along with each stroke. Abby nodded, feeling the tension lower as her desire rose.

"And I'm not sure if you heard," Freya continued, her voice taking on a sensual quality, "but I'm pretty good at getting questions answered."

Abby couldn't help but let a smirk float to her lips, but as quickly as it did, the heavy anchor of reality pulled her back into a frown. "I wish it were that simple."

Freya brought a hand to Abby's chin and lifted her face up. "We'll figure this out, Abby, I promise," Freya said. As if to seal the pact, she leaned in and gave Abby a kiss. It was light, but it still set off rockets inside Abby, and she had to fight to keep herself upright. She brought her hands to Freya's waist, at first to steady herself, but then the soft curves of Freya's body were begging to be explored, and she let her hands follow the path up Freya's side, along her shoulder blades, across the nape of her neck, down her arm. She could feel Freya's breath quicken under her palms, each exhale a soft plea for Abby to continue her exploration.

The sound of raised voices outside the door burst the tension like a pin in a balloon. Wandering hands fell to a neutral place at their owners' sides.

"We should probably go," Abby said. She held her arms in place but couldn't keep her eyes from trailing down to Freya's half-open blouse which exposed shapely topography caressed in pink lace.

Freya glanced down with a smile and then, almost regretfully, worked the buttons closed. "You're right. Heads will be rolling, and I want to make sure they are the right ones." After fastening the last button, she turned to open the door.

But before she reached the door handle, she stopped and turned back to Abby. Her eyes were soft with the glaze of lust and limerence, but Abby watched as the creases of her smile seemed to harden into concern. "Abby ... with everything else happening, we should probably keep this between us."

Abby felt a lump rise in her throat as she imagined herself trying to explain to Riley or Naomi or, frankly, anyone, what had transpired. She nodded. "I couldn't agree more."

Freya smiled and she leaned in, letting her lips brush against Abby's. "See you soon."

Before Abby could reply, Freya was out the door. Alone in the quiet for the first time since she woke this morning, Abby's mind finally had time to catch up with her body. She could do nothing but stand in the spot where Freya had left her as the last few minutes came rushing back to her. None of what she was remembering seemed like reality, yet her cheeks were still wet with tears, and her lips were still tingling with the pressure from kisses.

Eventually, she wandered into the hallway and followed the signs back to the makeup room, where her purse and ice-cold cup of coffee were still waiting for her. She sat down in the stylist's chair and rummaged through her bag until she found her phone. Twelve new voicemails, five of which were from her mother, and twenty-eight new texts. It seemed that everyone she knew had watched this morning's nightmare.

She closed all her notifications and went to the reminders app on her phone.

*Destroy all comfortably-sized underwear.*

# Chapter 16
## *Freya*

"Hi."

"Hi."

IT WAS FRIDAY NIGHT AND ABBY WAS STANDING AT
Freya's door for reasons that Freya wasn't one hundred
percent sure about.

Two days after the wedding—after their kiss—a message
had flashed onto Freya's screen.

> ABBY: Hey. We should talk

Talk about what? Their kiss? Will and Naomi? Their
opinions on the impact of macroeconomic conditions on
income inequality (of which she had many)? She was worried
that asking, "talk about what?" would make it sound like she
didn't think they had anything to talk about. In fact, she felt
that they had a lot to talk about, macroeconomic conditions

included. She decided to try a more subtle approach that she hoped would suss out the answer.

> FREYA: I agree. Phone call?

The reply came quickly and so did the unexpected flutter in her core.

> ABBY: I was thinking...dinner?

Dinner sounded like a let's-talk-about-us date. Was there an "us"? Despite all that had happened in the last 48 hours, that was what had occupied her thoughts the most. Not only that the "us" involved Abby, but that it involved another woman.

She'd never kissed a woman before, but not because she'd never had the inclination to. The thought had crossed her mind, even slipped into her fantasies a few times, but she had always brushed it off as a rogue impulse.

But that kiss.

It was the HD version of a kiss, richer and deeper than anything she'd experienced before.

Was that only because emotions were high, or was this more than a rogue impulse? How could she know? What would she do if she found out?

Another message rolled in.

> ABBY: Do you know Chez Moi in the West Loop?

Indeed, she did. It was a very cozy and very romantic spot tucked off the city's bustling Restaurant Row. It was exactly the kind of spot for a date, which was exactly what she couldn't be spotted doing with Abby. Photos of her over a candlelit meal with some Girl Friday would make the social media rounds before their dessert did. It was exactly the kind of clickbait she didn't need, especially now with the chance that INN would consider her to take over for Kent James. The thought made her breathless with anxiety and she typed a response before she had time to think about it.

> FREYA: How about dinner at my place instead?

Reading her very much sent and very much marked as seen words on the screen, she felt another meteor shower of anxiety. Dinner at *her* place? What was she thinking? Why couldn't her anxiety-induced typing have led her to suggest a less conspicuous restaurant, like the ones she went to constantly with business associates where no one would think twice about seeing her? Dinner at her place meant, well it meant ... dinner. At her place. It couldn't get more date-y than that. What if this wasn't a date? But also what if it was?

Maybe there was still time to offer some other options.

There wasn't.

> ABBY: Friday? 8?

She didn't know what to do but agree. So, she did.

> FREYA: Friday. 8.

Friday had been only two days away, but it had been

long enough for Freya to recapture her composure. Dinner at her place. No big deal. She had people over to her place all the time. She was an excellent cook and an even better host. Abby had probably suggested dinner to put an end to things in the safety of a public place, to avoid a scene. Not that Freya was the type to put on a scene. Besides, she knew that whatever this was, well whatever that kiss was, it wouldn't go anywhere. She had gone too far in her career, was too close to achieving what she'd worked so hard for, to let some scandal take her down. There was too much at stake. Her agent's words haunted her: she needed to be squeakier clean than she had ever been.

Dinner at her place. For talking. Not a problem. She picked a business casual outfit, a fitted pair of navy black slacks, a white sleeveless blouse, and a burnt orange cardigan that said, "let's talk." For dinner, she went with a brown rice and mushroom baked risotto, a utilitarian dish that came out of the oven ready to eat but also happened to be one of her go-to dishes that she knew she could knock out of the park. When 8:00 p.m. on Friday rolled around, she was feeling calm, confident, and ready to talk.

~

SHE OPENED the door and saw Abby in a low cut, ruffled, black jumpsuit, accentuated by a chunky black necklace, razor thin high heels, and cotton candy pink lipstick, and all of that flew out the window. The jumpsuit hugged Abby's waist, reminding her, vividly, of the feel of Abby's hips in her hands only a few days ago, of the roadmap of peaks and valleys that invited her to explore the landscape of Abby's body. Freya nearly had to hold onto the door jamb to steady herself as one of those "rogue impulses" gripped her.

"Can I ... come in?" Abby asked, bringing Freya's thoughts back to the present. *They were here to talk*, she reminded herself.

"Yes, of course." She stepped back and motioned for Abby to enter. Her home, a rehabbed 1880's brownstone on a quiet street on the northern edge of the city's famed Gold Coast, had been visited by dignitaries and movie stars, all of whom had expressed their admiration for the interior. The open plan of the first floor, coupled with the remaining Victorian touches of stained glass and vaulted ceilings, gave the impression of walking into a cathedral. Large globe chandeliers hung from the ceiling, leading the way from the sprawling living room to the lengthy dining room, to the over-sized kitchen.

Until this very moment, Freya had delighted in bringing people to her house and watching their reaction, but as she welcomed Abby into her home, she was overcome with nerves. Was the house too big? Too ostentatious? Why had she let the interior designer leave so much open space? It looked empty, even a little cold. What exactly was it about Abby that had her spinning over a house she was incredibly proud of?

"Your home is stunning!" Abby said, once again bringing Freya back to the moment.

"Thank you. Dinner should be ready shortly, if you want to sit over there." She motioned towards her marble island lined with a row of bronze bar stools.

"It smells incredible," Abby said as she followed Freya into the kitchen. Freya had an overwhelming desire to turn around and take in Abby moving in the flirty fabric of her jumpsuit, to watch what it teased and revealed as she walked. Instead, she focused on getting a pot holder and opening the oven door.

"It's one of my favorite recipes," Freya said, lifting the lid off the Dutch oven and inspecting the contents. She reached for the carton of vegetable broth and added a dash more before covering it again. "I learned it from a chef who has this tiny seven table restaurant in the South of Italy. A really interesting guy with a fascinating story."

"Fancy," Abby replied. "My recipes mostly come from Instagram, or the restaurants I order delivery from."

Freya couldn't tell if the heat was coming from the oven or her cheeks. "Sorry," she said, closing the oven door. "Sometimes I forget that not everything I do needs a backstory."

"Oh, no, I didn't mean ..." Abby stammered. "Not much of what I do has backstory. Therapy is confidential, obviously, so I don't have any stories from work and, well, you've seen enough of the Confession Cam interviews with my friends to get a sense of what the rest of my life is like."

Was it possible that Abby was nervous too? That Abby was feeling insecure? Of all the feelings she had tied to Abby over the years, insecurity had never been one of them, but then again, Freya wasn't one for insecurity either.

"How about a drink?" Freya asked, closing the oven.

"I'd love one," Abby replied.

Freya walked over to a large oak bar cabinet in the dining room. She tugged open the heavy wooden doors to reveal a series of shelves lined with bottles, glasses, and other bartending accoutrement. "Are you a fan of cognac? I know this really fun take on a Sidecar from—" she stopped herself from finishing that sentence. Was she always so pretentious? "I also have wine and beer." She bit down on the corner of her lip to keep from exhaling a loud breath.

"I'm always down for a good cocktail," Abby said.

Freya reached for the cocktail shaker and then walked to the refrigerator for ice, passing behind Abby on the way. The jumpsuit was backless, and Abby's hair was pulled back into a high ponytail, leaving an inviting canvas of soft skin and curves. Freya's thoughts accepted the invitation and suddenly she was picturing the feel of her fingers brushing down Abby's back, the sensation of Abby shivering under her touch, that scrumptiously delicate whimper she'd been replaying over and over.

They needed to talk.

"Are you ..." Freya said before she even had a question to ask. She needed to change the subject and fast. "Comfortable?" She opened the refrigerator and scooped a handful of ice into the shaker, grateful for the rush of cool air. "Why don't you take a seat on the sofa? I'll be over with our drinks in a second."

"Sure," Abby replied as Freya walked back to the bar cabinet and began measuring out the ingredients. She stood up, and this time Freya caught a glimpse of her as she walked towards the sofa. The view did not disappoint, and she let the seconds drag on as she watched Abby's hips sway with each step.

Abby sat down on the sofa and looked up, catching Freya's stare. She whirled around to the task at hand. "How has your week been?"

Freya wanted to bang her head against the wall, but she

substituted by vigorously shaking the cocktail shaker instead. Her literal job was to ask questions and that was the best she could come up with? Yes, Abby, how has the week been where your best friend was accused of adultery and left at the altar on national television and you kissed someone you've always hated? She wanted to take it back, but it was too late. The question was out there.

"It's been—" Abby paused, giving some understandable thought to her answer, "Tough. I haven't talked to Naomi since, well, you know. She said she was going to her parents' house and that she needed some time. I feel so bad. I don't know what to do for her. I want to give her space but, also, she's my best friend and I absolutely don't want to give her space. I don't know what she needs from me right now. Actually, is it okay to talk to you about this? You're not going to put it on the news or anything?"

"This is all strictly off the record," Freya assured her.

"Have you ... talked to Will?"

Freya poured the contents of the shaker into two low ball glasses. "I haven't. I told him to take the week off, or however much time he needed. I know how you feel though; I keep wanting to check in on him, but I'm not sure if I should or if there's something else I should be doing. It feels like no matter what I do, it might make things worse."

"Exactly! At the same time, it seems like things are getting worse on their own. The internet is an absolute dumpster fire. Which is saying a lot for the internet. Have you seen all the Team Naomi and Team Will stuff out there?"

She had. Wilomi had been burned to the ground, and out of the ashes, two factions had risen. Team Will, who believed Will had been cheated on, and Team Naomi, who believed she had been set up. NGN couldn't have been happier. Leading up to the wedding, they had been holding planning meetings and focus groups to figure out how to keep the Wilomi enthusiasm going after the nuptials. This fiasco was an executive producer's wet dream. Despite her best efforts, and she had given it her all, they weren't shying away from the story like Freya asked. They weren't respecting Will and Naomi's privacy. They were cashing in any way they could. Freya wasn't about to tell Abby any of that. Instead, she said, "Yes, unfortunately," as she walked back to the refrigerator to get a handful of chilled whiskey stones from the freezer.

"It's been less than a week and you can already buy swag on Etsy for whatever team you're on. It's gross. But at the same time, I know that if I were some schmo who didn't know anything other than the twenty second videos I watched on TikTok or whatever, I'd probably get myself a few stickers and maybe a tote bag. There was a pretty hilarious one featuring Riley in a full telenovela gasp which, honestly, when this is all over, I might actually order anyway. But that's beside the point. There's no way we're going to convince the public to do anything other than lap up this tragedy, and I wish there was something I could do for Naomi and Will. I care about both of them, and I know the truth has to be in there somewhere. And ... you probably wanted to know if I'd been to any relaxing yoga classes this week or if I ate a particularly good salad when you asked how my week was, didn't you?" Abby put a hand to her forehead and grimaced. "Sorry, sometimes I have a habit of going off on rants."

Freya chuckled as she walked back to Abby, one drink in each hand. As she approached the couch, Abby scooted down to make room for her. Not a lot, though. As she sat, their legs brushed together, sending a jolt through Freya's body. She handed Abby her drink. "It's worth ranting about."

"Cheers to that," Abby said, raising her glass. They clinked glasses and sipped. "Have you heard anything at all? I believe your exact words were, 'we'll figure this out, I promise.'"

Freya felt another rush of heat rise up her neck as she recalled saying those words as Abby's body was pressed up against hers. In that moment, she would have done anything to ensure that Abby would find her way back into her arms. "I'm looking into it, but it's not that simple, and, to be honest, I'm not even sure Will wants me to, and I don't want to go digging up something he's not ready to hear."

Abby sighed. "You didn't really mean what you said before, that you think Naomi did it?"

Freya tugged the corner of her lip in between her teeth as she considered her answer. "I honestly don't know what to think. I've looked at those photos a thousand times."

"Me too."

"Naomi's face is so perfectly left out of every photo and that conveniently placed newspaper? It feels intentional."

"Right?"

"At the same time, I've seen thousands of photos where you just can't quite make out the face of the person in question."

"Okay, but you know Naomi. I mean you two became—" Abby swallowed. "Friends, right? You know she wouldn't do this."

Freya gave a shake of her head. "I wish I could, but in my line of work I've learned that anyone is capable—"

"Enough with your job," Abby interrupted. "Sorry, but Naomi isn't a story you're working on. She's your friend. Will is your friend. What does your heart say about your friends?"

Freya brought the glass to her mouth and took the longest sip she could manage. She didn't make decisions with her heart. Her heart hadn't gotten her to where she was. She looked at the facts, she looked for the truth, she looked for the best option. Her heart? She'd stopped listening to that a long time ago. At Abby's directive though, she paused and allowed herself to listen to that quiet voice in the back of her head, just for a moment. "My heart says ... that Naomi loves Will."

Abby clapped her hand on her leg and then pointed at Freya. The sparkle in her hazel eyes was captivating. "Exactly. She loves Will. If she loves Will, she wouldn't be running out on him the night before their wedding. So, then what?"

Maybe it was the Sidecar taking effect or one more whisper from her heart, but she said, "Then it's not really up to us, is it? It's up to Will and Naomi to decide if they want to fight for each other."

"Damn." Abby paused to take a pull from her drink. "I hadn't thought of that, but you're spot on. Even if someone uncovers the truth and exonerates Naomi, there's a rift between them. Naomi didn't fight for him, and he didn't fight for her. In the end, it won't even matter unless they start the process on their own."

"It sounds like the 'then what' part is that we try and help them see that they need to start fighting."

"Have you ever considered being a therapist? It seems like you have a knack for it?"

Freya cracked a smile. "I think that was just beginner's luck."

"Alright, I'm giving Naomi a week and then I'm driving up to Michigan to drag her out of bed and get her into fighting shape."

Freya didn't see herself bursting into Will's apartment, but she was willing to at least talk to him. "Maybe I'll invite Will out for coffee," she said.

"We have to at least try. Don't we?"

Freya nodded. Abby nodded. They both took a drink, eyes meeting briefly and then darting away.

Finally, Abby broke the silence. "This is ... weird. Us, working together like this? I mean, we ..." she trailed off with a chuckle.

*We hate each other*, Freya wanted to say, *right?* Instead, she set down her drink and asked another question. "Is this what you wanted to talk about when you said let's talk?" Her voice came out so much softer than she had expected. She'd meant to be direct, to get to the point, but instead she found herself feeling like she had stepped onto a creaky old bridge that threatened to plunge her to the bottom of a canyon.

Abby retreated into her drink. She took a sip and then a gulp. "Well, yes. I mean, sort of. I mean, um, I thought we should also talk about ... wow, um, why does it feel like I'm a teenager on my first date?" She took another drink and then set down her glass. When she looked up, her expression had changed. It was subtle but her eyes weren't sparkling anymore, they were searching, and her cheeks were tinged with a touch of color.

That was it. That look was all it took to raze any last semblance of business casual "let's talk" from Freya's mind. Just like in the hallways of NGN, it became impossible not to kiss Abby. To wait another second felt like a death sentence. She leaned in, and just as quickly, Abby moved forward to meet her.

Their lips touched and the swell of relief and desire that came over her was so consuming she nearly had to break the kiss and catch her breath. Then Abby let out a little sigh of pleasure and the swell became an intense drive to hear that sound again, hear it louder. She teased her tongue along Abby's lips and, without hesitation, Abby opened her mouth, inviting her to deepen the kiss. As their tongues met, Abby rewarded her with a little moan and brought her hand to Freya's neck, pulling her somehow, impossibly, closer.

Freya's body couldn't keep up with her mind, which was already envisioning everything she wanted to do to every inch of Abigail's body and every sound she wanted to elicit. Not daring to break the kiss, she reached her arms around Abby, enjoying the fulfilled promise of Abby's backless jumpsuit, and guided her until she was lying on the sofa.

As she brought her lips to the hollow of Abby's neck, she thought she heard the timer going off in the kitchen over the sound of Abby's purr. Dinner was going to have to wait.

# Chapter 17
## *Abby*

ABBY AND RILEY WALKED DOWN THE LONG CORRIDOR TO Naomi's childhood bedroom,

"I really think it could help!" Riley protested.

"Would you let me handle this?" Abby replied in an over-the-top hushed tone.

"Why do you always get to be in charge of everything?" Whether by choice or obliviousness, Riley missed her cue to talk quietly and responded at full volume.

Abby slowed as she approached Naomi's door and looked at Riley. "Let's make a deal. When your best friend from Hebrew school locks herself away at her parents' house for two weeks and you have to drive up to Michigan to see her, I will let you be in charge."

"I don't have a best friend from Hebrew school!"

"So?"

"That makes your deal null and void because I can never meet the requirements!"

Abigail pursed her lips and raised her eyebrows in a way that she reserved purely for Riley, and they knew it.

"What? Why the evil eye? All I'm saying is that I can be a productive member of this support group. My advice is as valid as yours."

She crossed her arms. "Let me guess, your advice involves a copious amount of sex."

"Maybe."

"With a copious amount of people."

"Possibly."

"All of whom are strangers."

"You make it sound so awful when you say it in that tone of voice," Riley whined. "Besides, correct me if I'm wrong—"

"You're wrong," Abby interjected.

"Okay, I'm revoking your right to correct me. As I was saying, I'm pretty sure that the last time we were in this situation, my advice was that she get laid, and that was exactly what she did, and it worked out splendidly." They paused and then added, "Granted, by setting her up on a date with Will, we created this current situation, but that's really beside the point since we solved her original problem of being sad over Simon. Which, sure, I'll admit was only a temporary fix that may have slightly blown up in our faces, but it worked in the short-term, didn't it?"

"For the love of—" Abby turned in front of Riley to block them from the door and then whispered, "This is exactly what I'm talking about. Can you please not mention Will or Simon when we go in there?"

From behind the door, Abby heard shuffling.

Naomi cracked the door open, squinting as the light from the rest of the house flooded in. "Would you like to come in?"

Abby turned around and grimaced. "Sorry," she said. "They ... showed up at my place unexpectedly as I was leaving. I told them I was going to Michigan, but apparently they didn't care."

"You underestimate me, Abigail," Riley said, smoothing their eyebrows. "I saw it on your calendar when I was going through your computer and cleared my schedule accordingly."

Underneath her unkempt curls, Abby spied the hint of a smile on Naomi's face. Although she had initially been annoyed when Riley invited themself along, she was remembering now that they were always good medicine.

Naomi grabbed a sweatshirt off a chair in her room, draped it over her shoulders, and stepped out into the hallway. "Why don't we go into the den?" She led her friends down the stairs of her parents' home and into a large room padded with thick carpet, window-sized oil paintings, and two large couches. Abby took a seat beside Naomi while Riley sank into the sofa across from them.

As everyone settled in, Abby examined her friend, who only two weeks ago had been glowing with excitement to start her new life with her love. Now, her face was gaunt, accented by dark circles under her eyes, but it was more than that. Her entire body seemed to have hollowed out. Her shoulders were slumped, her hands limp, and her gaze empty. Abby wanted desperately to scoop her into her arms and hug her until the life came back into her, but she knew that Naomi wasn't the scoop and hug type.

As if to prove that point, Naomi turned to Riley. "Are those glasses new?"

"Thank you!" They threw their hands up in the air. "How is it possible that you are the first person to say anything to me today? I'm beginning to wonder why I even spend time with you people." They gave Abby an accusatory stare from beneath their lenses.

Abby shrugged, doing her absolute best not to show that she had been taking pleasure in not acknowledging Riley's new look. Today, they were wearing a remarkably unremarkable outfit of jeans and a plain, gray T-shirt, their brown hair was gel-free, and a pair of black glasses rested on their face. For anyone else, it would have been just that: unremarkable. On Riley, the look was louder than a tornado siren and she couldn't stop herself from having some fun with it. "I just figured you were getting old," Abby said.

Riley gasped. "How dare you! I'll have you know I'm making a statement."

"What statement is that, exactly?" Abby asked.

"Something you said inspired me, actually. You said this could be my most radical look. After a crisis of faith, I realized that they can take my life but they can never take my fashion. The studio cut and dyed my hair but instead of giving up I have chosen to embrace the mundane. Today, I am average." They adjusted their glasses. "But the greatest average that ever existed."

"You truly rival some of the great philosophers," Abby said, flatly.

"I didn't realize that they made homes this nice in Michigan!" All heads turned as Becca strode into the room wearing Daisy Dukes, a midriff halter, and jean stilettos.

"Be—" Abby stammered. "What? How did you even find ..."

Rebecca dropped her purse next to Riley and then followed suit. "Riley told me."

"Riley!"

Riley held their hands up innocently. "Don't blame me!"

"Why shouldn't I blame you?"

"Because you shouldn't."

"Don't be mad, Abby," Becca said, shuffling through her handbag like a magician looking for a rabbit in a hat until she pulled out a tube of lip gloss. "These last few months have taught me a few things, like how I need to spend time with people who have worse lives than me. It makes me ... happier. I mean, forget Naomi—look at you, Abby. Are you wearing the same outfit you had on yesterday?"

Abby felt her face ignite like a forest fire. When she'd hurried out of Freya's house at seven that morning and drove home, she'd been planning to shower, change, have breakfast, and *then* leave for Michigan. Maybe squeeze in a nap too, since she hadn't actually gotten much sleep. The past two weeks had been nothing but sleepless. Since she'd kissed Freya, or Freya had kissed her, or whatever exactly had happened that day at the studio, she'd suddenly found herself ... *in* something. Infatuated with every curve and bend of Freya's body. Intoxicated by what Freya did to her own body. Incomplete when they kissed goodbye. In total shock that every text, every word, every touch from Freya—Freya!—made her heart flutter. Mostly, though, she was in Freya's bed every night, simply giving in. Those nights seemed timeless, marked only by long conversations, laughter, and well, lust. When each morning came, she found herself wondering what she had gotten herself into. And how. And why. And ...

She had been ready to start another day of exhaustion and introspection, but as she parked her car on her street, she saw Riley walking out of her lobby, two cups of coffee in hand.

"There you are!" They had shouted, doing the don't-spill-the-coffee shuffle. "Oh my God, I'm so glad I came back down. We must have just missed each other."

Riley was the last person she had been expecting to see, but they had a knack for appearing when she least expected them. It was one of their best and worst qualities. As they approached the car, she begged her exhausted, un-caffeinated brain to give her a solution. She could simply tell Riley the truth. Up until last week, the only secret she had been keeping from Riley was that she hadn't listened to Taylor Swift's *1989* album because she wasn't a Swiftie. There was nothing she couldn't tell Riley (except the Taylor Swift situation). There would be some teasing but if anyone could understand jumping into bed with someone, it was Riley. Riley wouldn't judge, so much as relish, which was fine. She could handle some relishing. It would be so nice to finally stop skulking around and have someone to talk it through with.

Riley was good at keeping secrets when they *really* needed to, so when she grabbed them by both arms, she made sure that they were looking into her eyes when they promised. Riley was also Riley. Twas always a chance, partic-ularly with a secret this gossipy, that they would let it slip. The last thing Naomi needed in this moment was to hear about how her best friend was sleeping with her ex-fiancé's boss.

It was what she and Freya had already agreed on: don't say anything right now. As she mentally reviewed her options, she returned to that conclusion. When Riley reached her car, she'd quickly brushed her fingers through her hair and then rolled down the window and gave a truthful excuse. "I wish you'd called! I'm actually on my way to Michigan to see Naomi."

"Perfect! Then you'll definitely need this coffee and a support buddy. I don't have anything else to do this weekend anyway," Riley replied, not missing a beat. They jiggled the passenger side handle. "C'mon, open up."

Her brain had refused to provide her anymore assistance. The coffee looked so inviting. She'd unlocked the doors and hoped no one would notice anything was amiss. But she was out of luck.

"What's this?" Riley interlocked their fingers and held them to their lips. "That's not the face of someone who forgot to do their laundry. That's the face of someone who was doing very bad things at someone else's place and didn't have time to change afterward. Come to think of it, you haven't been around at all this week."

Abby adopted what she hoped was a believable look of offense. "What are you talking about? I met you for lunch two days ago!" Abby said.

"Met?" Riley scoffed. "More like I went through your calendar, figured out when you'd be at your office, and forced you to go out with me."

Abby frowned. "I need to come up with better pass-words," she said under her breath.

"Not that I would call it a lunch, since you hardly touched your food," Riley added, sounding hurt.

"I told you I wasn't hungry!" Abby exclaimed, feeling like an injured seal being circled by sharks.

"Hold on now." Riley raised a finger for silence and then

let it drop until it was pointing directly at Abby. "Disappearing all week. Wearing the same clothes. Not eating lunch? Oh my God. I've seen this before. Abby's in love!"

Abby's mouth opened and shut several times before any noise came out. "I—" she stammered, feeling her face reddening even more. "I am not!"

"Oh yeah?" Naomi asked, her eagerness a transparent attempt to keep the attention off herself. "Then where have you been?"

"I was ... in ... mourning," Abby said, her mind churning like rusty cogs as she desperately sought an answer. "For you. Who can think about a thing like clothes and lunch after what Will and Simon did to you?"

Riley gave a gleeful squeak. "You said Will and Simon. You heard it, didn't you, Naomi? Abby kept telling me not to say Will or Simon in front of you and then she's the one that goes and says it. You all heard it, right? Will and Simon? Straight from Abby's lips?"

"Yes, we get it. Thank you, Riley," Abby said. There was no backhoe big enough to dig the size of hole she wanted to crawl into.

"It's okay, Abby." Naomi was clearly trying to sound reassuring, but the quiver in her voice gave her away.

Riley tapped the toe of their sneaker against the mahogany carpeting. "I want to make sure that everyone heard it because Abby acts like I'm always the troublemaker. But around her, everyone is a troublemaker, because it's impossible to keep up with all her rules. Even she can't!"

"I heard it!" Becca confirmed, smacking her freshly glossed lips together.

Abby gave Naomi an apologetic smile. "I didn't want to bring them up ... if you weren't ready to talk about it."

"Since we have, I want to know what's been going on!" Riley adjusted their glasses, clearly prepared to get down to business. "While Abby's been in, er, mourning, I've been out of the loop. Well, except for Team Naomi gossip, of course."

Naomi blinked. "Team Naomi?" she repeated, sounding unsure.

"Well, of course! You don't think I would follow anything Team Will, would you? I mean, okay, occasionally I check out their Facebook group to see what everyone is saying. But I would never join anything TW related—I don't want to bump their numbers, which, I have to admit, are always a bit higher than the TNs. And sure, I was in Will's wedding party, so it's likely I would be a celebrity among the TWs, but that hasn't stopped me from being a TN all the way."

"I didn't realize all that was going on," Naomi said, her voice tired and hesitant. "After everything ... happened, I started getting all these messages. Just vile stuff. I didn't know what to do, so I shut down my social media."

Abby could see Naomi's fists squeezing closed. "We don't have to talk about this. I didn't come here to make you talk. I wanted to make sure you were okay."

Naomi rubbed her thumbs over her clenched fists. "It's okay. I've been trying not to think about it too much, but maybe it's time I start."

"Have you ... heard from him?" Abby asked hesitantly.

Naomi gave a sharp shake of her head. "I can't imagine he'd want to talk to me. Not after what I did."

"You can't blame yourself."

"Sure, I can." She swallowed hard, but her words still came out shaky. "This entire thing is my fault."

Becca clicked her tongue. "You think you could have stopped some maniacal stalker from trying to frame you?"

"Maniacal stalker?" Abby's brows cinched together. She'd given this a lot of thought over the last two weeks, and discussed it ad nauseum with everyone in her life, including Freya. She was confident that there was only one, clear, answer. "Please, we all know who was responsible for this."

"Here we go again," Riley said. "We were arguing about this the whole way over. I don't see why it has to be Simon simply because he was in the pictures."

"Yes, it does!" Abby looked at Naomi. "You know it's him, don't you? You heard him at Rosh Hashanah. He said he would do whatever it takes to get you back."

"Whoa, hold on—" Riley held up a hand, their forehead nearly wrinkling with distress as they looked at Abby. "Simon showed up at Rosh Hashanah? And you never told me?"

"Us!" Becca interjected.

Naomi blanched and pulled her knees up to her chest. "Don't be mad at Abby," she said. "I made her promise not to tell anyone. I didn't want you guys to be upset."

"He dropped by unannounced to try and win Naomi back." Abby said, grateful that it was finally out in the open. "He said he had changed."

"Yeah," Riley said with a sarcastic huff. "And the Pope is an atheist now."

"You don't think he could have masterminded this whole thing, do you?" Naomi asked, hugging her arms around her legs like she was clinging to a life raft. "I mean, what if he was framed, too?"

"It's possible," Abby said, throwing in a retroactive attempt to soften her approach. It was more than possible. It was exactly the kind of manipulative bullshit that a narcissist like Simon would pull. Also, it didn't matter what she believed. It mattered what Naomi believed and what she was going to do about it. "I think the real question that you need to ask is, who has the most to gain from breaking up your marriage? When you consider that *and* the fact that Simon was in the pictures, then the image starts to get a little clearer."

"Oh—try that again," Riley said, taking off their glasses and holding them out toward her. "Only this time, take the glasses off halfway through."

"Not now, Riley," Abby scolded. As Riley dejectedly put their glasses back on, Abby's phone dinged loudly in the silence. Then again.

"Sorry," she said, reaching for her phone. Her intention had been to silence it, but she stopped when she saw the name on the screen.

JULIE MCCOY (3 Messages)

She told herself that she could wait and open them later, but then the notification updated to three messages and she couldn't stop herself from unlocking her screen. A little peek, that was all.

> JULIE MCCOY: I don't know how I'm supposed to work under these conditions. Trying to research a famous actor's connection to a cult while thinking about the places your lips have been recently…

> Or where mine will be this evening…

> It is not going well.

Abby hoped her friends hadn't heard her involuntary intake of breath. That was all it took, a few words, to make her entire body ache. One particular part of her body more than others.

She fired back a message.

> ABBY: I suppose you think it's easy trying to give good advice to Naomi when you're sexting me?

The response came back within seconds.

> JULIE MCCOY: Sexting?? I am so not sexting you. Teenagers sext and I am not a teenager. I am an adult producing artfully crafted copy describing the myriad ways I am planning to make you come tonight.

The corner of Abby's lip lifted into a smirk.

> ABBY: Ohhh, I see. So, if I were to tell you that right now I'm thinking about that delicious sound you always make the first time I slip my fingers inside of you…

> JULIE MCCOY: Oh now that would be sexting.

"I see how it is," Riley said, their voice snapping Abby's attention back to the room. "You can get your text on during this serious moment, but if I want to help you be a little more Perry Mason, I get yelled at."

"Okay, sorry," Abby said, locking her phone. She cleared her throat. "As I was saying. I don't know if it was Simon, but we have to start somewhere, or we'll never get any answers, and he seems like a good place to start."

This made Naomi shrink even further into the sofa. "What's the point in looking for answers? What's done is done. Will is never going to talk to me ever again and I'm going to die alone and hated by the entire world."

"No way, Naomi." It was said with such strength and finality that Abby had to check to make sure it was, in fact, her sister who had said it. "You're one of the strongest, most amazing people I know, and I'm telling you that you're simply not allowed to give up because of a man."

Abby was tempted to check her sister's body for blinking lights or whirring sounds that would suggest that she had been replaced by a robot. She tore her gaze away from Becca and back to Naomi, who looked about as taken aback as she was.

"This may be the first time I've ever said this," Abby said. "But Becca's right. You have to keep fighting. You have to choose yourself so that in the end, no matter what, you know you did everything you could."

Naomi's eyes began to sparkle with tears. "How do I do that?" she asked, her voice cracking

Abby let her head fall back against the sofa cushion, and stared at the ceiling. She hadn't thought that far ahead. She traced the crown molding with her eyes as she tried to take that next step. "You're sure a hundred percent sure that there's no one who can verify your whereabouts?"

Naomi nodded.

Riley rubbed their hands together, as if inspired by the

challenge. "Did you post any stories on Instagram that would show where you were? Preferably selfies?"

"No."

Becca cocked her head to the side. "Not one selfie the entire night? How is that even possible?"

"Did you make a call?" Riley asked. "I'm sure they could, like, triangulate your whereabouts or something, right?"

Naomi gripped the edge of the sofa until her knuckles were white as silent tears began to run in rivulets down her cheek. Her chest rose and fell with fast, almost fearful breaths. "I went out," she whispered.

Abby exchanged the quickest of glances with Becca and Riley. "Okay, where were you?"

"I can't ... tell you." She buried her face in her knees and let out a deep, heartbreaking sob.

Abby wasn't afraid of tears. Tears to her were like a frying pan to a chef. They were an implement of her trade, and an important one. Tears brought a release of emotion and access to new feelings that allowed her clients to talk, to have breakthroughs, and even to efind relaxation and comfort after pain. But Naomi wasn't a client, and no matter how many times Abby saw her cry, she couldn't see it through her therapist lens. It was her friend, hurting, and it hurt her too. She reached over and rubbed Naomi's back silently, letting her know that she wasn't alone.

When her crying eased, she said softly, "You know you can tell us anything."

"I know," Naomi said, looking up and wiping her eyes with her sleeve. "I've been so afraid to tell you. Abby, I made such a mess of everything."

This time Abby gave Riley a knowing look. "Yeah, you're

in good company," she said. "Thankfully, we're a safe space for making mistakes."

"As long as you don't mind us making fun of you later," Riley added.

Naomi made a noise somewhere between a laugh and a sob. "That's fine," she eventually said.

Abby patted her back. "So, tell us, sweetie. Maybe we can help."

"It was ... Simon," she managed to say before dissolving into tears again. Everyone's eyes widened, and she waved a hand at them, dismissing their assumption. "Not like that. He called me a few days before the wedding."

"Called you? About what?" Abby asked, her shoulders tightening as she tried to figure out where this was going.

She tried to calm her ragged breathing as she answered. "Do you remember, a year after he and I got married, we bought that plot of land up here in Michigan?"

Abby thought for a minute and then nodded. "Oh yeah! You were going to build a vacation home. I was still living off ramen noodles in that studio apartment and wondering where I had gone wrong in my life."

"Simon was going to build the house by himself, but, no one will be shocked to hear, he never did."

"What does that have to do with anything?"

"Technically, my parents bought it. I mean, we gave them the money, but they put the land under their name. It was some stupid tax thing that Simon insisted on. So, when we got divorced, it was the only thing he couldn't take from me, not that he didn't try. He didn't have a legal leg to stand on, and I had given him everything else without a fight. I couldn't give up that silly little plot. Then, right before the wedding ... Simon ... called. He said that he saw me on the news. He said ..." She sniffed and rubbed her nose with her sweatshirt. "...that he could see that Will and I were truly in love, and that he would leave us alone."

"Let me guess," Abby said. "There was a catch."

"He wanted me to sign over the land to him. It seemed so easy," Naomi said, her voice quivering again as she tried to fight back another round of tears. "I should have known better, but I agreed. It was such a small price to pay."

"Why didn't you say anything?"

Naomi rested her cheek on her knees and stared at the wall. "I think ..." she said, "I think I knew it was a mistake, but the idea of having him out of my life forever was too great an opportunity to pass up. I knew you'd try to talk me out of it."

"Did you end up signing the papers?"

She squeezed her eyes shut and then opened them again. "Yes, at least I thought so. I met with his lawyer. I got a call from him right after you left, and he said Simon wanted the papers signed right away, and that he would meet me at a café down the street. I should have known that something was up but ... you were gone, Abby, and I ... I wanted it over. I was afraid of what he would do if I said no. So, I left and met the lawyer." She paused before continuing. "That's why I couldn't say anything at the wedding."

Frustration ripped through Abby's chest. "What do you mean? You had proof!" It came out sounding angrier than she had intended.

"Come on, Abby, proving that I wasn't cheating by admitting I was lying and sneaking behind his back wouldn't have made things any better. Besides ..." She picked up a throw pillow from the couch and buried her face in it. "It wasn't real."

"What wasn't real?"

Naomi kept her face hidden as she talked. "Him, the lawyer. I checked. I knew you were going to want to use him as my alibi, so I went to look him up and there is no him. There is no Kevin Freemont of Wilson & Ellis. There isn't even a Wilson & Ellis. It was all a lie."

"Well," Becca chirped. "On the upside, that means you still have your property, then, doesn't it? Do you think maybe Peter and I could—"

A thought popped into her head that was so startling, Abby gave a little cry and flew off the sofa before she could stop herself. "The alarm!"

Shocked, Naomi opened her eyes and looked at Abby.

"Sweet Mother Mary, Abigail Meyer." Riley clapped their hand to their heart with the fervor of a silent movie actor. "Is that really necessary?"

"Oh, stop acting like you tied your corset too tight today and listen!" Abby reprimanded. "The alarm! In my office! You said it yourself, Naomi, I wasn't there when you got the call from the lawyer. You think it's a coincidence that it went off the night you needed to be without an alibi?"

"Yeah, but didn't you say it was going off all month?" Riley asked.

Abby pointed at them. This was the missing piece. The thing that had been niggling at her since this all went down. She tried to speak as quickly but as clearly as she could. "That's exactly it! It *was* going off all month, but since the wedding, it hasn't been triggered once. I'll bet you anything that was Simon testing out how long it would take me to get

to my office and handle things with the police. And no"—
Abby held up a hand toward Riley who was slipping their
glasses off their face—"I do not want your glasses as I say
this."

"I'm only trying to help," they pouted.

"Think about it, Naomi," Abby continued. "Simon
decides he's going to ruin your marriage by making it look
like you cheated on Will, but he needs to make sure that you
are totally off the radar so no one can vouch for you during
the time those pictures were taken. He concocts a surefire
way to get you to sneak away in secret. He has you meet with
someone with a fake name, so even if you do admit what you
were doing, you can't track them down later to prove it."

The trio watched her, silently, as she paced.

"Then he just needed a time when you'd be completely
alone and—" She slapped a hand to her mouth and then let it
slide down her face. "Oh my God, the bustle!"

"I'm not following," Riley said.

"No? Don't you remember the dress episode when the
bridal attendant told me to drink and practice bustling the
night before the wedding, so the muscle memory was fresh?
We talked about it, Naomi, and you said that's what we
would be doing. All the issues with the alarm at my office
started *the day that episode aired*." She gave a knowing shake
of her head. "He knows where my office is; he's even been
there—remember? He came for the little office-warming
party that Riley threw me when I first started my practice. I
remember because that's right before you were going to serve
him papers for the divorce, and I was so afraid that I would
let something slip."

Riley snapped their fingers. "That's right! We even

talked about how grown-up you were with your very own alarm system."

"Right! He knew what to do. He knew when to do it. What I can't figure out is how he got into my office. The door was always open but there was no sign of forced entry."

"I can answer that," Naomi said, sitting up a little. "He copied the spare key off my key ring. I can't believe I never thought of it. He was always insisting on having a copy of all my keys—Abby, remember I had you change your locks after we broke up? I didn't think about your office key. It never occurred to me ..." She shook her head.

"Of course!" Riley bounced up and down excitedly. "So, he has the key. He can set off the alarm without doing any damage that might raise actual suspicion. Then he does a bunch of practice runs before the wedding so he knows how long it takes you to get there, handle everything, and come back. Then the night before the wedding he set the alarm off at the same time Naomi *happens* to get a call from this lawyer."

Even Becca was beginning to get into the crime-solving spirit. "Then all that was left was to take some pictures in front of your place with a Naomi lookalike and shoot them off to NBS!"

"Brilliant!" Riley declared before adding, "Incredibly twisted, but brilliant."

Naomi smiled but the smile wasn't on her face for more than a few seconds before it was wiped away by a sudden realization. "Yeah, but even if we could prove this, what good would it do anyway?"

"There has to be something," Riley insisted. "Couldn't you sue Simon for slander or something?"

"For what?" Naomi gave a forlorn laugh. "For going out with someone who looks like me from behind? Besides, I don't want revenge. All I want is to get Will back, and there's pretty much zero chance of that happening. Whether or not I was in those pictures, I still lied to him, and he hates me for it."

"You're right, Naomi," Abby said, plummeting back onto the sofa beside her. This was the moment she had been waiting for. The one Freya had talked about. It wasn't about who did it, it was about Naomi choosing Will. "You should give up now."

Naomi wrinkled her nose. "You make it sound so awful when you say it like that," she said.

Riley nodded at her. "She has a way of doing that. I think it's her tone of voice."

"It's not my—" Abby started to protest but then decided not to take the bait and turned back to Naomi. "I'm trying to point out that this helpless maiden thing is not for you."

"Me?" Naomi looked closely at Abby to make sure she wasn't indicating someone else. "I am not being a helpless maiden."

Abby hummed as if considering her argument. "I see," she said. "So, then you're not locked in your room, waiting for your knight in shining armor to come to you?"

Naomi gave a little groan as her body went limp and she toppled back onto the armrest of the couch. "Why do you think I didn't want you to come see me? I don't want to hear this!" She covered her face in her hands as she let Abby's words sink in. Finally, she pulled her hands away. "So let me guess. You think that if I want to have Will in my life again, I need to win him back instead of lying around in my room feeling sorry for myself."

Abby didn't say anything, but her smile won in the battle for control over her lips.

"I hate your advice," Naomi said but there was a spark in her eyes that indicated that even though she hated the advice, she knew there was a nugget of truth in there. "But let's suppose, hypothetically, that you were right. What now? I mean you said it yourself: Simon went out of his way to make sure I wouldn't have any way to prove where I was that night."

"Well, you didn't teleport there," Riley said. "Somebody must have seen you go to and from your apartment."

"What about at the cafe?" Becca suggested. "Didn't you have a waitress?"

Naomi closed her eyes, trying to recall if she had had any interaction with her server. "I never went inside. I tried calling the attorney when I got there, and the number was out of service. I waited outside the restaurant for a while, but it was pretty obvious no one was coming." She opened her eyes.

"Did you take a cab or rideshare?" Riley asked.

"No, I walked."

"Did you stop at an ATM?"

"No."

"A convenience store?"

"No."

"Any kind of store at all?"

"And seriously, not one selfie?" Becca added.

"No!" Naomi looked crestfallen, like the ember of hope

Abby had inspired began to fizzle out again. "I can't believe I managed to make myself completely invisible."

Abby crossed her legs. "Okay, but I think we're missing the point here. It's not about proving to him that it wasn't you in those photos, although we can work on that too. I think what's more important is speaking your truth."

Naomi looked at Abby, waiting for more.

"As the adage goes, our secrets make us sick. In the end, it was the secrets that really caused the problems, right? Simon had all the power because he could control the narrative."

"I guess so," Naomi said.

"What if you take that power away from him by not hiding or being ashamed anymore? You have nothing to be ashamed of. There's no shame in marrying a man who turned out to be something else than what you thought. There's no shame in the fact that you tried to protect Will from danger. There's no shame that you met with that lawyer, hoping it would help your marriage get off on the right foot."

"You're saying that I should tell him ... everything."

Abby nodded. "If he's going to give up on your relationship, then let him do it with all the facts. Let him face the truth of what you've been through and what you were trying to do. No matter what he decides, you can be free of all those secrets once and for all."

"Free," Naomi repeated, sounding like she could taste the word as she said it. "Well, what I've tried up until now hasn't worked too well for me, so I guess there's no harm in trying this."

"You know," Becca said. "When I told Peter about those other boys, I felt so much better."

"Except for the part where you didn't tell him; he figured it out on his own," Abby replied.

Becca made a huffing noise. "Whatever. I told him with my *actions*, Abigail. My point is that once it was out, that's when things started to get better."

"How am I supposed to tell him anything when he isn't talking to me?" Naomi asked.

"Oh, that's easy," Riley said. "Text him."

"I have. He hasn't responded to any of them."

Riley adjusted their glasses. "Yes, but reading texts and responding to them employ two entirely different muscle groups."

"I don't think it's physically possible for a person to not read a text," Becca confirmed.

Riley pointed a finger at Becca. "Exactly."

"What if he's blocked me?" Naomi said.

"I'd bet my therapist's license that he hasn't," Abby said. "He's hurt—but he loves you. I don't think he's going to cut you out of his life completely."

Naomi tugged her phone out of her sweatshirt pocket. "I just ... text him," she said, a hybrid of a statement and a question. Heads bobbed in confirmation around her. "And you'll help me?" More bobbing heads.

Abby watched as Naomi pulled up her text messages to Will, where at least a dozen unanswered texts were stacked like Lego, and started typing. *Dear Will...*

It took nearly an hour to craft only a handful of sentences, but they were raw, vulnerable, and powerful. They would finally lift the veil for Will and, more importantly, let Naomi reclaim her voice. When Naomi hit send, there wasn't a dry eye in the house.

Naomi smiled the first truly genuine grin that Abby had seen from her since her wedding day. "Thank you. I don't know what's going to happen next, but for the first time in a long time I feel like I'm in the driver's seat. I'm in a car with four flat tires and a smoking engine, but I'm driving it."

Abby gave Naomi a tight hug, hoping to transfer her love, relief, and joy to her friend. "We're always here for you."

"I know," Naomi said, squeezing her back. "I'm so lucky."

"Does this mean you're coming home?" Riley asked. "We're all overdue for a trashy TV marathon."

Naomi released the hug. "Yes, because I'm going to need some distractions to keep me from checking my phone all the time. I love my parents, but that's not in their skill set."

"Do you want to drive back with me?" Abby offered.

Naomi shook her head. "My car is up here, and I need some time to pack and let my parents know what's going on. I haven't told them any of what I told you and I probably should."

Abby nodded and gave her friend another hug.

As she walked back to her car, she checked her phone and saw another message from Freya waiting.

> JULIE MCCOY: When do you think you'll come by this evening?

The simple question made her stomach flip. Riley and Becca were several paces behind her, so she tapped out a quick reply.

> **ABBY:** We're leaving now so probably by about 10 or so.

> **JULIE MCCOY:** We? I thought you were going up there by yourself.

> **ABBY:** 😔 Yeah I did too. And then Riley and Becca showed up. It's a theme in my life.

> **JULIE MCCOY:** Well, come by my place whenever you get in. I'll leave a key to the back door under the mat.

Freya's house was bigger, better, and most importantly, Riley didn't have the keys to her place and Naomi didn't live down the hall, so it had been an easy decision to keep all her rendezvous at Freya's.

Abby put her phone back in her pocket. "Riley, I think you should drive back with Rebecca."

"Why is that exactly?"

*Because it's a three-hour drive home and I would like to get to Freya's as quickly as possible and not have to drop you off first.* "Because you're the reason she was here in the first place, so you should have to suffer the consequences of your actions."

"Rude," Becca interjected.

"Fine," Abby said. "It makes sense. Their place is on the way to yours."

"I normally like being treated like a piece of meat but in this case, it's not fun," Riley said.

Becca wrapped an arm around Riley's. "See now you've made Riley feel bad. Of course, you can ride with me, love."

Any sense of guilt Abby had was buried under the avalanche of excitement of getting on the road.

Sometime after ten, she pulled up at Freya's. The sky was already midnight black, a sign that even though it was spring, it was still early in the season. She took the keys out of the ignition but stayed put, turning on the overhead light and reaching for her purse. She pulled out a recently-purchased cosmetic bag stocked with makeup essentials. Using her visor mirror, she began reapplying and refreshing as best she could with the minimal light.

She had barely retraced her eyeliner when she heard a tap at her passenger window. She jumped, but the initial fear was immediately replaced with glee. She quickly unlocked the doors.

"Maybe I am a teenager after all," Freya said as she slid into the passenger seat. "I saw your car and I didn't think, I just ran outside."

Abby didn't think either. She leaned across the seats and kissed Freya voraciously, drinking in the still-new but becoming-familiar taste of Freya's mouth. Freya clutched her and let out an impossibly, addictive throaty purr that Abby wanted to hear again. And again. Right away.

She pushed out of her seat and, with a sexual-fueled deftness that she didn't know she had, slid across to the passenger side until she was straddling Freya. Still entangled in a kiss, she braced herself against the headrest of the seat with one hand while she let her other hand find its way to the button of Freya's jeans. The button practically popped open on its own, leaving Abby free to slide her hand down further until she could feel the rough texture of lace. She traced the edges, running her fingers underneath the fabric, promising, teasing, with each pass until she heard that delightful purr again.

"Wait," Freya said, pulling back. "Not here. Let's go inside."

Abby leaned down until her face was nestled in the crook of Freya's neck. "That's kind of where I was headed," she murmured playfully as she planted a line of kisses under Freya's ear. This time when Freya let out the purr, Abby's lips literally vibrated with Freya's pleasure.

She felt the cool rush of air as the door swung open. "I have plans for you," Freya said. "And they're difficult to accomplish in this car."

"It's not the most comfortable I've ever been," Abby admitted as she twisted herself out of the passenger seat.

Freya jumped out after Abby and took her by the hand, pulling her into the house. She felt like a teenager, too, giggling as they struggled to unlock the door in between kisses, barely getting it closed again before their clothing fell to the floor.

# Chapter 18
## *Freya*

FREYA'S BEDROOM WAS DARK AND SILENT, SAVE FOR THE dance of moonlight coming in from her window and the sounds of slowly quieting breaths. She and Abby were entangled, arms and legs and sheets, in such a way that she couldn't tell where she ended and Abby began. Strange as it was, she liked that feeling. It was becoming less strange by the day and more like Abby was a puzzle piece that she hadn't known she was missing. Abby made her feel complete in a different way than she'd experienced before. Yes, because of the sex. The mind-bending, otherworldly orgasms were definitely something she'd never experienced before, but it was more than that. It was what happened after. When they were simply together, talking or even not talking, she felt more herself than she ever had. It was as if Abby was able to see her for who she was and for some reason she was able to truly be who she was. Each morning when Abby headed home, it left her feeling empty, like she had been wrapped in a cozy blanket that had been abruptly ripped away, and she found herself counting down until she could nestle back into the warmth and comfort that was Abigail Meyer.

She looked over at Abby, her face still rosy, her skin damp and glistening in the moonlight. "Penny for your thoughts," she said.

Abby smiled. "I was thinking about my conversation with Naomi today. Or yesterday. Whatever time it is." She lifted her head to peer at the small clock on Freya's nightstand and then let out a small groan of protest. "We've officially crossed the line into Monday."

Freya rolled onto her side and propped her head up with a hand. "I didn't get to ask how it went with Naomi."

Abby stared at the ceiling. "I think it went really well, actually. Not that I would ever wish something this horrible on her, but I almost feel like maybe it needed to happen to help her find herself. I think maybe for the first time ever, she's really going to step into who she is, not who she thinks she needs to be or has to be. By the time she left, she almost looked happier than I've ever seen her." She looked over at Freya. "Did you talk to Will?"

"On Friday." She nodded. "I can't say that Will looked happier than I've ever seen him, though. He seemed more contemplative than anything. But we have a different relationship, and I don't have magic therapist powers."

"Hey, contemplative is good. As long as he's cogitating, then maybe ... there's hope."

Why did it feel so nice, so damn good, to have this woman in her bed, while they recounted their days, and worked together to help their friends? She felt this nearly uncontrollable urge to nestle up to Abby, to make sure every inch of her body was touching Abby's. She loved the way

Abby responded to her touch. Sexually, of course. The way Abby moved and writhed and enjoyed Freya's body on hers was new and exhilarating, but it was more than that. It was everything in between. It was the way Abby's body folded into hers. Whether they were holding hands or cuddling on the couch or nuzzling in bed as they drifted off to sleep, Abby made Freya feel like she wasn't supposed to be anywhere else except right there. It was the most incredible sensation that made her feel ... made her feel ...

"Now it's my turn. Penny for *your* thoughts," Abby said.

Freya startled, realizing she had been staring silently at Abby for an indefinite amount of time. "Uh," she stammered. "Thinking about what we were talking about. How about you?"

Abby smirked. "I don't know why, but I was thinking about high school."

Freya hopped on the change of subject. "What about? I don't have many fond memories from that time."

Abby propped her head up in her hand. "Really? That was the last thing I was expecting to hear. You were literally *the* most popular girl in school."

"Well, sure," she responded.

Abby laughed. "Okay, you could have argued that a little bit more, but continue."

Freya shrugged. "But just because people like you doesn't mean they like you for who you are."

"Damn. Deep thoughts so early in the morning."

Was it deep? It had always been a simple truth to her. It sparked a thought and she rolled on to her side so she was facing Abby. "It's..." she stopped.

"It's what?"

"This is going to sound so stupid."

"Well, now you have to tell me."

Freya chewed on her lower lip, contemplating whether she really wanted to finish her thought. "I think it's the main reason I hated you so much in high school. I was so jealous of you."

"Me?" The disbelief on Abby's face was almost comical. "You were jealous of me."

"Yes!" Freya said with a laugh. "You got to be ... you. You didn't have a lot of friends and you dressed kind of weird and you were in literally the nerdiest after school club—"

"I am really hoping there's a compliment in there somewhere."

"My point is that you were friends with the people you wanted to be friends with, lifelong friends like Naomi. And you wore what you wanted to wear because you liked it. And you joined the anime club because it made you happy. And you were out of the closet, getting to be yourself, and dating who you wanted to date. You had this amazing life and this crazy confidence that I didn't have, and it made me so angry."

Abby brushed a strand of hair from Freya's forehead as she took this in. "I was jealous of you too. You were a cheerleader who had all the friends and all the attention and all the cutest clothes, but it never occurred to me that the things you had were the things that were making you miserable."

Freya gave her an impish smirk. "Miserable might be taking it a little far. Don't get me wrong, being popular had its perks." Abby gave her shoulder a gentle push and Freya chuckled. "But no, I never ever felt like I could be myself. I knew if I was then I'd risk losing everything. I wasn't brave enough to do that, but you were. You still had people who loved you. Like the actual you. It's funny though, if you'd asked me back then, I don't think I could have told you all that. I only knew I hated you."

Abby bent forward and kissed Freya gently. "And now?"

"Now?" Freya inched closer and kissed her back, still gentle but now with a twinge of hunger on the edges. "I don't know what to think. The things I hated about you are the things that ..." her voice trailed off. "They're ..." she tried again, and then stopped.

"I think I know what you mean. I've spent these last two weeks trying to figure out which was real. My feelings before, or now. Like, can you really love something about a person that you hated before?" She snapped her fingers. "Just like that? Can it all change?"

Freya wasn't sure what to focus on. The question or the sprinkling of the word *love* into the conversation. Maybe Abby noticed, too, because she didn't give Freya too much time to think about it.

"Or," Abby said, pulling Freya to her. "Do I need to stop asking questions and start having my way with you?"

It was definitely the latter.

~

At some point, they must have fallen asleep. Her only indication was that the moonlight had been replaced by early morning rays and she didn't remember that happening. She tried to go back to sleep, but the sun was glowing so bright through her lids, she knew it wasn't going to happen. She rolled over and her tired, sore muscles greeted her, followed by a rumble in her stomach; both of which she wasn't surprised by, given the amount of physical activity she'd participated in during the night.

Abby had rolled to the edge of her bed, her back turned to Freya and a tumble of her auburn hair splayed across the pillow. Freya couldn't resist and inched closer to Abby until she was tucked against her back, her face nuzzled into Abby's neck. She inhaled the intoxicating scent of sweat and shampoo and ... Abby. Earthy and soft, like a dewy morning.

"Morning," she heard Abby mumble. "Again."

"Sorry, I didn't mean to wake you," Freya said, planting a kiss on her neck.

Abby reached behind her and pulled Freya's arm across her body, locking their snuggle into place like a seatbelt. "Actually, I think the sun and my achy body did that all on its own. We might be acting like teenagers, but I'm definitely still in the body of an adult that isn't used to quite so much ... activity."

"We were pretty active last night, weren't we?" Freya said with a laugh.

Abby rolled so she was face to face with Freya. "Last night? I believe I confirmed we were busy well into the morning."

Freya's stomach gave a grumble of agreement. "I definitely worked up an appetite."

"After how much you ate out last night?" Abby replied, the grin evidenced in her voice.

Freya let out a pained noise. "That was terrible."

"That was amazing," Abby responded, tossing her pillow at Freya and then sitting up. "Now let's go put some food in that belly."

Freya tugged herself out from underneath the sheets and

sat up, slowly, giving her body time to acclimate to the altitude change. "Food sounds amazing."

"And coffee."

"And *coffee*," she repeated, with extra emphasis. She looked over her shoulder where Abby was sitting on the edge of her bed, stretching her arms over her head. "You stay. I'll go make us some coffee and something to eat."

"I was kind of hoping we could hit up that juice place I spied down the street. I feel like my electrolytes could use a little loving." She stood up, scooping up her underwear off the floor. "That is, assuming we can piece together where all my clothes are," she said, stepping into the bathroom.

It was true, these last few weeks her house had become a scavenger hunt after their sexcapades. Move a sofa pillow? Bra. Pull out a dining room chair? Dress. Close the bathroom door? Shirt.

Abby poked her head out of the bathroom. "Actually, do you mind if I borrow something of yours? Riley ambushed me yesterday, so I didn't have time to go inside and pack a bag which means I'd be going on day three of wearing the same thing and that's crossing a line for me."

"Of course," Freya said.

"Something forgiving!" Abby called as she dipped back into the bathroom. "My curves are a lot ... curvier than yours."

Freya walked to her dresser and pulled out her comfiest Lululemon leggings and matching top. "Yeah, and I love those curves." There was a Wilhelm scream inside her head as soon as she said it. There it was. Again. That L word. Only this time she had been the one to use it. Or maybe she was overthinking the whole thing. Neither of them had used the word towards each other, only to describe things *about* them. Merely a turn of phrase.

She wasn't even sure she had a word to describe the way she felt about Abby or how Abby made her feel. The only word that came to mind was home. Not even her current home or the home she'd grown up in. A cozy Thomas Kinkade painting of a cottage in the woods illuminated by a rosy sun speckled sky kind of home. A crackling fireplace and fuzzy blankets and mugs of hot cocoa kind of home. It wasn't a home she knew or had ever wanted and yet it was the feeling she got when she was with Abby. It was different than love, at least as far as she could tell. It was its own special thing. Which was fine by her. Everything about this situation was its own special thing.

Silently, she placed the clothes on the bathroom counter and scurried away to pull more clothes out of the dresser for herself. Once she was dressed, she scouted for her phone, finding it in the back pocket of her jeans, which were sprawled on the floor. She plugged it in and sat on the edge of her bed to do the standard morning skim. When she opened her e-mail, though, her eyes were immediately drawn to a message from her agent.

She only read the first line before she bolted straight up. "Holy shit," she said loudly.

"What's wrong?" Abby appeared at the door, dressed in Freya's clothes and finishing up a ponytail.

Freya's forced herself to read the e-mail, slowly.

*Freya,*

*Great news! Just got word that you're on the list to replace*

*Kent James! They want to meet with you next week to discuss the opportunity. Apparently, the wedding special is what pushed you to the top. It showed your versatility beyond simply being a news journalist. They want someone who can find the truth and also go viral. I told them they ain't seen nothing yet.*

*Congrats!*

*Kiara*

Freya read and reread the e-mail and continued to read the e-mail even as she talked to Abby. "INN is considering me to replace Kent James."

"What?" Abby squeaked, doing excited bunny hops into the room "That's incredible, congratulations!"

Freya looked up, stunned with disbelief and excitement. "It's not a done deal yet but it's still ... wow ..."

"This is so exciting!" Abby clapped her hands exuberantly. "I'm so happy for you! What a way to start the week. What does that mean, what's next?"

"They want to meet with me, to discuss," Freya put air quotes around *discuss*. "I have no clue what that means or how many candidates I'm up against."

"None that stand a chance," Abby replied, giving Freya a kiss on the cheek. "Now we definitely have to go out for breakfast, so we can celebrate! C'mon!"

"Let me reply to Kiara really quick," she said, and set her thumbs to work tapping out an answer and her availability next week. With the incredibly satisfying *whoosh* sound that signaled her e-mail was on its way, she walked into the living room to find Abby bent down and looking under the sofa. "Any idea where my left shoe is?"

Freya grabbed her keys which had been tossed on the floor near the door. "I think I saw it ..." Freya opened the door and retrieved Abby's shoe which was lying on its side on the porch. "Yep. I vaguely remember noticing it was there last night."

"I'm not even going to try and understand how I didn't notice losing a shoe before I got inside." She slipped it on with a laugh.

"Next week I want to try that little bagel place a little further down the street," Abby said as they left her house. "Is it any good?"

"To be honest, I haven't really been to any of the places in my neighborhood," Freya said. "I'm not home that often."

Abby gave a playful gasp of shock. "This will not stand. You're in such a cool pocket of the city." She raised an eyebrow in mischievous defiance. "Challenge accepted. I'm going to see to it that you start patronizing your local businesses."

"Did you mean that to come out so menacing?"

"Maybe." Abby's whole body grinned back at her, and Freya had half a mind to kiss her right then and there.

"Freya!"

The sound of Brian calling her name was like an X-acto knife tearing into her cozy, sun-speckled, cottage painting. Or, more aptly, like a meteor ripping through the painting and destroying everything within a sixty-mile radius.

In her exhaustion, giddiness, and absolute stupidity, she had left her house with Abby. Here they were, early on a Monday morning, no more than a block from her house, laughing and flirting with each other, when Brian lived in the penthouse suite of a high rise only five minutes from her, where other execs, her other co-workers, lived, too. What had she been thinking?

She'd gotten lazy. Forgetful. She'd lost herself in dream-scapes of homes that didn't exist. There was no cottage in the woods; that was a painting invented in someone's mind. Reality was here and now, and it was walking right toward her, waving a chubby hand. Her body buzzed with anxiety, leaving her with a ringing in her ears.

"I thought that was you," Brian said, as he came closer.

"Good morning, Brian," she said with the most pleasant smile she could muster, taking a small side-step to create more distance between her and Abby. A part of her hoped that Brian wouldn't recognize Abby, but that was quashed as quickly as she thought it.

"And one of our NGN stars, what a surprise! It's nice to see you Abby," Brian said, extending a hand.

Abby reciprocated. "Oh, have we met?"

"This is one of the executive producers of *Nightly Global News*," Freya explained, not meeting Abby's gaze.

"I guess we haven't, but it feels like it, since I've seen a lot of footage of you in the past few weeks," he said, his delivery coming off creepy rather than flattering.

"Oh, have you?" Abby replied, in a questioning tone.

Freya needed to end this as quickly as possible before Brian started taking a closer look at the two of them and noticed their morning hair or the fact that Abby was wearing an outfit that he had definitely seen Freya in before. "Abby had some, um, new information regarding the situation with

Naomi and Will, so we were on our way to discuss it over coffee."

If Abby reacted to this lie, Freya couldn't tell.

"I like it. If we can be the ones to break the story of what really happened, that would be gold. Well, I won't keep you then. I was on my way to the bagel shop before I head into the studio, but why don't you stop by my office later today to tell me where we stand with that."

Freya nodded. "Will do," she said.

He gave her a two-finger salute then gave Abby a quick glance. "Nice to officially meet you, Abby."

"You too," Abby replied, then gave him a closed mouth smile. She watched him until he was far enough away to be out of ear shot. "That guy seems like a real winner. I bet he's a delight to work for."

Freya's mind was too far away to hear what Abby said. The icy wind of vigilance was blowing through her, freezing over the warm feelings she'd been basking in these last few weeks. She had been distracted and it had nearly cost her.

Abby lifted her eyebrows into an inquisitive arch. "What's wrong?"

Freya pursed her lips, not sure what to say. Maybe there was a way to figure this out. She needed to clear her head; she needed time to think. "Wrong? Nothing."

Abby crossed her arms, a non-verbal *I'm not buying that.*

Freya let out a sigh. Of course, Abby wouldn't let it go that easily. They were going to have to have to have the conversation she had avoided as best she could so she could hide in her bubble for a little longer. Time was up. "Abby..." Freya had said her name many times—as a growl, as a threat, as a joke, as a moan, as an invitation, as a giggle but never, never as a sigh. Not this kind, laden with sadness and regret.

"What is it?" Abby asked, starting to look more concerned. "Was it what you told that guy? I don't care that you said we were meeting to talk about Will and Naomi. Your personal life is not your work's business."

The more that Abby pressed, the more she tried to understand, the more Freya felt like her body was turning to ice. "I can't," she said, her throat thick.

Abby's brows came together slightly like she was trying to make out the image on a Magic Eye poster. "Can't what?"

Freya ran her hands like a windshield wiper across her face, trying to wash away the barrage of feelings and thoughts.

"Freya," Abby said, putting her hand on Freya's arm. "What's going on?"

Freya moved her arm away. "I should have talked about this sooner," she said.

"Talked about what?" Abby asked. "You're going to have to narrow that down a bit, because I'm literally compiling a Wikipedia-sized catalog of potential problems ranging from cancer to alien abduction."

Freya took a deep breath. "Remember when I asked you not to tell anyone about us?"

Abby nodded. "Sure."

"I wasn't doing it only because of everything that happened to Naomi and Will. I did it because ... I can't let anyone know I'm bi." Saying it out loud hurt worse than she expected, and she felt tears threaten to surface. "No one knows. Hell, I barely knew. I mean I knew, I think I always knew, but it's not something I ever allowed myself to entertain. I never thought I would, either, in a world like we live in. Relationships and love, they're dangerous enough without throwing in homophobia. That's why no one can know, Abby. Especially now with this incredible opportunity on the horizon. I can't be spotted walking around with you."

Abby, on the other hand, seemed to relax. "Is that all? Listen, I don't mind if you need to keep this private. We can keep things low key. No local stuff. We'll stick to places and neighborhoods where people don't know you."

Her skin prickled with frustration. "That's the problem, Abby," she said sharply. "That's what you don't understand. What you've never understood. Everyone knows me. Everyone. And they're all paying attention to me. It started in high school, and it's never stopped. People are always watching me and judging me and it's up to me to live up to their expectations. Only it's so much more than in high school. People on the street take pictures of me, sometimes even the paparazzi hang around. Whether we go to a cozy café down the street or on the other side of the city, someone will see us and word will get out fast."

"Whoa," Abby said, holding up a hand. "Is that what you meant last night when we were in the car and you said, 'Not here'? And why you always ask me to come in the back door of your house? And why we've ordered take out every night I've been over?"

Freya didn't know what to say. Maybe if she had told Abby from the beginning, she could have avoided this. But now, having it laid out bare, it sounded so much worse.

"Okay," Abby said, clearly trying to give herself time to process this information. "So, alright—we find a way to make it work. When we're out together, we'll make sure there's no

PDA. No behavior that could be construed as anything other than platonic. We keep our relationship just in the inner circle."

"No," Freya said so viscerally that Abby stepped back slightly. "You're not listening to me."

"No, what?"

Freya's hands clenched. "No inner circle. No one can know."

Abby's face registered a look that said maybe, finally, she was starting to understand why this, none of this, ever had a future. "What are you talking about?"

"No one can know, Abby. Not even Riley or Naomi. One slip is all it takes. One photo. One text. One email. And it's all over." Freya's words came faster and faster, fueled by a rush of fear. "This can never be more than what it is now—a secret." When Abby didn't say anything, she continued. "I should have said something right away. I wanted to. I just ... couldn't help myself."

"If I want to ... be with you ..." Abby said haltingly, like she was reading off a delayed teleprompter. "I have to keep it a secret. From everyone in my entire life. Forever."

"I'm sorry," Freya said. She was, but the Band-Aid was off and there was no turning back. "It shouldn't have to be this way, but it is."

"But a secret from everyone? From my best friends? From my mom?"

A bolt of anger sliced through Freya. Where was understanding, therapist Abby now? Why couldn't she see? "You live in a different world than me."

"A different world? You think I don't face discrimination?" Abby demanded, the softness and understanding in her eyes hardening.

"Not like I do, no." Freya's voice was taut like a guitar string wrapped too tightly. "If one of your clients finds out you're gay and they don't like it, they can stop seeing you. If someone finds out about me... it won't end with that person. It will end up on TV, on Popsugar, on Instagram. It becomes a story and suddenly people are boycotting me and the station and then my chances of taking over for Kent James drop to zero. Abby, I could even lose my job."

"*Could* being the operative word. You also *could not* lose your job."

"Could is not something I'm willing to risk. Not for anyone."

"I see," Abby said, bitterness creeping into her words. "So, everything we talked about last night didn't actually mean anything. You're exactly the same person you were in high school. Still too afraid to be yourself. Apparently, you like all those things about me, about how I'm myself, as long as they don't affect you at all."

As hard as she tried, Freya couldn't stop the tears from welling in her eyes. She set her jaw. "Abby, that's not fair."

"Isn't it? You preach to other women about how they need to take a stand. How did you put it in your book? 'You are royalty. Put on your crown and fight for your kingdom.' Isn't that what you said? Well, what about all the people out there who need to see a strong, beautiful, successful queer woman take her crown? You have a chance to make a difference. You have a platform to inspire millions, maybe to bring about some real change. You can *be* the Julie McCoy of your own story, be, what did you call her, a trail blazer?"

"You act like it's so easy," Freya said, her voice raw. "You don't know what I've been through to get here, and you have no idea what I stand to lose. You can't even begin to understand."

"Oh," Abby scoffed. "I can't begin to understand. Why, because your life is so much more important than mine?"

"Yes. It is, okay?" Freya said in a hushed yell. "You're right, I inspire millions of people. What I do matters. I can't throw it all away."

"Of course, you can't. You'll always choose popularity. Except instead of hating me for being myself, you're doing something worse. You're expecting me to join you in perpetuating this broken system that is continuing to hold people back and force them to lie about who they are."

"No, that's not what I'm expecting," Freya said. According to Newton's First Law of Motion, an object in motion stays in motion, and this was never truer than in this instance when Freya's mouth spoke what she didn't want to say: "I'm expecting you to leave."

Silence exploded like tear gas, making it impossible to breathe, to speak, to see, and it wasn't until she heard the footsteps that she realized that Abby had done just that.

# Chapter 19
## *Abby*

"I HAVE MET THE LOVE OF MY LIFE," RILEY SAID, SLIDING into the diner booth next to Abby with such force that her coffee cup clattered in protest.

"Riley!" Becca exclaimed. "Thank God you're here. I might as well have been sitting with two dead bodies." She gestured toward Naomi and Abby who were now sandwiched in the middle of the booth.

Abby shot her sister a well-worn look of irritation.

"Well, get ready to live again because Luke ... no, wait, Leon ... er, whatever. His name doesn't matter. What matters is that he's so beautiful, it's not safe to look at him without sunglasses, and we are soulmates."

"You don't know his name?" Abby said.

"Names aren't important when you are connecting on a transcendent level of the soul," Riley told her. "Besides, it was too noisy in the bar, and I couldn't quite make it out."

"I thought that other guy was your soulmate. The guy from last week. Dan or David, remember?" Naomi took a sip of her coffee, which had been sitting untouched on the table for so long it had to be barely lukewarm enough to tolerate.

"Turns out it was Darren. I was close. But no," Riley said, glancing out the window, wistfully recalling their brief romance. "That was a love that was not meant to be. We were two cars passing in the night."

"Ships," Abby said.

"That makes zero sense. Why would ships be on the road?"

Abby let out a sigh, but not the usual amused exasperated sigh she gave Riley. The sigh wasn't really about Riley at all. The sigh was the deep, empty cave inside her chest that had opened up a week ago, when she had walked away from Freya. She hadn't seen or heard from her, although she had seen and heard her everywhere—an absolute nightmare side effect of dating a celebrity who was on commercials, billboards, ads, commentator recaps, and just plain on her TV basically every night. Not that she was likely going to have the opportunity to date someone famous ever again, but should that chance arise, she was going to respectfully decline.

Thankfully, and yet not thankfully, she'd had plenty to distract herself with. Her brush with fame meant that she was the new "it" therapist in Chicago and she'd had to hire a virtual assistant to help her manage her client intake.

Then there was Naomi. While she had returned to the city, things hadn't gone as they had hoped. Even though she had done her best to speak her truth—not only to Will, but by making a few concise statements online—and then move on, the internet wasn't so ready to let go. #TeamNaomi and

#TeamWill were still some of the top trending hashtags, nearly a month after the wedding.

Abby, Riley, and even Becca had done their best to help divert her attention, but there was only so much they could do and only so many trash TV marathons they could sit through. Naomi was still receiving daily messages from fans and haters alike, and intrusive reporters popped up everywhere she went, making it nearly impossible for her to go five minutes without being reminded of what happened.

Abby's own broken heart seemed inconsequential compared to what Naomi was going through, so she dove into her work and into caring for Naomi, using them as a balm to hide from the pain she felt. It worked pretty well, except every once in a while, the howling winds of sadness would escape from her mouth in the form of a loud, despondent sigh. No one had noticed, or at least no one had said anything, yet on several occasions, Naomi had given her a look that suggested that she had in fact noticed and was in fact going to say something. It was the look that she was giving Abby right now.

Abby really didn't want Naomi to ask—but also, she really did. She was desperate to tell her best friend what had happened. She wanted to tell all of them. Not that she would even claim to know what had happened. From start to finish, none of it made sense. She wanted her friends to tease her and comfort her and make it all make some damn sense, or confirm that it didn't make any damn sense so she could call it a fugue state and move on.

Naomi's lips parted, but before she could speak, her phone buzzed on the table in front of her. When she let out a little gasp, Abby looked down to see what the screen said.

FACEBOOK

*Will has tagged you in a live video*

She looked at Naomi and then back to the phone.

Naomi's hand trembled as it reached for the phone. "It's probably a mistake," she said, but she clicked the notification. Facebook loaded and instantly a video started playing.

"—giving this a few seconds to go live. And hopefully Naomi will see it. I'm not sure if there's a way for me to know for certain." The image of Will was pixelated but clear enough.

"Oh my God," Naomi said aloud.

"Is that Will's voice?" Riley leaned over her arm and peered at her phone. Becca craned her body towards Naomi.

"What is he doing?" Abby asked no one in particular.

Naomi didn't answer, she just kept watching.

"Umm, so, I had this whole speech planned but now that it's actually time, I'm realizing it's all wrong and sounds so stupid. So, I'm going to wing it," Will said. He was walking somewhere. Down a sidewalk, the picture bouncing with his steps. "I know everything is a mess, and I know that I'm part of the reason for that. I'm not going to act like I didn't have every reason to be angry or hurt or confused. Finding out your fiancée has been married before and that she might have been cheating on you with her ex when you're seconds away from taking your vows is, well, calling it a nightmare is an understatement. But I get that abandoning you wasn't the right move either. No matter what was going to happen next, we should have done it together."

"O-M-G. Is he live-streaming this?" Becca asked, yanking Naomi's arm.

"It looks like it." Riley pointed at her screen. "And it's

public. Look at the viewer count. There's over 10,000 people watching this right now."

"Shh!" Abby shushed.

"It took me a while," Will continued. "But I get why you didn't tell me about Simon. After everyting happened, Freya sat me down one morning and told me I needed to wake up and see that I was throwing something important away without even trying to understand it or fight for it. I didn't see it that way at first. But when I read your text, I finally started to put it all together. It wasn't only that I wasn't fighting for us now, but I had never fought for us. I was comfortable being the good guy who loved you, but good isn't *safe*. And I never showed you that I was safe enough to weather this with you. In fact when push came to shove, I proved that I wasn't. I ran away without listening to you, and without trying to find out what was happening with you or why you didn't feel like telling me was an option. I won't pretend to even begin to understand what you've been through. I've never had to run from my past. I've never had to live in fear of the next knock or text or phone call. I've never had someone go to extreme lengths to manipulate and control me. I've never been let down by a system that was supposed to protect me. If I had, it would take a lot for me to trust someone enough to share it with them and I think I would do anything I could to build a new life without those things, even if it meant keeping it hidden from someone I loved."

The viewer counter was approaching 30,000. Heart and thumbs-up emoji were floating across Will's face in a steady stream.

"Once that hit me, I knew if there was any hope for us,

then it was time. I needed to step out of my complacency and it was going to begin by getting to the bottom of all of this no matter what that meant. I work in journalism. Finding the truth is supposed to be my job. So that's what I set out to do. Though, it was Freya—who I should probably note has no idea I'm doing this—she was the one who cracked the case. We sat and scoured those photos for any hint or clue we might have missed. She's the one who noticed that in one picture you can see someone looking out the window next to your apartment, holding a cat."

"Mrs. Pachenkis?" Abby practically shrieked.

"I knew who it was right away. I'm guessing you do too. So, I got her phone number and called her. She doesn't have a TV, much less the internet, so she wasn't aware of what had been happening with us, but she did have a lot to tell me about that night. She said she'd heard you leave. It was dark and she did not approve; she wanted me to tell you, by the way.

"She watched out the window as you headed out down the street, then she saw a car park in front of your building and a woman get out. She said she had long hair like yours. A minute later, two men showed up. They walked to the grassy area across the street and one of the men stayed back and took pictures as the other two walked together. She didn't like what they were up to, so she wrote down the license plate of the car."

"Go Mrs. Pachenkis!" Abby slapped the table. "I can't believe it. Next door to us this whole time!"

"From there, everything fell into place. Freya was able to help me get the license plate information. The car was owned by a woman, a server and aspiring model, who'd answered a Craiglist ad for a moonlit photoshoot. She'd been given a time, date, address, and a non-disclosure agreement. When she saw the pictures and people claiming it was you, she thought she couldn't say anything, or she'd get sued. Luckily, it only took us a little digging to find out that the NDA was with a non-existent law firm, in other words, completely null and void. I can now publicly say that she has confirmed she is the woman in those pictures and that the man she was with, the man who hired her was ... Simon Phillips."

Naomi covered her mouth as a sob of relief welled up.

"Holy mother of petticoats and peep toe shoes," Riley said.

"Yes!" Abby clapped her hands. "This is unbelievable!"

The viewer count was well over 100,000 now and rising at an exponential rate. Comments were racing along the bottom of her screen.

*Maggie Levy* Yaaaaas

*Alex Garcia* #TeamNaomi all the way. I knew it

*Tina Patrick* Who's the model? Is she single?

*Marie Bree* @ChristyWright are you seeing this?

"PerezHilton is legit live tweeting about this right now," Becca said, looking at her own phone.

Will was still walking, and he paused to navigate across a busy street. "Once I knew that, I needed to figure out what to do with it. I could tell you, but I felt like you deserved something bigger. No one should have to live through what you went through. There's nothing I can do to fix that, but I thought maybe I could help even the scales a little. I can't exactly recreate our internationally-televised wedding, but I figured with our current popularity I could put this out publicly. I can also put myself out there, publicly. Which seems to be working," his eyes flicked down and he gave a nervous chuckle. "250,000 people watching. Jesus. Okay. Um. Right. So, I'm going to try not to think about that while I keep talking.

"I should have never walked away that day, Naomi. I should have trusted you. I should have stayed by your side while we figured this out together. But I ... left you in front of everyone. So, I want to give you the chance to do the same thing to me."

"Where is he going?" Abby heard Riley say. She glanced at his surroundings; the buildings and streets had given way to grass and trees.

"I want to pick things up where we left off. I want to put everything that happened behind us. I love you, Naomi, and I want to be with you. And I mean *with* you. Every step, not only when it's easy. I'm sorry it took this long for me to find my way here. And I understand if it's too late and you don't want that anymore." The image dipped and blurred and then settled as it was propped up against something. Will took a seat on the ground, leaning up against a large gray stone. Behind him, Lake Michigan bobbed lazily.

"He's somewhere on the lake?" Abby said.

"I know exactly where that is," Naomi said, her voice breaking. "It's where he proposed to me."

"Here I am. I've brought a good book and I'm going to spend the afternoon right here. Whatever my fate, it will be broadcast for everyone to see, which only seems fair. If you don't come, I promise you won't hear from me again, but I really hope you do."

Naomi looked up at her friends who were all staring back at her.

"You're going to go, right?" Becca went first.

"You have to," Riley said. "This is literally *the* most romantic thing that anyone has ever done."

Abby waved at them. "Don't push her. She needs to make this decision on her own." She put a reassuring hand on Naomi. "You don't have to do anything right away. You can think about this and decide what you want when you're ready."

Naomi looked up from the phone, her lips moving silently until finally a small whisper came out. "I want to go to him," she said slowly.

Becca and Riley both applauded enthusiastically.

"Oh, thank God," Abby said immediately. "I didn't know how long I was going to be able to act neutral."

Dazed, but clearly fueled with a rush of adrenaline, Naomi looked resolutely at her friends. "I'm going to go to him," she said again, this time without hesitation.

Riley jumped out of the booth. "Well then what are we waiting for? Let's get out of here!"

Becca was right behind them. "We're pretty far from the lake; he's going to be sitting for a while."

Abby swiped at Becca, trying to pull her back, and missed. "Whoa—who said we're all going with her?"

"Please, Abby," Riley said. "You know you want to go. You can stop trying to be so level-headed already."

Abby dropped her head back and laughed. "You're right; who am I kidding? Let's go already!"

Moments later, they were in a cab, with Naomi in the

front seat giving directions to the driver while Riley, Abby, and Becca coached her from the back.

"What are you going to say?"

"Here, do you need lip gloss?"

"Do we need to get Mrs. Pachenkis a present?"

"Do you even want to know the watch count now? No, you don't. Don't look."

"But don't run to him. You're going to be all red and out of breath."

"Don't you kind of wish it was raining right now? That would be so movie perfect."

"Let me rephrase. You *need* lip gloss."

Naomi left the lip gloss and everything else as the car pulled up and she practically fell out as she ran across the large green expanse. Abby followed, but as Naomi reached the large rocky stairs leading down to the lake, she slowed her steps.

"This is exactly why I told you to take those pole dancing classes with me," Becca said. "You need to be in good shape for important moments like this!"

"No, hang on," she said loud enough to halt Riley who was a few paces ahead of her now. "Let's give them a little space."

"Space! I don't wanna give them space," Riley said, shoulders slumping in tandem with their adolescent whine. "I thought we agreed we were going with."

"Let's just give them a few moments to themselves," she said before whipping out her phone and giving them both a mischievous smile. "Besides, we can watch them from up here and still eavesdrop."

Riley tossed their head back and groaned. "Fine, but

after this I get to force you to make at least five immature decisions. At least five, Abigail."

"You've got yourself a deal."

"I want that deal too," Becca said.

"I'm not entrusting you to make any decisions in my life," Abby said, tapping Facebook open and pulling up Will's feed. They reached the top of the stone steps just as Naomi reached the bottom and they watched in real life and on the screen as Naomi dropped to her knees and kissed Will.

He wrapped his arms around her and when he pulled away, they heard him say on Abby's phone, "I'm so sorry. I love you," before he was smothering her in kisses again.

"Yaaas, girl!" Becca shouted.

Abby wanted to scold her for interrupting the moment, but instead she found herself unable to resist joining in. "Wooooo!" she shouted down at them, waving her hands in the air. Riley added in with hollers and clapping of their own.

Still holding on to her, Will broke the kiss to look up at where Abby, Riley, and Becca were standing, further back. "I see you brought company," they heard him say on the camera. He waved at them, and they waved back.

Naomi looked directly into the camera of his phone. "I think my three don't really compare."

Will laughed. "I don't know about you, but I'm so ready to be done with the audience. I want to start over. With you, and only you." He took her hand and kissed it.

"Let's do that then," she said. She reached over to the phone and the image went dark.

*This Live has ended.*

"Ahh, dammit," Abby said.

"See, this is why making mature decisions is always a bad idea," Riley said.

"All we get to do is watch two tiny figures make out, which is boring." Becca sighed. "If I wanted that, I'd watch porn on my phone."

Riley sighed. "Good lord, are they going to come up for air at any point? Oh, I can't take this anymore." Riley cupped a hand around their mouth. "We've been really patient while you made out! I need to know what's happening!"

"For once, I'm with Riley on this one!" Abby yelled.

"Because of this beautiful moment, I'm choosing to ignore how you worded that," Riley said back to her.

Naomi's beaming face could clearly be seen as she shouted, "We're getting married! Again! Right now!"

The screaming that ensued scared the nearby seagulls. The trio made their way over to Naomi and Will, who pulled themselves up to standing in time to receive the volley of hugs.

"You're getting married like now, now?" Becca asked.

"Now, now," Naomi confirmed.

"We already have the marriage license," Will said. "We just need an ordained minister to marry us and two witnesses."

"I think the three of us can handle those things," Abby told him, too caught up in the moment to think of any objections.

"How do we do this, then?" Will asked.

"Here's the plan," Naomi called the troops to order. "Will, you go change into your suit. I'll go home and change into my wedding dress. Riley, you're in charge of alcohol.

Becca, you get us some flowers. Abby, you figure out how to get ordained. We'll meet back at my apartment in an hour."

"You've put the right person in charge of the right job," Riley said.

"I'm less excited about flowers," Becca said with a sigh. "I'd rather be in charge of finding strippers. Are you sure you don't want a quick bachelorette party first?"

"I'm sure," Naomi said with a smile.

Will leaned down and kissed the top of her head. "Me too."

"Well," Abby said, "If we've only got an hour, we need to get moving! Come on, Naomi. We'll share a ride back."

She wasn't positive Naomi's feet were touching the ground as they walked to the road and got in a Lyft.

"I'm no-words-for-it thrilled for you right now," Abby said. "This is the happiest happy ending I could have wished for you."

"It's really happening, right?" Naomi said, taking hold of Abby's hands. "I'm not dreaming?"

"I can pinch you to make sure."

"I'm good!" She laughed.

In what felt like only a blink of an eye, they were stepping off the elevator of their apartment floor. Abby walked to her door and unlocked it. Opening the door, she brushed her fingers across her mezuzah and then her lips and said, "Give me a few minutes to figure out this ordained minister thing. Just come over when you're ready."

For the second time that day, she heard Naomi gasp loudly.

"What is it?" Abby turned and time stopped as she took in the scene in front of her. Her eyes followed a trail from the barrel, to the strong hand clutching the gun, to the black shirt, to the sharp jawline, until finally, she was looking into Simon's face.

Simon was looking back at her with brutal, unruly eyes that narrowed as they met hers. Everything about him was taut, and he quivered and twitched, as if every sinew in his body was pulled to its end, ready to snap. He waved his gun at her, urging them both backward until they were inside her apartment. Keeping the gun trained in their direction, he stepped in after them and slammed the door shut.

Naomi stood facing him, her shoulders rising and falling. When she finally spoke, her words were like the sound of a heart being rendered into pieces. "Simon ... no..."

Abby faltered as her thoughts took off like a pack of spooked horses. Could she scream for help? Could she run? Could she fight? Could she—

"Shut. Up." Simon spoke to Naomi through clenched teeth, his words more akin to a feral growl than English.

Naomi shrank under Simon's words. "Simon, please, just let Abby leave," she said, keeping her eyes down and her voice to a near whisper.

Abby was at her side. "Naomi, I'm not leaving you."

Simon's eyes flicked to Abby. "No, you never could, could you?" His arm jerked, and before she could react, the gun cracked across the side of her head. The blow stunned her, and she fell to the ground.

"Abby!" Naomi screamed as she knelt next to Abby and put an arm around her protectively.

Abby could feel a warm trickle down the side of her head. *Move!* she commanded herself, but her muscles wouldn't respond.

"Get up," Simon commanded, indicating Naomi with the barrel of his gun.

Naomi flinched but then something else happened. Instead of shrinking back, her body seemed to expand, and Abby could feel Naomi's trembling give way as she took in a long breath. For a second, Naomi held her breath and the room seemed suddenly, eerily, void of all sound. Then, with an exhale, Naomi rose to standing, squaring her shoulders as she did. "Simon, put the gun down," she ordered. "It's over."

A glassy sheen of tears came over his eyes, and he sucked in air sharply through his teeth. "It's not over. Not after everything I did for you."

Naomi remained steady, holding her focus on Simon. "You think what you did back there was for me?"

He pulled at the collar of his shirt. "I told you I would do anything to get you back. It was working. I was going to get you back until he," he waved the gun to his left, presumably indicating Will, "ruined everything. If he could have left everything alone, it would have worked, and we would have been ... we could have been ..." He faltered, his voice cracking over the words.

"No, we couldn't have been. It's over."

"It's not over. You are mine, Naomi. You have always been mine."

"It's been over for a long time, and nothing you can do will ever change that. I did love you. Nothing will ever change that either. You were my first kiss. You were my first love. I built a life with you. But that's over."

"It isn't over!"

"I think you know we can never go back."

"Stop saying that!" Simon shoved the gun forward,

pushing it into Naomi's chest. He let out a noise, an angry, heaving cry, as if he were fighting against the rush of fury and pain that threatened to crush him.

Abby looked around, desperate to find a way to stop him. She was dizzy but she could move a little now. Maybe she could reach for his feet, pull him off balance but it seemed too dangerous. Caught off guard, he could pull the trigger and hurt Naomi.

Naomi moved calmly as she placed her hand on the barrel of the gun. "I know that you love me too. Which is why I know you won't hurt me."

Simon's frame seemed to ripple, and the gun trembled in his hand.

Naomi's voice dropped to a gentle whisper. "It's okay, Simon. It's over now."

Abby couldn't be sure how long it took for Simon's arm to lower, but it seemed to happen in slow motion, the gun dropping in imperceptibly small increments until finally it was out of sight.

An odd rattling noise came from the door, followed by the most beautiful, welcome sound in all the world.

"I can hear voices in there, Abigail Meyer. I've come bearing alcohol and I won't be left out, so if you're not going to let me in I'm going to use my key to enter whether you like it or not."

Before anyone could react, the door flew open, crashing full force into Simon, who toppled forward, the gun flying from his hand and sliding across the room.

Part of Riley's head poked through the doorway. "What the hell have you got in front of the door?"

"Riley!" Abby shrieked their name as a shout of relief

and a cry for help. Simon, still blocking the door, was on his hands and knees, disoriented, but quickly regaining his senses.

"Calm down, I've brought wine." Riley's arm shot out, clutching a bottle of Merlot.

Ignoring the thundering ache in her head and the rush of nausea, Abby leapt up, ran to the door and snatched the bottle of wine.

"Excuse me!" Riley yelped at her.

She raised the bottle and without giving herself time to think, swung it as hard as she could onto Simon's head. She heard a sickening cracking noise, and his body slumped to the ground.

Riley's face disappeared and then the door began opening farther, pushing against Simon's unconscious form. Once it was open a few inches, Riley slid themself through and into the apartment.

"Do we need to talk about this key thing, because—oh my God!" they said, their eyes finally making their way to the floor. "Is that—are you—what the hell happened here?"

"I think flowers are more expensive than a stripper." Becca, bearing a bouquet of flowers, walked into Abby's apartment. "I really think it would have been better—what is going on here? Why is there a man on your floor?"

"That's Simon," Riley said to her. "And that's a gun. And that is your sister who says she's fine but there's literal blood running down her face." They nodded toward the bottle in Abby's hand. "And that's my bottle of wine which was used to subdue him."

Abby, still clutching the wine bottle, felt her legs begin to quiver underneath her. "I'm fine," she insisted. She put out a hand to catch herself but the wall couldn't prevent her knees from buckling and she dropped to the floor.

"Oh my God, we need an ambulance," she heard Naomi say as the room started to spin and then darken until there was nothing but black.

# Chapter 20
## *Freya*

FREYA SAT AT A LONG CONFERENCE TABLE, THE WOOD polished to such extremes that she could practically see up the noses of the six INN Executive Producers, two attorneys, and her agent, sitting at it.

The meeting had been going on for more than three hours and had felt like a combination of an audition and psychological warfare. Luckily, she was well prepared for both. Maintaining a pleasant but unreadable smile while still looking interested was a tool of the trade she had mastered years ago. Her agent had done extensive research on each person at the table prior to their meeting, ensuring that Freya was equipped with the information she needed to tailor her answers to the individual and to the group as a whole.

"As you know, Kent James was adept at striking a fine line between balanced commentary and journalism. It was a style that polled well with our viewers, who valued his opinion, but at the same time wanted room to make their own decisions. INN is hoping to continue that tradition and I'd be interested to hear how you feel you might approach that," said Executive Producer Ron, sixty-seven, twice divorced, currently single, two children, one grandchild, beloved elder at his Lutheran church, frequent donor to the Republican Party, and avid gardener.

Freya knew that 'balanced commentary' was just another way to say 'family friendly'. "Absolutely, Ron. As they say, if it's not broke, don't fix it. I think James has laid out a great roadmap for delivering what the viewers are looking for. I don't have any interest in getting political or trying to turn what Kent James built into *The Daily Show*. I'd work closely with the producers, like I do now at NGN, to bring the same quality content that James has delivered for four decades. The only way I might approach it differently is to use my personal style to bridge the gap between the generations. The older generations expect a trusted figure to deliver the news, while the younger generations, many of whom have cut the cord and are getting their news online, look for more personable experiences, almost like a friend delivering the news. I'd suggest that we take a similar approach to what NGN did with the wedding special and create content for TV *and* social media. As you've seen in my work and on the wedding special, I have the skills and the personality for both."

"And the looks," Andy, in-house attorney, thirty-nine, married, one son, country club membership holder, frequent gambler, said. The men in the room chuckled.

Freya smiled. "Thank you," she said, not meaning it. "So yes, I can bring a more professional style to cable news and a more casual style to social media, which could result in bringing in an entirely new audience base that INN has not connected with yet."

What she was proposing wasn't rocket science, but it was risky. INN prided itself on being a traditional news source. Kent James had modeled himself after Walter Cronkite, "the most trusted man in America", and it had won him the top spot at INN. She was betting on the fact that INN was also struggling with dwindling numbers and was looking for something different but safe. She wanted to prove to them that she could be both.

To her relief, heads and eyebrows bobbed in approval.

"Well, I think that about wraps things up. Thank you for coming in today, Ms. Jonsson," Bob said, closing his leather portfolio. The room followed suit. "You can expect to hear from us within the next few weeks, one way or the other."

"Thank you," she said. "I look forward to it."

Everyone stood, and after cordial hand-shaking, she and her agent were escorted to the elevators. The moment the doors closed, her spine melted and she relaxed up against the wall. "I'm not sure how that went," she said to Kiara. "How did it go?"

"You were absolutely killer. You had them on the edge of their seats the entire time," Kiara gave her an enthusiastic pat on the back. "That little social media bit at the end? I was worried you weren't going to get to use it, but you snuck it in right at the last second. I think that's what's going to seal the deal. You're a social media darling and they need that right now."

The elevator dropped them off on the first floor. "I hope you're right," Freya said as they stepped outside onto a frantic New York city street.

"I know we've only done guest appearances and smaller

bookings up until now, so you haven't really seen me in action, but trust me. My gut never lies."

"Mine doesn't either, but it's all over the map on this one."

"That's because you can't use your gut on yourself. That's like trying to tickle yourself. Can't be done. You'll have to trust mine instead." Kiara lifted a hand to hail a cab. "I will be calling you with their offer in a few days, and then we can begin negotiations, which is my favorite part." Kiara smacked her lips like she was savoring a tasty dish.

"Ugh, give me a hostile interview any day."

"That's why you've got me. You do your job so that I can do mine." A yellow cab swerved across traffic and pulled up in front of them. "You deserve a drink on me. I know a great bar in SoHo that I think you'd love."

"I actually need to head to the hotel and do some work," she replied, pulling out her phone. She blinked as she took in her screen. One hundred and sixty-two e-mails, sixteen missed calls, four voicemails, and fourteen texts waiting for her. Being unavailable usually led to a pile of missed communications, but this was excessive. This was 'you missed something important'.

"I did tell you to do your job so I could do mine, so I guess I can't fight you on that," Kiara said, sliding into the cab. "If you finish up or simply change your mind, text me! Promise!"

Freya waved absently as she unlocked her phone, trying to decide where to start first. She skimmed her email first. There were bursts of email chains from NGN staff in the last hour discussing "Follow up strategy" and "Station response" but scrolling through the dozens of emails, she

couldn't make heads or tails of what "live" they were referring to. A number of emails were from other journalists
asking her for a quote, once again referring to some Live on
Facebook.

She swiped up, hoping to find answers somewhere else.
She glanced through her missed calls first. One was from her
gym, several were from Brian, some from NGN numbers
with extension she didn't know, and two were from Will, the
last one from only ten minutes ago. She switched to voice-
mail. The transcriptions showed nothing helpful—just a lot
of "call me back" messages along with one "upgrade your
membership" offer. Finally, she went to her text messages.
This was the same hodgepodge as her missed calls. She
tapped Will's messages first, with the intention of asking him
if he knew exactly what in the hell was going on. But that
wasn't necessary.

> WILL: I can't believe you're out of town
> today. Don't think I haven't noticed that
> your calendar is mysteriously absent and
> you haven't talked about what you're
> doing. We're going to be discussing this
> further.

Freya smiled. She'd already told Kiara that she was
intending to negotiate Will as part of her contract.

> WILL: Here's the thing. I've been giving this a lot of thought and I decided I'm going to go public with what we discovered. I know that was always the plan but there's more. I don't want NGN to be a part of any of it. I don't want a curated story. I want to be real. I need to be myself, unedited. I need Naomi to see me putting myself out there. I checked with my lawyer and she said my contract with NGN doesn't cover talking about anything that happens after the ceremony. So I'm gonna go live on Facebook and just lay it all out and see if she still loves me.

"Wow," she said aloud. "Good for him." NGN wouldn't be thrilled, it would probably be a little messy, but—her mouth cracked open slightly. Follow-up strategy? Station response? Did that mean he had already...? She continued reading.

> WILL: Here's the part that might give you a little heartburn. I need to do it now. I've worked up the resolve to do this and I feel like if I wait any longer, I might lose it. It's not every day you invite the world to watch you get rejected by your ex-fiance that you ran out on. Ugh, I was really hoping you'd be around to tell me I'm doing the right thing. Or at least watch it. But you're doing something mysterious. I'm going to go live now so...wish me luck.

There were more messages from him, but she needed to know. Did he do it? What happened? Her chest crackled with happiness, pain, frustration, sadness. Had she missed it? She pulled up Facebook and went straight to Will's profile.

She watched the replay, sound blasting full volume. It was New York City, so no one cared. And based on the view numbers, a good chunk of them had probably seen it anyway.

"I want to start over. With you. And only you."

"Let's do that then."

When the screen went black, Freya found she couldn't stop the tears that had welled up. It was beautiful and raw. It was human. It was exactly what Will wanted. Not curated, not whitewashed, not even safe. He hadn't known what was going to happen when he started that video. In some ways, he still didn't. NGN was working on a station response right now which might include, "You went rogue and we're firing you." He'd risked it all for Naomi, and not even to win her back, only to do right by her. If Freya didn't know Will, if she hadn't been with him, seen him struggle, and come back, she would have wondered if it was all staged. But it wasn't. It was real. Their love was real and strong enough to survive something this big.

She wiped at the tears on her cheeks and then went back to her text messages.

> WILL: OMG did you see it? She came!
>
> We're going to get married RIGHT NOW before anything else can stop us. This is killing me, where are you?

Freya checked the time stamp. Only an hour ago. Maybe there was a chance she could reach him and at least attend by video? She hurried on to the next message to make sure she didn't miss anything else before calling him.

> WILL: Something's happened. I was really hoping you'd pick up. I want you to hear this first before it gets picked up.

Will had tried to call her only ten minutes ago. Maybe there was a delay in the wedding, and she would still have time to watch it.

> WILL: Naomi and Abby went back to their building to get some stuff. Naomi's ex-husband was there waiting for them. With a gun. They subdued him. But not before he hit Abby with the gun.

Freya had to clutch the phone harder to keep from dropping it. She tried to read the words over the sound of blood pounding in her ears.

> WILL: She's unconscious and the EMTs are rushing her to Northwestern right now. We're following behind.

Freya tried to take a breath, but her lungs refused to expand. Or maybe there was no more air for her to breathe. She couldn't tell.

> WILL: I know it's probably not my place and maybe I have no idea what I'm talking about. But come home.

# Chapter 21
## *Abby*

A knock at her hospital room door woke Abby out of a doze.

Before she could respond, the door swung open, and her friends tumbled into the room like they were falling out of a clown car.

"How are you?" Naomi was the first to her bedside. She inspected the bandage around Abby's head, wincing in sympathy. "They wouldn't let us in to see you any sooner."

"They wouldn't let *you* in any sooner," Becca said, plopping down at the foot of the bed. "I was allowed because I was family, but Mom said I might not be 'helpful' and went in without me."

Abby had laughed until her head throbbed with pain when her mom told her she'd made Becca wait in the visitor's area.

"I love her, but her voice makes me feel like I have a skull fracture most days, I can't imagine what it would do to me if I actually had one," she'd told Abby.

"Your mother tells us they're releasing you today?" Riley moved to the front of the pack.

She nodded. "Finally!"

"Finally?" Naomi replied, "You've been here twenty-four hours and literally have a crack in your skull."

Abby raised a studious finger. "But the non-dangerous kind."

"I don't think that's a thing," Riley said.

"Okay, well, the less dangerous kind. The kind that requires brief observation, which has occurred, and then rest at home, which I happen to be exceptionally good at."

Naomi smiled at her, but there was more than relief at the good news in her expression. "Then, if you're feeling up for it, we were wondering ..." she looked over her shoulder, where Will was standing.

"We were wondering," Will continued for her, "if you'd like to marry us."

Abby made a noise somewhere between a guffaw and a gasp. "Here? Now?"

Naomi grinned, a surprisingly gleeful expression after everything they had been through. "If there's one thing I've learned from all this it's that I can't let Simon or anyone else hold me back. If I'd listened to you from the beginning, maybe we wouldn't be here today. But here we are, and I don't want to put my life on hold anymore. I don't want to let one more thing interrupt our future. We want to get married. Right now."

Abby felt like she should be level-headed about the request and talk them through it. Get married here? In a hospital room? After they had been through a traumatic event together? While she was still in a hospital gown? Shouldn't they take more than one day to process it all?

Instead, she let out a laugh that was accompanied by tears of joy and spoke her own truth. "I can't think of anything else I'd rather do right now."

"While we were in the waiting room, we took the liberty of registering you as an ordained minister." Will held up his phone, which displayed a digital certificate from the Universal Life Church bearing her name. "You're good to go."

Becca held up a bouquet of slighty drooping flowers. "I've still got the flowers from yesterday. I would have gotten fresh ones from the hospital, but I'm saving that money for a stripper. Everyone is saying no stripper, but I think there's a stripper in our future."

Naomi took them in one hand and held Will's arm with the other hand. "Okay then, third time's the charm?"

Abby swung her legs out of bed and then stood up, wobbling slightly. "Oops, maybe I'll stay seated for this," she said, sitting back down. She attempted to brush out the wrinkles from her hospital gown and then gave up with a hearty laugh. "How do I look?"

"Perfect," Naomi said.

The crew rearranged themselves so that Naomi and Will were standing in front of Abby, flanked by Becca beside Naomi and Riley next to Will.

"Hang on," Abby said. She tugged the hospital sheet from her bed and handed one end to Riley and the other end to Becca. "Hold your arms up. This won't be your dream Jewish wedding, but at least we can have a makeshift chuppa."

Becca and Riley obliged, lifting their arms to drape the sheet over the couple. "I can manage for about sixty seconds, so you'd better get a move on it." Riley said.

"Great, let's get you married," Abby said, placing her hands in her lap resolutely. "Now does anyone know what that means exactly? Like, what am I supposed to be doing here?"

"You have to witness us sharing our wedding vows. That's it. I looked it up," Will said.

"Like the 'I do' part?"

Will nodded.

Abby laughed at the hilarity and the perfection of it all. "Given your history with nuptials, I feel like I need to get to that part really fast, but I really want to say something first." She looked from Naomi to Will as the words flowed out of her. "You two have overcome so much and yet you've managed to still end up here. With each other. I can't think of any couple more prepared to face life together than you two. So, let's make that happen already. I think it goes something like this—Will, do you take Naomi to be your lawfully wedded wife? Isn't there more?"

"Something about honoring, cherishing, and dying, right?" Riley suggested.

"Yes, all those things. Do you?"

His entire face smiling, Will turned to look at Naomi. "All those things and more, yes. I do."

"And Naomi, do you take Will to be your lawfully wedded husband? And all those things?"

Naomi's laugh was full of all those things and more. "I do. Absolutely."

"Well then, by the power vested in me by, I'm assuming,

the state of Illinois, I now pronounce you husband and wife!" Will and Naomi began to lean forward for a kiss, but she held up a hand. Wait!" Abby grabbed the Styrofoam cup from her lunch tray and gulped the last sip of 7-Up from it before dropping it on the floor.

They stared at it for a moment, before Will caught on and, lifting his foot, smashed it under his shoe. They kissed, under their bed sheet chuppa and shouts of "Mazel tov!"

"Quick, everyone sign this!" Naomi broke the kiss and ran over to her purse, pulling out their marriage license. Laughing, they crowded around Abby's bed and jotted down their signatures.

"That's it!" Naomi said when the last signature was complete. "We're married!"

"Time to celebrate!" Riley reached into their satchel and pulled out a bottle of wine.

Abby made a choking noise. "That's not the wine that I used to—"

"God no, they took that away CSI-style. You didn't think I'd purchase one measly bottle of alcohol, did you? I don't do that on a boring average day, much less on a wedding day." Riley set the bottle down and then dove back into their bag like Mary Poppins, pulling out three more bottles and an opener.

They hurriedly drank out of hospital paper cups, laughing and toasting and then hiding the evidence moments before hospital staff arrived to discharge Abby.

"There's a little bit of a crowd outside the hospital," a nurse told Abby as she helped her into a wheelchair.

"A crowd?" Abby repeated, looking back at her friends

who were following behind her like an entourage while she was wheeled down the corridors.

"Yeah, news media," the nurse said. "They've been parked outside for the last few hours now."

Riley's phone practically teleported into their hand. "Literally what is happening right now? It's all over the interwebs!" They swiped vigorously across their phone. "Simon's attack, the arrest, Abby's hospitalization. How did I miss this?"

"We were a little busy talking to the police and worrying about Abby," Naomi said.

"If you can't multi-task in the twenty-first century you might as well be dead," Riley replied.

"We're going to need lip gloss," Becca said. "Especially you, Abby. Although I'm not sure how much it's going to help. You're a mess."

"Thanks," Abby said, devoid of gratitude.

"You're the newsman, Will, what are we supposed to do?" Riley asked, pausing at each reflective surface they passed to adjust something on their body. "I am so not ready for an on-camera appearance."

Will's shoulders raised and lowered. "I guess we keep it simple?" he said. "Thank them for their concern and say we're ready to move past everything. Or we find out if there's a secret back entrance."

The appeal of not having her post-hospital couture look plastered on the internet was high. "Still," Abby said, finishing her thought verbally. "There's something about closure. Like it or not, the public has been on this wild ride with us. It might help us in the long run if we let them know we're fine and moving on."

"See this is why being friends with a therapist is helpful," Naomi said. "She's got a point. I know we said we wanted to leave the audience behind, but maybe this is how we make that happen."

Will nodded as they approached the sliding doors.

Outside, Abby could clearly see the throng of reporters on either side of the doors. "Then we're agreed?"

If anyone responded, she didn't hear as the doors whirred open and the barrage of questions tumbled in as reporters surrounded them. The nurse pushed her over the threshold and then stopped, allowing her to stand up. "Good luck," she might have heard the nurse say.

"Abigail, how are you feeling?"

"Can you tell us exactly what transpired in the apartment?"

"Wilomi, now that you've reunited, what's next for you?"

"Abby, Naomi, will either of you be pressing charges for the attack?"

"Naomi, any response to the people who stood by you during all of this?"

Cameras flashed as Naomi came alongside her and spoke with a firm voice. "I think I speak for all of us," she said, and the crowd went silent, "when I say that I'm ready to put all this behind me. We're grateful for everyone's support, but we've spent enough time in the public eye and we're really looking forward to doing whatever is next, privately." She looked at Will, then Abby. "Right?"

Abby gave her arm a squeeze. "I believe that about covers it, yeah."

The reporters seemed to take their statement as an invitation because the battery of questions started up again immediately.

"Can we expect any further statements from you?"

"Will you be communicating with your fans at all going forward?"

"What exactly is next for you?"

Abby glanced at Naomi. "This is the part where we just go, right?"

"I think so," her friend replied.

She started to take a step forward when another question rang out from the crowd. "Abigail, what can you tell us about your recent breakup?"

It was the question that first stopped her in her tracks. Her breakup? No one knew about that. Who would be asking a question like that? She started to convince herself that somewhere between the head injury and the medication she'd misheard it. Then she saw the flash of golden hair.

There, crammed in between the cameras and microphones, was Freya Jonsson.

The sudden attack of stars in her vision and weak knees weren't from her injury this time. "I ..." she stammered, her thoughts skittering so quickly in every direction she didn't bother to try and catch them.

Freya pushed her way closer through the crowd. "Does staying out of the public eye mean you wouldn't date a public figure?"

Every molecule sizzled with disbelief and, at the same time, a euphoric delight. Was this really happening? Was it really Freya? Was she really saying what it sounded like she was saying?

She looked at her friends for guidance but immediately

realized that they would have nothing to offer because they had no idea about her relationship with Freya. As she turned back, it briefly registered that they didn't look astonished or confused. Instead, they were huddled together, mouths open, faces lit up like Christmas morning. Over the din, it sounded like Riley was saying, "It's happening!"

Right as the observation turned into a question, her eyes met Freya's again and all other thoughts fell away. She couldn't stop the smile that rose to her lips. "I think I could be talked into making an exception for the right person."

As Freya moved toward her, she wasn't entirely sure if the reporters had stopped asking questions or if she had simply stopped hearing them. "Can someone be the right person even if it took them a long time to get to a place where they were ready to be the right person?"

The only answer she could think of was a question. "Are you sure?" Freya was close enough now that she didn't have to shout. "Your career. Everything you've worked for. Your whole life. I know I said a lot of things, but I don't want to be the reason—"

Freya grabbed her hands. "When I didn't know what had happened, when Will said there'd been an attack and you were on the way to the hospital and I didn't know if you were alive, it just," she laughed, "it just became so obvious that none of that matters. Abby, I don't want to waste one more moment hating you, or being afraid of what might happen because of who I am. Maybe my career will go up in flames and maybe it won't. Maybe my life will get turned upside down and maybe it won't. Maybe I'll make a difference in the world and maybe I won't. You were right. It's time for me to put on my crown and fight to be who I am. With you. Because I love you."

Looking into Freya's eyes, Abby could clearly see herself, at fifteen, on the first day of high school, snarling as Freya strode down the halls of Northwest High. Had she loved Freya from that very first second? Or had her love grown so gradually that she hadn't noticed when it took root? How long had she tried to convince herself that she despised Freya when deep down, she adored every inch of her?

Suddenly, visions of their encounters, clashes, and kisses flashed before her. In her mind's eye, she watched the threads weave impossibly together to bring her to this very moment. She smiled and wondered if that fifteen-year-old girl would have ever believed that she would end up here, in front of all these people, saying with all her heart, "I love you, Freya Jonsson."

# Epilogue

@usweekly Those rumor mills can finally stop spinning. Freya Jonsson, award-winning journalist, just came out of the closet. Follow us for more updates as they become available. #truelove #GaykingNews

@JennyfromNH Can't stop crying and rewatching @TheFreyaJonsson kissing her love. #happycomingout #GaykingNews

@laurastweeeeets We shouldn't have to have dramatic coming out stories in the 21st century, but since we do, this is the one. Romantic AF #gaykingnews #PutOnYourCrown

@carlikor_abroad @TheFreyaJonsson thanks for reminding me what's really important. #PutOnYourCrown

@AmeliaKnits_96 I'm living for this. @TheFreyaJonsson wherever you go, I will follow. #gaykingnews

@DiplomiALLIEcy Okay even with all this #gaykingnews I still want to know more about the mysterious neighbor that cracked the #Wilomi case. I WILL NEVER BE WHOLE UNTIL I KNOW WHO THEY ARE

*Cosmopolitan.com*

*Top Stories*

*Freya Jonsson Makes Royalty Of Us All*

When Freya Jonsson went all *Notting Hill* on us, she basically broke the internet. What will come of her career, we've yet to see. But what seems clear is that wherever she lands, she won't be alone.
Read More...

*Wonkette*
*Meet the Sexy Geniuses Behind the* Take My Dicktation *podcast*

One morning, we woke up and the number one podcast on iTunes was something called *Take My Dicktation*. If you haven't heard it—well first of all, how? Second of all, give it a listen. Just don't do it with your kids or your mom around. But definitely do it if you want a good laugh accompanied by surprisingly insightful conversations on life, fashion, spirituality, politics and—obviously—dicks. It's a tumultuous time out there, with tensions making cancel culture and the block button a regular part of our lives, so there's something refreshing about popping in your AirPods and entering a world where everyone is welcome but no one is safe.

Co-hosts of *TMD*, Riley Tahara and Becca Rhein, are not shy about talking about themselves on the show, but we thought we'd see if we could get a little more from them in a one-on-one interview.

*Wonkette*: What exactly was the inspiration for your podcast?

*Becca Rhein*: Well, um, mostly dicks.

*Riley Tahara*: We're both extremely well versed in them. From different perspectives, though, which is where the real magic comes in.

*W*: But you don't only talk about dicks in your podcast.

*RT*: That was an interesting turn of events. If you go back and listen to our original episodes, we were pretty focused on that topic. But when we started taking listener questions, we began getting dick-adjacent questions. Which kind of opened up our subject matter.

*BR*: Well dick-adjacent and also Wilomi-adjacent.

*W*: Which brings me to a big question. How much do you credit your affiliation with Wilomi to the success of your podcast?

*RM:* Can you call it just an affiliation when I provided the wine bottle that subdued Naomi and Abby's attacker?

*BR:* Yeah, somehow we've become ancillary characters in all of that when actually, we were major players.

*RT:* Ancillary, nice.

*BR:* Peter and I have been playing professor and student lately.

*RT:* You know, if you really think about it, our friends are the ... ancillary characters. We're the reason any of this happened in the first place.

*BR:* O-M-G how did I not put that together before? If it wasn't for me, Naomi wouldn't be with Will.

*RT:* And if it wasn't for me, Abby and Freya wouldn't be together.

*BR:* Okay, that might have been your idea, but it was really a group effort.

*W:* Wait, what was your idea? What was the group effort?

*RT:* Umm ... I think the point you're really missing is that we're the heroes in this story. So, if we get to reap any rewards with a little podcast popularity, it's hard-earned rewards.

>> Page 2

Reddit.com
I Am Freya Jonsson, journalist, AMA

This is technically an AMA to promote my upcoming book. But I'm happy to talk about whatever is on your minds. So go ahead—ask me anything!

I'll start at noon CT. Tweet verification from @TheFreyaJonsson

Booksniffer23
Can you talk about your decision to leave traditional journalism and start your own online news outlet?

FreyaJonssonReports
In my first book, I encouraged women to let their voices be heard, but I realized that I wasn't truly practicing what I was preaching. In my quest to build a career within the confines of traditional journalism—truthfully, to build a life within the confines of traditional expectations in general—I lost my voice. I wasn't willing to sacrifice that anymore. So, I took a huge leap, left it all behind, and started producing my own content. Our Voice, Our News was supposed to be short, casual, videos that covered important stories that were getting left out of the major news networks. I started on TikTok and planned to move to some longer form content on YouTube down the road. It turns out people are hungry for this kind of on-the-ground journalism that isn't being driven

by advertisers and out of touch execs. The response was so huge and the following grew so fast that my "down the road" approach wasn't an option. I was able to secure some funding so that Will could join as the first Our Voice, Our News staff member, and we got to work laying the foundation for a news outlet that would make room for all the voices out there, not just the loudest ones. In a few short months we've added three more staff members and have a lot of new projects in the works. It's been one of the most humbling, but exciting, rides of my life!

View Entire Discussion (3.8k comments)

Tumblr.whathappensinvegas.com

They've managed to stay out of the limelight, but that doesn't mean we're not still obsessed with #Wilomi. Anyone know if the reports of the baby bump are confirmed yet because, hi, I need to know. #TeamBabyWilomi

73,493 notes

Book Review—The New York Times
http://www.nytimes.com/section/books/review

Non-Fiction
*She Loves*

*Modern Romance* meets *Eat, Pray, Love*. In her follow up book to *She Speaks,* Freya Jonsson teams up with her wife, therapist Abigail Meyer, to take us down a path that we didn't even know we needed to walk. Interviewing celebrities, sociologists, influencers, even normal folks like us, they explore the stories, messages, battles, and triumphs of the female quest to love and be loved. Swiping right (or left) will never be the same after you understand how far we've come and how far we still have to go.

# Acknowledgments

This book started as an idea over twenty years ago, so I've had a lot of time and a lot of reasons to give up. But because of many amazing people who supported me, I didn't.

Tina Beier and Alexandria Brown at Rising Action Publishing Collective, I can't believe I am so lucky to work with such talented and inspirational women who saw far more possibilities and potential for this story than I ever dreamed.

My friends and family, it's been a long road getting here, and through all of it you read, re-read, brainstormed, listened, cheered, believed, and never gave up until I crossed the finish line.

Mom, a lot has changed since you read my very first draft all those years ago, hasn't it? I couldn't have imagined where life would take this story or me, but I knew you would always be there.

Jane, you literally willed this purple book into existence, not only with your magical powers but with your creative powers that you shared whenever I needed help.

Leigh, you helped me become the person who could become this author.

Team Girls Who Travel, you are truly the most incredible group of women, and I can't believe I get to work with you every day. You all stepped up whenever I needed time to write and gave me a place to share my excitement (looking at you, Book Sniffers!).

My incredible husband Mike, your love and unwavering support is in between every page.

Clark and Rosie, while I am proud of this book, I am and always will be proudest of you.

My wonderful readers, thank you for being part of Abby and Freya's adventures. Thank you for being a part of my adventure and for giving me the chance to share my creativity with you.

And finally, in Judaism, we say a special blessing to acknowledge and celebrate the first time something happens. This debut novel is certainly a first worth acknowledging:

*Baruch Ata Adonai, Eloheinu Melech Haolam, shehechiyanu, v'kiy'manu, v'higianu lazman hazeh*

*Blessed are You, Lord our God, Ruler of the Universe, who has granted us life, sustained us, and enabled us to reach this occasion.*

# About the Author

Arden Joy turned to writing at an early age as a way to create a world as unique and different as she is. Today, she still focuses on telling diverse stories that reflect her colorful life as a queer, Jewish woman and the beautiful spectrum of people in it.

She lives in Chicago with her husband, two children, and dog. When she isn't chasing after her little ones or stirring up trouble for her fictional characters, she runs Girls Who Travel, an award-winning community redefining travel to be inclusive, sustainable, and empowering for all women.